B E S T
G A Y
EROTICA
2005

B E S T
G A Y
EROTICA
2005

Series Editor

Richard Labonté

**Selected and
Introduced by**

William J. Mann

CLEIS
PRESS

Printed in the United States
Cover design: Scott Idleman
Cover photograph: Celesta Danger
Text design: Frank Wiedemann
Cleis logo art: Juana Alicia
First Edition
10 9 8 7 6 5 4 3 2 1

"Doll Boy" © 2004 by Jonathan Asche, reprinted with permission from *Playguy* (August 2004), where it first appeared in different form; "Romulus" © 2004 by Bruce Benderson, first appeared in *fab magazine* (January 2004), excerpt reprinted with permission from *The Romanian* (Payot & Rivages, 2004); "Derelict" © 2004 by Steve Berman, reprinted with permission from VelvetMafia.com, Issue 9, where it appeared in different form; "Yang-Qi" © 2004 by Teh-Chen Cheng, reprinted with permission from *Best Gay Asian Erotica*, ed. Joel B. Tan (Cleis Press, 2004); excerpt from *My Name Is Rand* (Suspect Thoughts Press, 2004) © 2004 by Wayne Courtois; "This Little Piggy" © 2004 by Jim Gladstone, reprinted with permission from *Love Under Foot*, ed. M. Christian and Greg Wharton (Harrington Park/Southern Tier Editions, 2004), where it appeared as "Days of Wine and Toesies"; "The Strange Château of Dr. Kruge" © 2004 by Drew Gummerson; "Wrestler for Hire" © 2004 by Greg Herren, reprinted with permission from *Wanna Wrestle?* (STARBooks, 2004); excerpt from *Voodoo Lust* © 2004 by M. S. Hunter; "The Bad Boys Club" © 2004 by Michael Huxley; "My Place" © 2004 by Alpha Martial; "Old Haunts" © 2004 by Jay Neal, reprinted with permission from *American Bear* (December 2003–January 2004); "Wake the King Up Right" © 2004 by Mike Newman; "Kindled by Vowels (An Epistolary Seduction)" © 2004 by Ian Philips and Greg Wharton, reprinted with permission from *Satyriasis: Literotica2* (Suspect Thoughts Press, 2004) and *Johnny Was & Other Tall Tales* (Suspect Thoughts Press, 2004); "Face Value" © 2004 by Scott Pomfret, reprinted with permission from *In Touch for Men* (January 2004); "Surf" ©2004 by Andy Quan, reprinted with permission from *Best Gay Asian Erotica*, ed. Joel B. Tan (Cleis Press, 2004); "Pink Triangle-Shaped Pubes" © 2004 by Alexander Rowlson, reprinted with permission from *fab magazine* (January 2004); "Get on Your Bikes and Ride!" © 2004 by D. Travers Scott, reprinted with permission from *Law of Desire*, ed. Greg Wharton and Ian Philips (Alyson Books, 2004); "The Thanks You Get" © 2004 by Simon Sheppard, reprinted with permission from *Just the Sex* (Alyson Books, 2003); "The Bigg Mitkowski" © 2004 by Davem Verne; "Gamblers" © 2004 by Bob Vickery, reprinted with permission from *Play Buddies* (Quarter Moon Press, 2004), originally appeared in *Playguy* (February 2004); "All at Sea with Master E" © 2004 by James Williams, reprinted with permission from *Blue Food* (www.bluefood.cc).

For Asa Dean Liles, again and always

For furry Percy, who winters well

And for Zach, new to the family

TABLE OF CONTENTS

Foreword
...Always More Than Erotic
Richard Labonté

The best sex is never really just sex. And it's always better when real bodies are involved. But in the absence of a body—and sometimes even in the company of one—sex is fun to read about, in all its infinite, glorious, messy, imaginative, soul-stirring variety. In assembling this collection for the past nine years, I sure have encountered variety.

That, and an amazing growth in the number of anthologies of erotic writing. Consider, for example, some of the crop of 2003–2004: *Fratsex* and *Escort Tales*, *Desilicious* and *Getting It!*, *Manhandled* and *Desire Lust Passion Sex*, *Quickies 3* and *Hard Men*, *Between the Palms* and *Bad Boys*, *Buttmen 3* and *Men, Amplified*—and those are only some of the collections *not* represented in *Best Gay Erotica 2005*. Stories were submitted or considered from most of them (as well as from the growing number of quality online queer fiction magazines, the now-venerable *Blithe House Quarterly* and the newer *Lodestar Quarterly*); that the stories here all came from elsewhere speaks to the splendid porn boom...it was a very good year.

Indeed, this year's judge, William J. Mann, moans in his

introduction about jettisoning so many great stories to make room for the even better ones in *BGE05*. I bookmarked a couple of hundred possible stories between *Best Gay Erotica 2004* and this year's anthology, and received a couple of hundred more original submissions. I selected forty-eight for William to consider. Any one of those few dozen would have done this book proud.

These best twenty-two savor the body erotic, from urgent tongues and salty lips down to the crusty cracks between toes; they celebrate body types from brick-shithouse hunky to fat and happy about it. If tickling is your thing, there's a tale or two; if muscles turn you on, pump your pleasure; if straight boys set you humming, there are a couple; if full nelsons and surfer boys get you off, come on in; if coy boys and scary scenes excite, enjoy—they're all here. But this isn't just a collection of fetishized body parts, super-sized fantasies, or hyper-masculine stereotypes. Fleshing out all the, well, flesh—what these diverse obsessions, deviancies, and sexual adventures have in common is the fact that the writers (several of them porn veterans and some of them talented newcomers) tell stories with character heft and emotional dimension. Just as the best sex is never really just sex, the best erotic writing is always more than erotic.

Erotic writing dabbles in the fantastic: Jay Neal's creepy "Old Haunts" and Drew Gummerson's science fictional "The Strange Château of Dr. Kluge," both surely not of this world, nonetheless arouse.

Erotic writing revels in memory: Michael Huxley's summertime of sex, "The Bad Boys Club"; Jim Gladstone's summer camp romp, "This Little Piggy"; Davem Verne's fable of Hell's Kitchen, "The Bigg Mitkowski"; Alpha Martial's boy toy fantasy, "My Place"—all draw on what once was, whether years ago or just last week, to entice.

Erotic writing relishes vibrant, one-on-one sexual sparking: Steve Berman's tender "Derelict," about two teens lighting a dark world with love; Teh-Chen Cheng's sensitive "Yang-Qi," about two rural men finding solace in a homophobic culture; and Alexander Rowlson's wise "Pink Triangle-Shaped Pubes," about a brave kid who flaunts his queerness, connecting with a bully still afraid of his own.

Erotic writing lusts after the athletic: Andy Quan's sun-drenched "Surf" and Greg Herren's cum-slicked "Wrestler for Hire," both realizing fantasies.

Erotic writing is electrified by reality: Bruce Benderson's "Romulus" and Ian Philips's and Greg Wharton's "Kindled by Vowels (An Epistolary Seduction)"—two slices of lives fueled by irrepressible connection.

Erotic writing is all about the accidental hot encounter ("Wake the King Up Right" by Mike Newman) and the impossible hot experience (the excerpt from *Voodoo Lust* by M. S. Hunter)—we should all be so lucky.

Erotic writing is all about indulging desire: in Wayne Courtois's excerpt from *My Name Is Rand,* an exalted new fantasy is explored; in James Williams's "All at Sea with Master E," a novice plunges deep into sexual depths.

Erotic writing is all about attempted rescue: in Scott Pomfret's "Face Value," a powerful man falls hard for an empowered hustler; in Jonathan Asche's "Doll Boy," a wealthy man wins the heart—or at least the body—of a teen virgin.

Erotic writing embraces self-image: D. Travers Scott's "Get on Your Bikes and Ride!" inverts the typical equation of neediness with sly eloquence: fat is proud, and furious.

And erotic writing has a sense of humor—exemplified by several stories, including Simon Sheppard's wry, sly "The Thanks You Get."

Twenty-two tales snatched from a universe of erotic possibilities. Have fun.

Some friends, both the older and the newer, are constant—a source of information, ideas, inspiration, and comfort: Nik Sheehan, Don Weise, Justin Chin, Lawrence Schimel, Kirk Read, Helyx Helyx, Andrew Currie, David Rimmer, Bryan Wannop, Frank Kajfes. So too are Felice Newman, Frédérique Delacoste, Chris Fox, and Diane Levinson, who keep Cleis Press purring, and who exude constant quality.

Richard Labonte
Perth, Ontario
September 2004

Introduction
All That Sex Stuff
William J. Mann

My very first published story was about jacking off. I wrote of
a kid who makes obscene phone calls and masturbates in front
of his mirror. Lots of "suck my cock's" and spunk shooting
onto glass and fingers greased up with Vaseline.

"You sure you want to make a name for yourself in this
way?" a friend asked me.

"What way?"

"Sex. With all this sex stuff."

I was a grad student, young and untried and eager to be
published. "I don't care what gets me into print," I said.
"Besides, how can I tell the story of a kid who makes obscene
phone calls without getting into a lot of sex stuff?"

Much of my early fiction is in fact permeated with sex
stuff. After that first anthology—the story was "Cords of
Love," later made into a short film by Dean Slotar called *The
Absolution of Anthony*—I started writing for porn mags.
I also contributed to all those endless early 1990s erotica
anthologies that Richard Kasak of Masquerade Books was
rolling out. I even won first place in an erotica contest spon-

sored by the late Scott O'Hara's *Steam* magazine, writing about sex between three generations of the same family. All that sex stuff was, in fact, getting me somewhere.

So when I wrote my first novel, *The Men from the Boys*, it was inevitable there'd be a lot of sex. I'll never forget the very first interview I did for the book. I was an anxious, first-time author going face-to-face with the Big Bad Press, personified by a serious-faced straight lady from the local newspaper of my then-hometown of Northampton, Massachusetts. "I've never felt so outside of a novel before," she said, taking me by surprise as she scolded me for having written a story that dared to not accommodate a heterosexual sensibility. "I mean," she said, her umbrage growing, "there was so much sex in it!"

Indeed, in the nasty review she published the next day, she wrote that there was, quite simply, "too much sex" in the book. I was devastated—it was my very first review!—until my editor rather astutely pointed out, "Saying there's too much sex in a book is not a bad thing. In fact, we can use it as a blurb on the cover of the paperback." We didn't, but his point was well taken: *The Men from the Boys* turned out to be a best-seller.

The moral here: Making a name for myself with "all that sex stuff" worked out pretty well.

Now, of course, I don't need to defend sexual writing— erotica, literotica, whatever—to those of you reading this book. You've picked it up because sex is part of the fabric of your lives. It's part of your consciousness, how you see and interact with the world. But there are still lots of people out there—reviewers, publishers, and prune-faced straight ladies like that one in Northampton—who don't see it that way. And ever since Janet Jackson's bustier busted out on national television, the forces of reaction, championed by the Bushies, have been clamping down everywhere and anywhere they can.

That's why works like this anthology are so important. Writing about sex is important for *all* people, but I think especially for lesbians and gay men and other nontraditionally heterosexual people. Our deviance—for that's what it is, a deviation from the antiseptic norm—is made out to be frightening and dangerous, something to be denied expression. But of course fear and danger are part of why sexual writing is so vivid and important. What turns us on? What is the line between desire and fear? Between safety and danger? Where do they intersect?

The answer is different for each of us. What makes the stories in this collection so powerful is their individuality, their iconoclasm, their distinct imprint on how each author experiences the erotic. When Richard Labonté asked me to judge this year's entries, I accepted without giving much thought to what I might be reading. In the old days, when I started out, erotica was usually written merely to get the reader off. But as the genre has evolved, it's become more focused on what all good fiction must ultimately be about: the telling of a good story.

Indeed, I was pleasantly surprised to find that the stories Richard sent me were, by and large, some of the most exciting and provocative I'd read in a long time. The quality of the submissions was incredibly high; I found myself truly regretting having to narrow it down to this final twenty-two, necessitating the elimination of so many fine pieces. I looked for a number of things in making my decisions: a diversity of experience, so that we didn't end up only with one type of story or character; a strong, unique authorial voice; and a narrative that engaged me—and yes, got me hard.

It's that immediate, visceral sexual response that distinguishes erotica from other forms of fiction. You don't have to be into S/M or wrestling or the joys of teenage sex to appreciate the power those experiences can have—not if the stories are told well, and if they compellingly convey the writers' own desire. That's what this anthology is intended to do: offer a wide-angle lens on desire.

I hope you enjoy the stories here, in all their quirky, individual deviance. I hope they make you consider your own fantasies, your own wells of desire. I hope they engage you, seduce you, and encourage you to write your own stories. And most of all, I hope they turn you on.

William J. Mann
Los Angeles
August 2004

Wake the King Up Right
Mike Newman

On the road from Baton Rouge to San Francisco, April, 1970

Kevin opened his eyes in the dim early light to find a man's face startlingly close on the next pillow. His fuzzy mind woke up in sections, like the windows of a dark house lighting sequentially as someone moves from room to room. He remembered Jerry getting into his car, he remembered Jerry's naked body in the shower, he remembered Jerry's cock going up his ass. There was a sunset over the Grand Canyon back there somewhere, and a campfire, and a fistfight. And Jerry's cock up his ass.

Asleep, his hitchhiker seemed younger than before, closer to Kevin's age, even boyish, with his dark eyelashes innocently knitted together and his lips parted slightly, showing the white of his front teeth. Kevin's morning erection stiffened. He felt like a spy, staring so intently at the unguarded face of a stranger he had picked up only two days before, now dozing inches from his eyes.

For the first time he noticed a slight asymmetry to Jerry's

face, a subtle mismatch of cheekbones that made one side look friendly and the other side seem stern, even cruel. One black eyebrow arched a bit more than the other. An off-center dimple marred an otherwise perfectly square chin. But it was mostly the eyes. Jerry's features shifted between angelic and crude as Kevin searched from one closed eyelid to the other. His hard-on throbbed.

Fucking mesomorph. You guys have all the luck. Your face is lopsided and you're still sexy. How could anyone be horny for a girl when a man is so...achingly...*male?*

The stubble Jerry had grown during their short time together dotted his jawline and spread down his throat. Kevin tensed his cock until it hurt. He wanted to lick the coarse, black bristles sprouting from the protruding Adam's apple.

I don't just want to fuck with you. I want to *be* you.

Kevin sighed. Trying not to jiggle the bed, he slipped from under the covers and padded, nude, to the bathroom, flipping on the wall heater as he passed it, watching his hard-on wag with each step. A window behind the plastic shower curtain let morning light into the room, making the old lion-foot tub and the checkered tile floor glow blue.

Squinting groggily, he stood at the toilet and pushed his erection down to aim at the bowl. It insisted on pointing out and up instead. Twisting it to the side only made it impossible to let anything out through the rigid tube. He moved to the bathtub and stood with his hands on his hips, cock high, waiting for the valve inside him to unlock from the night's sleep.

He yawned. He shifted his weight from one foot to the other.

He stared at the dimpled clot of his semen still clinging to the shower curtain, below the gap where he had torn the plastic loose from the curtain rod while Jerry fucked him up against the wall. His asshole tightened and his hard-on reared at the thought. He let a blip of gas pass, and took pleasure in the vibration. When his urine first stung at the base of his dick, he liked that, too. Crossing his arms and hugging his bare nipples, he brought back the image of the two of them pissing into the Grand Canyon side by side. Interior parts functioned, his most personal muscles loosened, fluid trickled inside him. He farted again, loudly, and forced out his first burst. A physical pleasure like a minor orgasm sent a shudder through him.

"Ah-h-h," he sighed, relaxing and flowing freely, playing with his private little golden arch, twisting his hips to sweep the stream up and down the tub. "My piss pistol," he whispered, repeating Jerry's name for it as he held it down level and squeezed off three strong shots that made satisfying splatters against the shower curtain across the tub. He shuddered again, farted once more, shook himself off, and laughed at his wickedness.

When he turned around he saw another streak of his cum across the mirror above the sink, trailing runny drips now congealed on the glass.

God, how many times did he fuck me? It's a wonder I can fart without leaking.

He used toilet paper to blow his nose and wipe his butt, which was clean and sore—properly sore, he thought, for a piece of personal equipment he had finally used right for the first time in all his twenty-one years.

Back at the ticking wall heater, he turned his behind to the warmth and cupped himself. His pouch had shriveled like a prune in the cold air but his erection still strained toward his navel. As the flame growled behind him and the backs of his legs baked, he surveyed the cabin.

Thick, dark curtains drawn over the front window blocked out most of the daylight, leaving only a halo around the edges that softly lit the rest of the room. Jerry's blue jeans lay wadded on the carpet by the table, then some balled-up socks, then Kevin's briefs next to Jerry's white boxers. He liked that, the trail of his first real night of debauchery leading to a bed with a naked man still sleeping in it. Kevin bent forward slightly to push his bare buttocks closer to the heater. His balls sagged in his hand.

Under the faded color photograph of the Grand Canyon, Jerry lay on his back with one arm crooked to his hairy chest, holding a corner of the sheet part way over his belly and hips. One muscled leg stuck out from under the tousled green chenille spread that half fell off the bed. Slowly pulling on his cock, Kevin watched the expansion of Jerry's chest as he snored.

My sexy sailor in the desert. I wish I could see you in your Navy uniform.

Even from across the room, Kevin could smell the cigarette butts that spilled from ashtrays on both bed tables, and stale whiskey, and suntan oil. The lampshade tilted up, exposing the light bulb left the way Jerry had turned it while they watched themselves dog-fuck in the dresser mirror. The empty Jack Daniels bottle lay on the floor below Jerry's foot, next to the motel towel with the brown smudge where Jerry had wiped Kevin's ass.

And Kevin gloried in it all. He lifted his elbow and took a long sniff of his armpit, the way Jerry had done while jacking off on the toilet the night before. He spit on his fingers and wet a patch of dried cum on his belly, then put it to his nose and smelled his own reconstituted semen. Gripping his hard-on, he closed his eyes and inhaled deeply.

"Me!" he whispered to himself. "Mine! This is what I want! Cock and cum and asshole sex with another man. This is what turns me on."

He longed to scoop Jerry into his arms, lift him up naked with the sheets and their dried cum and their undershorts and all the smells and all the booze and all the sweating and sucking and fucking and shooting off together, gather up the whole room and the night, and drag it with him all the way to California, and never let go of any of it forever.

He stepped through their scattered clothes and carefully settled onto the bed.

Fuck. I want to kiss you so fucking bad. His cock twitched in his hand. No, don't risk it. He'd be pissed again. He leaned over his hitchhiker's big chest. Has he got a hard-on under the blanket? He considered pulling the draped cloth away from Jerry's hand. No. I don't want to wake him up yet. This is too good.

The way Jerry had his elbow crooked over his body showed his black panther tattoo slinking down the outside of his thick arm, and on the inside a tuft of dark hair sprouted between the bulge of his muscle and his chest. The memory of that arm lashing out at his jaw made Kevin's heart thump nervously as he moved closer, getting his face back into an intimate proximity forbidden with another male. He bent down and put his nose and lips right up to the cleft where the underarm hairs curled out, and sniffed the acrid odor of his sleeping giant.

His dick stiffened in his fist. He whimpered out loud, "Muhhh!"

Jerry stirred. The big arm muscle bulged up and down as he twisted his forearm with his fist tightened. The glowering cat's paws moved. "Pant'er onna prowl," he croaked, with his eyes still closed. Kevin's hard-on grew slick in his hand. He kissed the tattoo.

"Mmm, yeah," Jerry sighed. "Turns me on." He flexed his arm again. "Lick all over it."

Kevin lapped his tongue across the cat and then sucked at the smooth skin. The mattress bounced as he masturbated shamelessly. Jerry raised his head and peered down. "You jerking off, man?" He laughed and coughed at the same time. "Over me?"

"Uh-huh," Kevin said, sitting back on his heels and displaying his erection to Jerry. "I've been watching you sleep. You aren't mad, are you?"

"Naw, I don't mind." Jerry yawned, distorting his words. "Nah affer—eeeeYUH—las' night. You beat off over my sorry bod all you want." He took a deep breath, put his fists to his shoulders, and raised his elbows up high. "Rub my belly," he grunted, arching his back.

Kevin put his hand under the blanket and made circles on the warm, hairy skin. Jerry squinted his eyes and twisted against the sheets. His abdomen hardened and then vibrated. Kevin laughed. "I can feel it in your stomach when you fart," he said.

Jerry grinned and squeezed out another. "You know, if I was king," he said, cupping Kevin's balls with his hand, "I'd put you on the payroll to be my own personal wake-up boy." His palm warmed Kevin's nuts. "Be your official assignment," he purred, tugging and fingering softly between Kevin's legs. "Jump in the sack with me every morning sportin' a big ol' boner like that, and then wake the king up right."

"You don't have to pay me," Kevin said. "Just tell me what to do."

"Okay." Boosting himself up with his elbows, Jerry punched his pillow behind his neck and looked down at the lump in the blanket. "First thing the king needs is a good scrotum scratch," he said, spreading his knees apart and making a tent. "King's always got itchy nuts first thing in the morning."

Kevin reached lower under the bedclothes and found Jerry's hairy bag, hanging down loose and warm and slightly damp. "Like this?" He nudged the soft pouch up with the back of his thumb and dragged his fingernails underneath, watching Jerry's face for approval.

"Yeah, like 'at," his king said, raising his arms and locking his fingers behind his head. The sour smell of his sweat blossomed in Kevin's face. "Get the right one now," he commanded, eyes narrowed to slits. Kevin fingered Jerry's right testicle with his nails. "Uh-huh. Now get upside the left one some more. Mmm-hmm. Now come right up the middle between the two of 'em. Yeah, right there."

Kevin's cock flamed in his fist as he felt another man's bare balls flopping about in his scrambling fingers. "Feels so fine," Jerry said, flexing his muscles and turning his face to sniff his underarm.

Kevin groaned. He leaned forward. He licked Jerry's open armpit, tasting salt on the fine hairs.

Jerry laughed. "King's wake-up boy is really throwing himself into his work," he said, twisting to reach for his cigarettes. "King likes that. Enthusiasm in the troops is a good thing."

"Muh!" Kevin moaned. "I'm so queer for your body it just makes me crazy," he said, running his hand back up the trail of hairs to Jerry's navel, inserting a fingertip into the knotty hole in his belly.

"Yeah, you got the main qualification for this job covered, I do believe." Jerry lit up and inhaled. "Play with my tits some," he said, blowing out through his nose as he dropped his lighter on the table.

With the sweet first puff of tobacco smoke filling the air, Kevin spread his hands over Jerry's chest and massaged the solid muscles. "I still can't believe you let me touch you like this," he said, circling his fingertips through the curls around the nipples. "It's so sexy that you're just kicking back and smoking while I feel up your body."

"You like that, huh?" Jerry put his free hand under the blanket. "Pull on my tits," he said, narrowing his eyes.

Kevin pinched Jerry's nipples and tugged at them.

"Harder," Jerry said. The blanket lifted and fell. "Harder."

Kevin got a better grip and stretched them out a full inch.

"Doesn't that hurt?"

Jerry squinted his eyes. "Uh-huh," he nodded. "'Specially when you do it for me. Two things I like to do when I beat my meat, is to suck on my tat and pull on my tits." He smiled shyly. "Gets me going real good when you do it for me." He took a puff and threw his head back to blow smoke straight up. "Harder," he breathed, tensing his chest.

Panting shallowly, Kevin pulled until Jerry stiffened and groaned, muscles bulging. He grimaced so alarmingly that Kevin slacked off the pressure, and Jerry slumped back against the pillow, grinning with his eyes closed. Kevin toyed with the two stubs, now red and elongated. "Your nipples get hard like little dicks."

Jerry looked down his chest. "Uh-huh. You got 'em sticking up like two little baby boners, huh. Standing tall." He licked his lips. "Just like the big guy down between my legs." The lump in the blanket rose and fell.

Kevin ran his palm down Jerry's chest, touching the bruise over his rib. He noticed a three-inch scar below it on Jerry's belly. Tracing it with a fingertip, he imagined Jerry in a hospital with a doctor slicing around inside his abdomen, taking out his appendix. He hesitated, envious that another man had touched a part of Jerry's interior that Kevin could never reach. He pushed the bedcovers down a few more inches, to the bare skin where Jerry's pubic hair began to bush out. "Can I see him now?" he whispered. "Can I see the big guy?"

Jerry pulled his hand from under the blanket and hooked his wrist behind his neck again. "You gonna be a good wake-up boy?" He took a slow draw on his cigarette. "Gonna treat the king's cock right?" He held the smoke out, butt end first.

"Oh, yeah." Kevin put his lips to it and took a puff. "I'm gonna be a real good boy."

"Okay. Head on down south and show me how good."

Kevin lifted the crumpled sheet and blanket.

Jerry's pale hard-on sprang up from the shock of black hair between his hips, standing tall indeed, robed and regal. Kevin scooted down by Jerry's side, kicking the blankets off the foot of the bed. His hitchhiker's manhood swayed proudly in front of his nose, smelling of Coppertone.

He touched a swollen blue vein. "This is the real king," he whispered. "Down here." The shape of the head showed through the foreskin. Kevin slipped it back until a circle opened and the tip peeked out, pink and glistening at the slit. "That's what you've got between your legs. The king of cocks."

"Think so?" Jerry held his cigarette down to Kevin's face again. "The king we all obey, huh." Kevin nodded and took a puff.

"Okay, whyn't you get all the way down there between my knees," Jerry said, stubbing out his smoke. He spread his legs apart. "Lemme teach you a trick with my dick."

Kevin curled up between Jerry's thighs, propped on one elbow. "Tell me what to do," he said, locking his legs around Jerry's calf.

"Can you suck your own cock?"

Kevin looked up from aligning his erection against Jerry's leg. "No," he said, and shrugged. "I used to try, but I can't quite get to it. Can you?"

"Nah. Used to be able to touch my tongue to it, back when I was skinny like you." He toyed with his nipples. "We'd all suck ourselves off if we could, huh?"

Kevin grinned. "I sure would."

"Okay, I'm gonna train you how I'd give myself a blowjob, if I could get my mouth down there to it."

"This is so queer," Kevin said, humping Jerry's calf. "We keep getting better at it."

"Yeah, champ, I'm working on that," Jerry said. "Here's the deal. Pull my foreskin up. All the way up over the head."

The fine skin rolled up in Kevin's hand and formed a pucker at the tip. Beyond it he could see Jerry staring down at it as he tugged his nipples out.

"Keep the hood up until I tell you, okay?"

He cupped Jerry's balls with his other hand, fascinated by their softly rolling heft, as Jerry's voice floated down to him. "Now open your mouth wide and put it as far down on it as you can go."

Looking up Jerry's belly and into his blue eyes, Kevin lowered his gaping mouth.

"Yeah," Jerry said, nodding and twirling his nipples. "Uh-huh, like 'at. Now close your mouth on it and give it a good suck. Get it good and wet."

Kevin engulfed it, an alien thing yet quite recognizable, a creature with a life of its own, vaguely reptilian, as strange in his mouth as a frog but familiar as a million secret orgasms in his hand. He wrapped himself around it.

"Ah-h-h, yeah-h-h," Jerry breathed. "Now, hold your mouth still and start pulling the hood down real slow, while you're sucking on it. Uh-huh, I wanna feel it roll back inside your mouth." Kevin obeyed, slipping his finger and thumb around the base and retracting the thin sheath through his lips.

Jerry sounded distant. "Go real slow, buddy, re-e-e-al slow. Mmmh! Quarter inch at a time. Peel it back. Eighth of an inch at a time. Fuck, sixteenth of an inch, oh yeah real slow."

Kevin could feel the foreskin withdrawing past his tongue, dilating around the head of Jerry's cock. When the knob popped free, Jerry groaned and put his hand on Kevin's neck. "Now!" he whispered, pushing down until the rounded head probed the back of Kevin's throat. He choked at first, but he held fast until he had to back off to breathe.

"Do it again, man," Jerry urged. Kevin obliged, running the foreskin up to loose folds between his lips, mouthing the whole thing, drawing the moveable skin down until it released the cockhead, then lunging forward to make it jab at his throat. He sputtered, his eyes watered, and Jerry's encouragement enthralled him.

"Get all over it, buddy," Jerry ordered, and he did. "Show me how much you love it," he whispered, and Kevin's erection burned against Jerry's leg. Kevin added flourishes, discovering he could retract the foreskin by pulling down on Jerry's balls, twisting his other fist around it on the upstroke, repeating, repeating, humping Jerry's hairy calf, knees clamped around him like a horny dog as he felt a slick spot spreading under his own dick.

The world receded. Kevin sucked grateful obscenities out of his sailor, teased him into helpless, plaintive cries, made him groan, "Yeah, Kev, buddy, oh fuck yeah like that!" then backed off to make Jerry collapse into breathless, trembling gasps of "More, man. More, buddy. C'mon, Kev, make me cum."

Cock connection. This is what I want. Complete connection with another guy's hard dick.

Knock knock knock.

Jerry jerked in his hands and hissed, "Shit!"

No! No! Not now! Kevin closed his eyes tight and pressed his face into Jerry's pubic hair.

"Room cleaning," a woman's voice came from outside.

Jerry cleared his throat and whispered, "I locked it last night."

"Nuh!" Kevin squealed through his nose. Go away! He's mine! Leave us alone!

But keys tinkled, the lock clicked, and the door swung open, just as Kevin raised his head and let Jerry's hard-on pop from his mouth. Sunlight glared around a girl carrying a stack of towels. She stepped inside, calling, "Hello?" Her brown face peered in past the white cloth. Her eyes locked with Kevin's.

"Oh!" she said.

Kevin stared back, too dismayed to speak. He realized that a strand of cum stretched from his lower lip to the tip of Jerry's dick, silver in the light, trembling with each thud of his heart.

"Oh!" the girl repeated. Then her voice lowered in comprehension, "Oh." Backing up, she bowed and mumbled, "Excuse, por favor, excuse, please." She bumped her elbow on the door and a towel fell on the floor before she disappeared.

Raised to be a polite Southern boy, Kevin considered briefly if he should pick it up for her. But her hand reappeared and snatched it up as she sang out, "Check-out time is eleven o'clock!"

The door slammed and the light dimmed again.

"Shit fucking almighty," Jerry muttered. "I know I threw that goddamn dead bolt last night."

Kevin wiped his lower lip, hesitated, and then licked his finger. Jerry rolled away and reached for the bed table. He squinted at his watch. "Fuck, man. It's after one o'clock. No wonder she's pissed." He got up and yanked the curtain open. "God damn it, she's heading straight for the office. She's gonna tell that old fart she caught us sucking cock. Shit!"

Kevin blinked in the light. "She's probably just going to tell him she can't get in to clean the room. Come back! I want to finish!"

"Did that bastard take my number down last night?" Jerry turned to him. "I showed him my Navy ID, remember? Did he write it down?"

"I don't think so." Kevin frowned. "I think he just looked at it." In the bright window light, he could see that Jerry's cock had gone completely soft.

"If that fucker calls the shore patrol, my ass is grass."

Kevin shook his head. "Jerry, we're in fucking Arizona.

There's no shore patrol at the Grand Canyon. I mean, for what, canoes? Come on back."

"Okay, the highway patrol. What if he calls them?"

Kevin remembered the cold stare the greasy old man had given him. "Oh, shit. He did write down my license plate number. And I know he caught on that I'm queer."

"Damn it! Now I can be blackmailed."

"What?"

"My security clearance. I told you, I work for the fucking admiral."

"So?" As Kevin stared at him, Jerry's neck and cheeks slowly reddened. "You're blushing," Kevin blurted.

"I'm brainwashed," Jerry muttered. He balled up his fist and smacked it into his palm. "Fuck! Now I'm a security risk, see? If anybody's tailing me, all they gotta do is talk to her." He bent over suddenly and grabbed their underwear from the floor. "Come on," he said, throwing Kevin's briefs to him. "We gotta get out of this dump."

Kevin wiped himself dry with his BVDs, watching dazedly as Jerry pulled clean shorts from his seabag and stepped into them. When Jerry's cock and balls disappeared behind white cloth, Kevin heard himself whimper. It was over. He sighed. His hairy animal now looked civilized.

"Jer," he began, but he didn't know what to say. Jerry looked up, stopping with one furry leg into his jeans. Kevin asked, "Can I, uh, borrow some of your underwear?"

Jerry pulled on his pants and tossed a second pair of his boxers onto the bed.

They dressed quickly, stuffing their things away unfolded, Kevin into his cardboard box, Jerry into his seabag. "Check for roaches in the ashtrays," Jerry told him, zipping his bag. While Jerry loaded the car, Kevin picked through the cigarette butts and then dumped everything into the trash. In the bathroom he swiped at the mirror and ran the water in the bathtub to rinse away the yellow puddle. He straightened the lamp in the main room, heaped the covers back onto the bed, kicked the dirty towel underneath it, and dropped the empty whiskey bottle into the can on top of the ashes.

Jerry came in and slapped the room key onto the dresser with a five-dollar bill under it. "That's, like, a week's pay in Mexico," he said, slipping on his aviator sunglasses. "Let's go."

At the door Kevin hesitated, looking back at the bed. He adjusted himself inside Jerry's loose-fitting boxer shorts. He flexed his asshole. He took a deep breath, smiled, and followed his new buddy out to the VW.

Yang-Qi
Teh-Chen Cheng

On a winter night, black and bitter as an herbalist's brew, old woman Kang gave birth to her first and only son. He emerged gasping and howling, his breath and body steaming in the dry, cold air. The baby gave off so much robust heat and energy that he nearly glowed.

They named him Yang-Qi.

By the time he could walk, Yang-Qi was toddling after his father's plow, flinging millet and barley by fistfuls into the freshly turned furrows. By twelve, he was proficient with a scythe and could cut and tie sorghum canes into bundles that he then sold at market, where he haggled harder than anyone else buying, selling, or bartering for their families' needs.

Although he carried himself like an adult while at the market, away from it he played and competed like all the other boys in the village. They raced laps around the pond and wrestled each other into submission for the fun and satisfaction of doing so. The boys teased Yang-Qi for having big square teeth and a wheezing laugh, but he didn't mind; he suffered no worse than his friends who had nicknames like Stink

Head, Fish Face, Fatso, and Dum-dum. They in turn called him Yang-Qi the Donkey.

Village life rarely changes. It moves like a cogged wheel turning a millstone. But boys change, gradually, almost imperceptibly. Their talk drifts from who could spit the farthest or eat the most pickled chilies to who could carry the most water pails furthest and fastest. Their lives were so guided by repetition and custom that new ideas entered their minds rarely and vaguely. They knew what they knew and were taught only what was necessary.

In this environment, Yang-Qi grew, slowly transforming from heavy-browed plowboy to strong-backed farmer. Like most of his friends, he developed a lean, defined body from working on the family farm, his skin retaining a year-round bronze. His unruly, cropped hair sprouted into glossy waves that curled about the nape of the neck when wet. The peach fuzz over his lip spread like moss across his cheeks and jaw, slowly stiffening into a rough beard that he kept shaven with a razor blade.

One hot day, after the morning fieldwork was done, Yang-Qi went to cool off at the pond. No one was there. By the way the sun hung in the sky he knew the market would still be busy for a while, so he swam out fully clothed to the sun-baked rock in the middle of the water. Once there, he stripped off his clothes and rinsed them clean before laying them out to dry on the tallest outcropping. He lay down on a shallowly submerged edge, pillowed his head with his hands, and enjoyed the scarce treat of being alone at the pond, the gentle water lapping along his hips, thighs, and between his legs. The heat beaming down and radiating off the rock made his scalp tingle, and something like a chill rippled down his spine, making his nipples hard.

A breeze skimmed across the water and over his body,

pleasantly tickling the hair in his armpits and groin. With eyes closed, he felt the water striders ricochet off his thighs and a dragonfly whiz around his upturned elbow. Soaking in all the vibrations like an antenna, his cock stirred and pulsed. Feeling hot, he splashed a handful of water over his crotch and stomach. The sudden coolness made his cock stiffen, throbbing, the foreskin drawing back from the plum-like head bobbing over his navel. He began jacking off—his balls, loose and hanging from the heat, jounced in the water. Beneath him the sun-warmed stone seemed to melt as the nudge and pull of small, insistent waves rocked him to and fro.

Suddenly, an unusual splash startled him. It was Dum-dum. He was treading water nearby, sending out ripples that broke against Yang-Qi's body.

"Don't stop," Dum-dum said, his eyes wide. Yang-Qi blushed hotly but he didn't stop. He got up on one elbow and continued to work his fist up and down his engorged cock.

Dum-dum swam closer. He held onto the edge of the rock with one hand, his other hand churning turbulently below the surface. His beefy shoulder twitched and flexed with the vigor of his pumping. Yang-Qi sighed and squeezed out a sparkling rivulet of his slick fluid.

"Taste it," Dum-dum said.

Intrigued, Yang-Qi did as he was told, having never thought to do anything else but smear the slippery stuff over his cock to ease the friction of his hands. He raised a glistening dab of it to his tongue.

"Good?" Dum-dum asked.

Yang-Qi nodded. It was like nothing he had ever tasted, at once faintly salty and subtly sweet. He milked his cock for more and stuck his fingers into his mouth. Then, with his spit-lubed hand, he jacked off some more.

Dum-dum squinted, suppressing a groan. His shoulders hunched in a concentrated contraction. He came so hard that he rose half out of the water, his thick pectorals and ribs flexing and glistening. He shook and shuddered three times before slowly sinking back down to his chin.

Yang-Qi watched his friend as if seeing him for the first time, fascinated by his broadly muscled torso and strong neck, his smooth, brown shoulders bejeweled with droplets. He felt his testicles draw up and the throbbing ache low in his belly like a light burning more and more brightly. His muscles clenched, and he clawed the smooth rock with his free hand for support. His hips bucked forward as volley after volley of white, hot cum splashed into the blue-green pond.

The light burning in his belly faded and Yang-Qi became aware again of the rock, the water, the sunlight sparkling on the surface. He looked at Dum-dum, who stared back, riveted, the reflection of water playing in his eyes. Yang-Qi sank onto his haunches and slipped into the water. As if suddenly self-conscious, Dum-dum blinked and swallowed. They gazed at each other in silence, the sun intense on their shoulders. Then Dum-dum uttered, "See you," and quickly swam back to shore.

Days passed, and Yang-Qi's curiosity grew. He was familiar with his own body, all the smooth and hairy parts, but he had never had another body to compare to nor to fill his imagination with, until now. During the day, mindlessly guiding the ox from field to pen, his thoughts would wander back to the pond with Dum-dum climbing out of it. He saw his friend gracefully stride up the bank, his broad back and narrow waist twisting slightly as he stepped out of the water. When he bent over to pick up his clothes, his pale, firm buttocks were thrust into the air like a white peach with a glistening trail of wet hair running down the middle. Yang-Qi remembered the back of his thighs and thick calves flexing as he inserted one leg and then the other into his loose pants.

In bed at night he aroused himself picturing Dum-dum in the pond, his thick shoulders and chest working as urgently as his hand pumping away underwater. He heard his soft voice saying, "Taste it," and he would bring his slicked fingers to his lips. He imagined over and over his friend's contorted face and tensed torso, his shuddering, and he would ejaculate into his hands cupped over the head of his cock. The first night he did this, he brought his smeared hands to his face and inhaled the deep musk of his own ejaculate, the scent like thousands of peeled and quartered persimmons. A thick dollop ran down his wrist and he lapped it up before it could spill onto the pillow. *Bitter-melon custard,* he thought as he rolled his tongue around in his mouth. If there were such a thing.

Two weeks passed, and the passion he felt turned into frustration. What nagged him most was the blank in his mind, the mystery hanging between Dum-dum's waist and knees. Picturing Dum-dum climbing out of the pond, droplets running down his back and legs, he would silently plead, *"Turn around! Please!"* but the event would play out unchanged every time, like the road to and from market. If he had only caught a glimpse of his friend—all of him—he would be able to imagine everything, and perhaps he'd be satisfied.

Washing up after work one day, Yang-Qi raised his arm and twisted his neck to inhale the heady scent from his own armpit. Sweat ran down his face to his lips and he wondered if his own smell and taste were unique or if Dum-dum would smell and taste the same.

The thought was maddening.

Driven to distraction, Yang-Qi decided to pay Dum-dum a visit. In all these years he had never sought anyone out on purpose, the days too full for planned diversions. He would catch his friends by happenstance, either at the pond or at the market, sometimes on the road. Now, his mind made up, he worried about what to do or say if he found Dum-dum. He came up with no reasons or excuses, but he plodded on anyway.

It was late in the day, the market would be empty soon, so Yang-Qi headed toward the pond. The only ones there were some younger boys shoving and tossing each other roughly into the water, playing Ruler of the Rock. "Donkey! Come play with us!" they shouted and beckoned. He waved back but shook his head, and marched around to the other side of the pond where a trail ran through the bamboo-covered hill to where he knew Dum-dum lived.

Yang-Qi had never gone into the bamboo forest, but he was resolute. He followed the trail up and around the side of the hill. At one point he looked through the bamboo and saw the blue-green pond, the rock, and the boys pushing and splashing. A perfect place to watch without being seen, he realized, but his thoughts were quickly interrupted by the sound of an axe striking wood. He resumed his pace.

A clearing appeared around a bend, and then a modest wood-plank house. Stripped logs lay in an orderly heap near where Dum-dum was swinging his axe, chopping another log into segments. He stood shirtless with his back to Yang-Qi, his legs splayed but planted firmly on the ground. Sweat darkened the waist of his pants.

Yang-Qi panicked and dived into the side of the hill, crouching in the tall grass. The resonant whacking of the axe disturbed the air. Slowly, Yang-Qi raised his head and eyed his friend, blood pulsing hotly in his neck and temples.

From chopping and hauling wood and bamboo all his life, Dum-dum had grown more thickly muscled than anyone in the village. Although he was almost a head shorter than Yang-Qi, Dum-dum's physique made him seem bigger all around. His solid thighs gave shape to his otherwise loose pants. His calves, bare below the rolled-up pants legs, were the size of pear-apples and looked just as firm. His upper back looked almost as wide as a door.

A sudden breeze caught the grass, sending ripples through the blades. A speck of pollen or dust tickled Yang-Qi's nose and he sneezed. The axe fell silent. He shrank and held his breath.

"Who's there?"

Thinking quickly, Yang-Qi answered, "Dum-dum, it's me, Donkey." He stood up, his heart drumming in his chest. "I was looking for wild ginseng. For my mother," he added.

Dum-dum dropped the axe and smiled. "They don't grow on that side," he said, stepping toward him. "I'll show you where you can find some." He reached out and pulled Yang-Qi up off the side of the hill.

Dum-dum excused himself to wash up at a water basin on the creaky porch. Watching him splash water on his face and feet, then wiping down his body with a wet rag, Yang-Qi almost forgot why everyone called him Dum-dum. Faint traces of the short, moon-faced boy with the wide-apart eyes and low forehead could still be found on this young man, his features still retaining some of his uncomplicated nature. But his confident air made Yang-Qi realize he certainly wasn't dumb.

"Come with me."

Dum-dum led the way up a steep hill behind the house. They cut through a dense swatch of old oak trees that gave way to more bamboo. Yang-Qi began to pant, sweat dotting his forehead. Dum-dum glanced back. "We're not far," he announced. Then he turned off the trail and began climbing through the bamboo thicket. Yang-Qi picked up his pace to stay close, not knowing where he was being led to and unsure, suddenly, of why he was there in the first place.

The bamboo opened into a small shady clearing, the ground covered in a soft layer of old leaves turning to mulch. A sparse scattering of ginseng poked their green leaves out of the soil to catch the filtered light, a few older plants sending up berry stalks.

Dum-dum looked at him expectantly, but Yang-Qi just stood there. He was caught lying and he knew it. His face flushed with embarrassment and his eyes burned with shame. Then Dum-dum took his hand. "I want to show you something," he said, and he pulled him into a dense bamboo grove.

A few feet into the grove, the tall bamboo having swung back into place behind them like a curtain, they came to a carefully cleared circle that had been maintained over a long period of time. A layer of dry green leaves carpeted the ground beneath them, the afternoon sun throwing down fluttering shadows of the leaves above their heads.

"No one's been here but me," Dum-dum said. "And now you."

Impressed, Yang-Qi walked along the perfect circle of bamboo and realized that what Dum-dum said was true. Not one smooth surface had been carved by a knife or snapped roughly in two, no sign of graffiti or horseplay. He turned to his friend and said breathlessly, "This is beautiful."

Dum-dum smiled proudly. Then, as if struck by an idea, he said, "Do this," and removed his pale cotton shirt, laying it on the nest of leaves. He laid himself down, put his hands under his head, and smiled up at Yang-Qi, waiting for him to follow suit.

Beautiful, Yang-Qi thought again, this time about his friend. He studied his body, the rise and fall of his rib cage and stomach as he breathed, the pale skin under his arms, and the thin wisps of wavy black hair in each armpit. His eyes followed the line of muscle flaring out from under his arms and tapering to his narrow waist, his navel winking from between the ridges of his abdominal muscles, up the furrow between his pectorals flowing into the sinews of his neck.

Nervously, he took off his shirt and spread it out beside his friend. But before he could lie down, Dum-dum reached over and pulled him roughly on top of him. He tipped his head and kissed Yang-Qi on the mouth. At first haltingly, then urgently, they sucked and chewed each other's lips and tongues, licked and bit each other's ears and necks. Walled inside the green and yellow poles with broken sunlight spotting their skin, they soon began to sweat.

Gradually, perhaps out of habit or instinct, the two began to wrestle. They grappled and rolled over their rumpled shirts, dried leaves sticking to their backs. While sucking on Dum-dum's neck, Yang-Qi slipped his hands into Dum-dum's and pinned them to the ground on either side of his head. He squirmed to get between Dum-dum's legs, hooked the back of his knees, and began to force his pelvis off the ground.

With a grunt Dum-dum bucked and flipped Yang-Qi unto his back. Like a shot he dove on top of Yang-Qi, grasped his pants, and yanked them hard, causing Yang-Qi's stiff cock to slap his stomach with a smack. Helplessly, Yang-Qi watched his pants sail through the air and catch on a bamboo branch high above their heads.

"Wait!" Yang-Qi cried, as if surrendering. Panting, Dum-dum put his hands up and allowed Yang-Qi to scoot up onto his knees.

"Yours," Yang-Qi demanded.

A small smirk crept across Dum-dum's lips. Slowly, he got to his feet. His loose pants were stretched out in front as if he had stuck a length of wood there. He stepped forward, the protuberance swaying and bobbing in front of Yang-Qi's face. A spot of wetness soaked the tip, and Yang-Qi recalled the taste of his own slick juice. He reached up and untied Dum-dum's pants. It slid off his narrow hips but was caught in front. With both hands, Yang-Qi lifted the soft sail of fabric off Dum-dum's rigid cock.

All those nights silently begging him to turn around, and now...Yang-Qi was reminded of tapered purple eggplant, elegantly curved cucumber, goose-necked gourds—things that he had never thought of as arousing before now took on a new significance.

Like the rest of his body, Dum-dum's cock was shorter than Yang-Qi's, but thicker. The shaft, which curved upward, tapered toward the head peeking out of the foreskin. A vein, like a fat earthworm, stretched out of his black pubic hair, down the center of the shaft, and disappeared into the minute folds of skin circling the crimson head. Below, his dark scrotum hugged the base of his cock like two braised eggs, smooth and brown.

Tantalized, Yang-Qi braced himself with his hands on Dum-dum's rock-hard thighs and planted his nose between Dum-dum's legs. He inhaled deeply, the sweaty musk igniting the air in his lungs. Dum-dum laughed and grabbed him by the hair to stop his burrowing. Instinctively, Yang-Qi opened his mouth and began lapping and then sucking on Dum-dum's balls, making him moan with pleasure.

As much as he enjoyed rolling those nuts around with his tongue and nibbling the tender sac with his lips, Yang-Qi inevitably worked his way up the underside of the shaft to the head of Dum-dum's cock. His mouth watered, saliva trickled out the corners of his mouth, and he plunged forward.

The taste and smell of him, the turgid flesh filling his mouth and throat...it was more than Yang-Qi could ever imagine. He sucked that cock ravenously, even reached around to wrap his hands on each hard mound of Dum-dum's ass to drive more of that cock into his throat.

Above him he heard Dum-dum catch his breath and sigh. One hand gripped Yang-Qi's shoulder, the other stroked the back of his head.

Yang-Qi sucked until he tasted the now familiar taste of

pre-cum. He pulled back and a silvery thread ran from his tongue to Dum-dum's cock.

"Your mouth is so warm," Dum-dum whispered, his eyes glazed lustfully. He bent down to kiss Yang-Qi on the mouth and pulled him to his feet.

Dum-dum pushed Yang-Qi up against the living wall of bamboo and began biting and licking his way down the side of Yang-Qi's neck, tongued and nibbled one nipple and then the other, then diving into his armpit. Yang-Qi swooned, melted, having never felt such intense pleasure. Dum-dum turned him around and came up from behind, biting his shoulder and running his tongue down the furrow of his back. Then he knelt, eased Yang-Qi's ass cheeks apart, and plunged his tongue into the dark, hot center. Yang-Qi grasped two bamboo poles for support, threw his head up to the sky, and let out a deep-chested sigh.

Everything happening was so new and unexpected. Yang-Qi became so hot that Dum-dum's body felt wonderfully cool, his palms like the flickering shade of leaves, his tongue like waves in the pond. Dum-dum guided his cock and balls back between his legs to lick and suck everything at once. Then he wriggled a spit-slicked finger into Yang-Qi's tight pink pucker and a flame of red and orange pleasure flared up in him like a struck match. He arched his back and thrust his ass out further. The more Dum-dum worked his finger inside him, biting his blushing buttcheeks and licking his nuts, the more he wanted, hungered for. A sensation rippled out of the pit of his stomach and Yang-Qi couldn't help but moan.

Dum-dum stood up and pressed something wet and fleshy against his quivering hole. Immediately Yang-Qi knew it was the engorged head of his cock, and was overcome with desire. He bore down. An explosion of lights and fireworks shot through him, his nerve endings crackling. He winced, held his breath, and waited for the stinging and burning to sputter out.

Dum-dum ran his rough but gentle hands all over his body, soothing him, easing him down. Gradually, Yang-Qi felt himself rearing back, the widening cock stretching him, filling him. Dum-dum spat where they were now joined and Yang-Qi felt it slide down his crack and drip off his nuts. Before he knew it, he was rubbing deep into Dum-dum's groin, the friction of pubic hair against his buttocks delicious. Dum-dum stepped forward, prodding Yang-Qi into an upright position. Yang-Qi hugged the bamboo, pressing his face and chest against the soothing coolness.

Dum-dum got onto his toes and began rolling his hips, his tapered cock sliding easily out and in. Yang-Qi moaned with each thrust, lost in the new sensations both outside and in. Becoming aware of the aching need to release his boiling juice, he grabbed his cock, now harder and more swollen than he had ever felt it, and pumped away frantically. Dum-dum pinched his nipples and began pulling his cock out and slamming it in with all his muscular heft.

The ache inside Yang-Qi radiated to a pulsing white. His muscles and joints locked in a massive convulsion as he sprayed his load, lashing the bamboo with fiery streaks. Just as the last gush of cum trickled over his fist, Dum-dum shoved up hard against him and yelped. He grabbed hold of the bamboo, pulled himself up deeply into Yang-Qi, and convulsed, his cock fluttering, throbbing, spurting inside him.

They remained joined for some time, clinging to the bamboo like a cicada emerging from its former skin. Then, gingerly, Dum-dum eased himself off. Yang-Qi turned and studied his friend, his sweat-glistening body and his flaccid but still swollen cock twitching sorely between his thighs.

Dum-dum looked down at Yang-Qi's own spent cock and said, "You *are* a donkey, you know," and Yang-Qi blushed.

They began getting dressed.

"I saw you at the rock that day," Dum-dum started,

reminding Yang-Qi of the view from halfway up the hill. "You should be careful no one catches you."

Yang-Qi pulled his pants off the bamboo branch in silence, thinking of the shame he'd have felt if he had been caught by anyone else.

"You should come here, where it's private," Dum-dum continued.

"I don't think I could find this place by myself," Yang-Qi answered truthfully.

"I'll bring you," Dum-dum offered. They smiled at each other and then laughed.

They made their way out of the thicket and back down the trail. Yang-Qi left his friend at his house and began the hike toward home.

"Come tomorrow," Dum-dum called after him. "You can help me pull bamboo shoots."

Along the way, Yang-Qi thought about the work that needed to be done the following day, and the day after that. For once he looked forward to the days and weeks ahead, rather than just floating along, season to season. And he'd see Dum-dum again, as invited. But now, strolling through the orange glow of the tiring sun, he savored the traces of Dum-dum on his tongue, on his hands, all over his body. He brought home a fresh crop of experiences that day, memories that he would enjoy all by himself later that night.

Pink Triangle-Shaped Pubes
Alexander Rowlson

It's forty minutes into geography class and you've glanced at
my chest five times. As soon as you realize that I'm looking
at you, you avert your gaze. You try to make me think that
you weren't looking at me, but I know the truth. I can see it
in your eyes. Every time you look at me, you turn into a deer
caught in the headlights. A blank expression falls across your
face as you think about all the dirty things that you want to
do to me, like taste my cum or tongue my hole. Whatever it is
that you fags do to each other.

You make me sick and I think that you know that. I think
that's part of the reason that you like me. It turns you on,
doesn't it? Oh! Caught you looking again, naughty little
boy. This time you're a bit bolder: I spy your little eye looking straight at my crotch. I'm half hard, so I decide to flex
my dick so it bulges in my pants. Didn't see that one coming,
did you?

You look at me, hopeful and nervous and timid. I look
you straight in the eye and mouth the word *fag* and watch the
pain and embarrassment wash over your face. You quickly

turn your head toward your paper and try as hard as you can to ignore me. I just stare at you from across the room.

Your hair is bright pink and the dye is coming off on the collar of your shirt. I imagine you in the shower for the first time after dying your hair. Half the dye washes out, staining all the hairs on your body. You even have pink triangle-shaped pubes. Thinking about this makes me laugh out loud. The girl in front of me turns around and smiles. She looks like a slut. I could fuck her. That makes me laugh too. I try to picture my cock pushing through her cherry-painted lips. I imagine grabbing hold of her ears and ramming my pole into the back of her throat, causing her to gag. She hasn't sucked as much cock as you have, so she doesn't know how to take it all in like a good bitch.

And then you start looking at me again. I know because I've been watching your eyes as they turned away from your paper and slowly made their way toward my leg. I try to catch the eye of my man Stan, and Stan's thinking the same. We look at each other and I point at you and mouth, *Watch*. I let out a whistle like a beer-bellied construction worker, causing you to look up. When you catch my eye I smooch my lips together and make kissing noises. Stan the man laughs, as do most of the kids around him. Half of them don't even know why they're laughing, but do so out of boredom.

The ruckus causes the teacher to stop writing out some tired passage on the blackboard and turn to the class in a half-assed attempt to make us be quiet.

You are mortified, and your public humiliation gives me a full hard-on. Your face turns bright crimson (just like your candy-ass hair) and your bottom lip starts to quiver. I know you won't cry, though. You haven't cried yet, and I've seen you get a lot closer than this. Like that time in gym, when me and Stan pantsed you in front of the whole class and you weren't wearing any underwear ('cause gay boys are such skanks) so the whole class saw your flaccid friend. But the best part was when the coach gave you trouble for being a perv and you had to run laps. I thought I'd see you cry then, but you didn't. And you're not going to now.

Your face is pretty when you look like this. You're pretty like a girl. I can't stop staring at you, and you can sense it. It embarrasses you even more and you squirm in your seat. I think about you sucking on my cock. You'd do it well. You've had a lot of practice. And, you've got those cocksucker lips. I can see your lips around my dick when I close my eyes. I start to flex my PC muscle, causing my cock to push against my pants and send shivers up my spine.

I remember the first time I saw your lips around a cock. It was at Queen's Park. Talk about the right place at the right time. I like going down there to watch; you never know what you're going to see, or who. I was leaning against a tree and watching some queers suck each other off in the shadows. I tried to match their rhythm with my hand as I jacked off. Some old geezer tried to swoop in for the kill, coming toward me and grabbing at my cock. I pushed his hand away, but he was relentless. Soon he had whipped himself out of his pants. I looked up at him and said, "You dirty fucking faggot!" and I spit in his face as I pushed him away. It was a good one too, lots of mucus. As he scrambled away, I made my way to another tree and watched the scene more closely.

I didn't know it was you at first because you had a hat on. The other guy had just come and you were standing up to get your turn. The hat hid your face, but as soon as your pants were around your ankles, I knew. Pink triangle-shaped pubes in the glow of the streetlight. I watched as you were getting your cock sucked, and kept on jacking off.

I shot into my hand, wiped it on the tree, and started walking up to the subway. I haven't been able to stop thinking about it since. Suddenly the bell rings. I gather my things and make my way out of class. As I pass you, I cuff you on the back of the head. You look up at me as I walk out the door and I wink at you.

Face Value
Scott Pomfret

I don't usually pay. But sometimes when the urge is on me
and my cock is hard and I've been pacing my apartment like
a panther and fingering my own ass raw—at those times I am
not afraid to pay. It makes me feel virtuous that I don't make
a habit of it.

A streetlight shines on the boys for sale. They're the ones
who are too old for Social Services to care about. The state
owes you nothing once you turn eighteen, so the boys cluster
on the sidewalk, a bunch of pistons at different ranges of the
stroke: some on the curb, some butts astride their backpacks.
Most leaning on the wall for display. You can take your time
picking among them, whatever you might want for the night.

The first time I saw Chevy, he stuck out from a hundred
paces. He wears two thin silver earrings. His hair collects
streetlight. His cheeks keep the last rose of his teens, and
his eyes capture something liquid and sullen. His ass is a perfect grab.

"I'm very bad," he drawls, and raises his arched eyebrows.
"And I'm very, very good." He licks his lips, so they shine. He

quotes a price that's too high. When I object, he says simply, "It's all about value, you get what you pay for. You got to pony up the coin." He turns sideways and exhibits his profile. Shrugs like he doesn't give a shit whether you buy him or not. Sweat gathers in the depression between his collarbones, trembles, and falls, drawing a neat wet line between his nipples. The other kids step aside to let him go first, bowing to the inevitable, and the fact that, once Chevy is out of the way, competition will be more favorable.

In my apartment, I can't take my eyes off the muscled belly, the smooth chest, the lean, angled hip to which my hand automatically strays. My own breath frightens me. My mouth dries and it is hard to breathe.

"I want you."

"I know."

He is wary at first, trying to sense what I'm looking for. Then, increasingly playful, he binds my wrists with my shirt as he pulls it over my head. He twists a nipple. He kneels at my belt, in a sudden hurry as he drags down my pants.

"Let's see what we're dealing with," he says and pulls my cock from my trousers. "Oh, very nice." He turns it over, sights down the shaft as if it were the barrel of a gun. "Very nice. You have to keep this thing registered?" He asks playfully. "As a dangerous weapon?"

He breathes hot fire until my cock is taut as a bowstring. He mimes a hand job, barely touching my skin. I reach down to force him, but he swats my hands away. He gargles my balls, and works his way backward, under me, away from my dick along the shaft to my ass. Where he bites me hard enough to make me jump.

He propels me to the bed. The base of his hand forces my lower back. His thumb-ring pings my spinal column. He lies on me with his cock in my crack.

"Is this what you want?"

"Oh, Jesus," I gasp, "fuck me."

"I'll fuck you like you've never been fucked," he breathes in my ear. His mouth sounds full. It is. A slow drool of saliva, like a long slow finger, drips between my shoulder blades. He spreads it with his lips. Then slides down my back until the same thick drool is froth in my ass. His finger rides up in me. He props my hips, reaches in under my sac. His wet hands make a mess of me.

"Do you like that?" Over and over he repeats the question, until I groan and twist and snap: "Of course I like it! Now wouldja fuck me, please!"

He turns me over as if he is ready. But when I face him, on my back, receptive, knees bent, he sits up. He lets me stare at him, a bemused smile on his face. He runs his hand over his body, like a shy, flushed girl—first at his neck, then touching his nipple and belly. He licks a finger and inserts it in his belly button. He lets the hand play at the fringe of his crotch. He brings the finger to his nose and sniffs. His cock is beautiful, a rocket twitching on the pad before takeoff, worn red in contrast to the golden rose of the rest of him.

"Do you want me still?" he asks.

I loop my ankles behind his thin hips and yank him down on top of me.

He becomes another person. He wields a condom the way a magician works a magic handkerchief: It just appears in his palm. He spreads my cheeks and begins to fuck me, angling his penis around to give himself some more space, gripping my knees hard to leverage himself inside. He butts me like a ram until my neck is crooked against the headboard. He climbs up on me until he is a long flat firm board, his hands gripping the headboard, anchoring his lower half. He fucks me like that, as if he were a bridge across my bed, his muscles taut, touching me with only his cock and the occasional wet kiss of slapped hips. When I can stand it no longer—and it goes on for days and nights; kingdoms are born, rise, and fall; stars burn and shoot off into the night; gods age and are forgotten—I tug myself off in a rhythmic hand-chatter to his deep grunts.

"I want you! I want you! I want you!" he says over and over, until I explode semen into my own chest hair. He thrusts three more times, hard, and then pulls out, and there's a barnyard stench of ass in the air. He studies me with a look so hot I twitch and shudder.

He spoons me with an embrace as light as a feather. His cock is a red-hot brand. I reach for it, but he knocks my hand away. "This is your night," he says. And I know he means: It isn't the point for him to get off, and besides he can save it for another trick.

Or for me, if I want to pay again.

We kill time talking. Chevy says he's from a little town in northern New Hampshire, where his mother is the town skank. She fucks the police chief for her yearly get-out-of-jail-free card. She fucks the mayor. "I hear she gives head almost as good as me," he says.

Chevy loves her. She's fierce on his behalf and proud. But he knows she isn't going to help him get anywhere. "She doesn't have the juice," he says. "It's too late for her. She doesn't know how beautiful she is."

Normally, I don't listen to a street kid's lies. My skepticism is a powerful prophylactic. But Chevy's so open in talking about love, and so good a talker, that his tale of sorrow infects me with sympathy. By the time he's done, I don't really want to fuck him. But I do. Can't give up this chance, 'cause I might not see him again, what with the turnover on the street being so high, and me not usually needing to pay for what I do.

I grab his ankles as if he were a baby and lift him up as if to diaper him. His asshole is a perfect flower. I smell him and taste him, and then flicker my tongue. He obliges with a few tender groans, a pant like a coal train, then I push my tongue as far into his ass as I can. When I fuck him, I take it slow.

"Must be a hard life," I say.

"Not really. One way or another, everyone sells themselves to get by."

I find it endearing the way Chevy likes to say hard things and call them the truth, as if to demonstrate that he does not blink in the face of life. As he assembles his clothes a little after midnight, I'm satiated, full of tenderness and mercy. And sorry about his skanky mother and tough rural childhood and his rabid ambition that's not matched to where he started in life. It's amazing how sympathetic an orgasm will make you.

Impulsively, I invite him to spend the night. Wave a hand at my apartment. "Not a bad place. Penthouse. Jacuzzi."

He glances at his watch, which never came off while we fucked. He mentions a fair figure for cuddling, and I agree to half that. At dawn, he resumes dressing.

"Don't go," I say. "I'll call into work, tell them I'm late."

"Can't," he says. "I only work nights. I have class."

"Class?"

He looks up, insulted. But that look dies away from practice; he has learned not to antagonize the johns. He explains he's in college, he pays for it with tricks, he's got to get ahead.

Yeah, yeah, yeah, I think. Whatever. And I invite him back for another night of fun. That night becomes another, and another after that.

By the third day, I'm embarrassed to admit that I'm half in love. I get hard at the sound of his voice. I had forgotten it's possible to fall in love like this, and scold myself for acting like a schoolboy with the captain of the wrestling team. Lord have mercy, I say to myself, you're forty-five years old.

With a forced, casual air—as if his answer did not matter one way or another—I ask at the end of the third date, "Chevy, why don't you come live with me? Seriously. Bring all your stuff."

It's the wrong thing to say and we both know it; play with it; tongue over, taste, test, sniff it.

I might as well have dropped an anvil on his toes. He looks at me a long, long time. Then he says, "I'm still going to work. I don't want to be dependent. Got it?"

I nod.

It's against his better judgment, and certainly against mine. But if he robs me, he robs me, I say to myself and I know I am lying and should run from this thing with my hands over my head and no look back.

"Someday," he promises as he moves in, "I'll pay you back. I'll give you the fuck of your life."

"You already did."

"The first night? That was nothing."

I am astonished. That first night has become everything to me. I think of it all the time. It seems impossible that he doesn't have the same sense that we were brought together by forces bigger than ourselves. It makes me horny just to think about it.

For weeks afterward, I have no clue what Chevy's thinking. I can't tell if he enjoys making it with me, or if it's just a series of mercy fucks. One night before he goes out, I suggest he quit his work. "I'll take care of the bills. What have you got to worry about?"

"I can't let you hold me back," he whispers. "I'm going places."

"Hold you back? Me? Hold you *back?* I'm legal counsel to three-billion-dollar corporations! I advise the governor! I'm in a position to help you. I know people in this town!"

"I don't need help. I can do it on my own. Besides," he

adds gently, "you're old. Me, I'm just beginning."

Old? Old? I look in the mirror, and a forty-five-year-old stares back at me, a complete stranger. I've never known anyone, let alone a goddamn prostitute, who was so capable of making me feel so suddenly like shit.

"Do you like me, Chevy?"

"Of course I like you."

"What do you like about me? What exactly?"

He nuzzles my neck, murmuring sweet nothings, joking about who else could pay the rent. I shove him away.

"I'm serious."

He stares at me for a moment and then says firmly, "I like you because I don't have to lie to you. Don't spoil that."

Sometimes, when I come home in the afternoon, the apartment reeks of lust and jizz and sweat and I know he's been bringing the businessmen home at lunchtime, which is against the rules of our arrangement.

"It's not businessmen," he says, modestly. "It's my professors." His wicked smile takes away the sting, as if it were all a big joke between us, we two men of the world. I force a smile, because I can't jeopardize the fuck of my life, which looms bigger and bigger.

Chevy is the only person in my life whose attention is worth getting. I beg him to tell me about his johns down to the very last detail, and I listen to these stories with the awed fascination with which one watches a train wreck.

At dinner parties, I watch Chevy work my friends. He listens long enough to be able to spout their opinions back to their face. He laughs at their terrible jokes. On the way home, Chevy admits that he gave head to the host in the back room for $250. "It was too good a deal to pass up," he apologizes. "Your friends have a lot of money," he adds admiringly.

"Fags always have money," I snap.

"I know."

"Of course you do. You're a goddamn prostitute!"

He says nothing.

"I want to watch you fuck someone," I propose.

His eyes shift toward me in the dark. "I don't know," he says warily.

"I'll pay."

"Let me think about it." He rearranges himself in the passenger seat, so his back is half-turned to me and his head is against the door. But in his reflection in the window, I see his eyes are restless. After ten minutes of pure silence, he advises, "Don't fall in love with the help."

"You're more than 'help' to me, Chevy."

"I know. That's the problem." He turns his face to me. The crease in his brow makes him more gorgeous than I've ever seen him. He offers a hopeless shrug. Chevy seems to have known long before me everything that I feel—even that I have fallen in love. He seems to have known these things so far in advance of me that it is utterly necessary to prove him wrong.

"Hey, Chevy, I'm not in love with you."

"Of course you're not."

"Get over yourself, Chevy. You're not *that* hot."

He flashes a wicked grin. "Get over myself? Would you get over yourself if you looked like this?"

One night, Chevy says, "Look, I've been meaning to ask you. I've got to do an in-call tonight. Do you mind making yourself...you know...scarce?"

I fiercely hope the john's some homicidal monster from whose clutches I can save him. I listen through the bedroom door to Chevy's champagne laugh. Bitterly, I remember him telling me, "The trick is to tell the johns what they want to hear—if they want to hear I'm with women, too, I tell them that. If they want to hear 'I love you,' I tell them that. If they just want to fuck, all the better."

I push the door. The hinge is perfectly oiled. They are on the bed together, sweating like a cold glass of lemonade in the summer sun. Chevy's gripping the headboard. His feet are on the john's chest. The john is staring down at where his cock enters Chevy as if he's sure he'll lose his way, or can't quite believe his good fortune at fucking such a perfect ass.

Chevy flashes me a quick, sharp look over the john's shoulder. Then he relaxes. He lets his mouth fall half open. He doesn't care if I respect him. *This is what I do,* his posture seems to say, *it should come as no surprise to you.*

I spank it as I watch, and don't clean up the jizz on the floor. I retreat from the room and pace the apartment, skinned and raw. The slightest city noise is an assault, a breath of fresh air is a screaming abrasive, the least murmur is a condemnation. Chevy does not love me. He will never love me.

After the john has left, I climb into bed beside Chevy. I smell the john's sweat. I see the crinkled foils on the floor next to the bed, a tube of uncapped KY next to it, with a lick of lube dangling from its opening.

"Give me the fuck of my life, Chevy," I demand. And then I begin to cry, surprising even myself. I don't usually pay for what I do.

He cradles my head, then pushes it down, down his perfect chest, down his chiseled abs, to the line of pubic hair. He presses his cock to the back of my throat. I am as hungry for him as I was on that first night. I would trade my soul for a fuck with him that does not end.

I lie on my back. He straddles my chest. His cock is in my face. His crotch has been buzz cut. At first, I suck him, but then he's fucking my mouth. His quaking hips explode into a one, two, three, as he rams his cock into the back of my mouth, performing a sudden inadvertent tonsillectomy. He takes his cock out of my mouth and beats my lips with it.

Then he straddles my face. His balls rest on my cheekbones. His shaft is like the bar of a jail cell and I follow it down to his ass and try to lick my way out. He sits on me, hard, and I think I'm going to be smothered in pure ass. The panic excites me. I bite and chew and my tongue finds its familiar way inside him.

He rolls me onto my belly. His hands lend an electric hum to my skin. The tip of his cock makes a home in me, slowly, insistently, a little more each time, until the whole of it is in me.

I am paralyzed. I know it's a mercy fuck, and I know he means for me to know. He's giving me this one last chance to win back my pride. To throw him out on the street where he belongs.

But pride loses to this one last chance to pretend.

"Tell me you love me," I choke out.

"What?"

"Tell me you love me." It seems a necessary ingredient of the fuck of your life.

He nibbles my ear. His breath is all fire. I am listening to seashells telling me dirty, ancient songs. I am listening to gibberish and magic spells. Obediently, he tells me he loves me. For a moment, I take those sweet words at face value. They are the worn, velvet soreness of a fucked rectum, the trembling animal heat caged in strong arms. They are what it means to make love.

I reach for myself. He is pounding hard now and my insides are soft and then he catches himself. He slows to a point so excruciating, I gasp. I push back against him, to get him in me again, where he belongs. My ass is suddenly empty and anguished. And I feel him, just at the door again, on the threshold of my ass. And his swelling makes me swell, and a fiery rush ignites there, spreads quickly up my shaft, in a heated circle from this one source, and I gush all over the sheets.

He pulls from me immediately, tears off the condom, and beats himself off. He sprays jizz all over me, like a champion athlete in a locker room shaking the champagne with a thumb on the mouth of the bottle, an outrageous celebration of his body over mine.

Gamblers
Bob Vickery

There's an empty seat at the blackjack table where Sam's dealing, and I quickly slide into it. I push two five-dollar chips in
front of me as he deals out the cards. Sam nods at me, and
smiles. "Hello, Al," he says, in his friendly baritone. "Nice to
see you again."

"Hi, Sam," I say. "Thanks. It's good to be back." This is
the casino that feels most like home for me on my frequent
trips to Reno, and by now I've got a nodding acquaintance
with just about all of the staff. Sam's my favorite dealer, big-
boned and easygoing, with a handy smile that flashes white in
his tanned face.

I glance around quickly at my table mates: a middle-aged
couple with matching aloha shirts, a leather-faced cowboy, an
old woman with gimlet eyes and a permanently bitter mouth,
and a kid with a Grateful Dead T-shirt and torn, faded Levis.

Sam's done dealing, and my face card is the queen of diamonds. I sneak a look at my down card. Two of clubs. Damn.

"Hit me," I say, and Sam hits me with a nine of hearts.
Things are looking up. "I'll stick," I say. Sam goes around the

table, ending with the kid, who stays with what he has. Sam flips over his cards. Two jacks.

"Fuck!" the kid mutters.

"Hey, watch the language," Sam says, fixing him with a look as he takes the kid's chips.

The kid just shrugs in disgust. I give him a closer look. He's young, barely out of his teens, and he looks like a punk: black hair greased and combed back, a surly baby face, eyes dark and contemptuous. The torso under his tight shirt is lean and muscled, and his bicep curls to a nice pump when he raises his cigarette to his mouth. I catch Sam's eye, nod toward the kid and raise an eyebrow. Sam rolls his eyes and shakes his head. *The kid's bad news* is his silent message.

The kid takes what's left of his chips and pushes them in front of him. "Okay," he says. "Enough dicking around. I'm going for broke." I put out my standard ten-dollar bet.

Sam deals the cards again. He deals himself an ace and a queen. "Blackjack," he says. The kid slaps his hand on the table. "Motherfuck!" he snarls.

"I warned you about the language," Sam says. "Keep it up, and you're going to have to leave the table."

The kid gives a bitter laugh. "Big fuckin' deal. I'm broke anyway." He stands up, and his chair tips over and crashes to the floor. He stalks away from the table and gets lost among the slots.

The old woman shakes her head. "Loser," she mutters. The others at the table nod in agreement. Still, I can't help feeling a little sorry for the kid. Some folks just don't know when to quit.

Later that night, out in the parking lot, I notice an old, beat-up Pinto parked next to my car, badly dinged and mottled with primer paint. I glance inside it as I unlock my door. The kid's curled up in the back, asleep. *Jesus Christ*, I think, shaking my head. I climb into my car and drive off.

Sunday morning, I check out of my hotel and head for home. I did all right this weekend, winning enough to cover my expenses and even walk away with a hundred or so extra dollars. As I approach the Highway 80 on-ramp, I notice a hitchhiker standing at the side with his thumb out. It's the kid who lost at Sam's table.

I don't normally pick up hitchhikers, but, I dunno, maybe because I have a little history with the kid I make an impulse decision and pull over. He grabs his duffel bag and hops in.

"Thanks, man," he says.

"Where you headed?" I ask.

"Bakersfield."

"I'm going to Modesto. That'll get you part of the way at least."

"Cool."

We make the introductions, and the kid tells me his name is Billy. We drive down the highway in silence for a couple of minutes. "What happened to your Pinto?" I finally ask.

Billy shoots me a sharp glance. "How did you...."

"I saw you asleep in it a couple of nights ago in the casino parking lot."

"Oh," he says. He looks out his window and then back at me. "I sold it at a used car lot." He snorted. "The sonovabitch only gave me a couple of hundred bucks for it."

Which you pissed away at the blackjack tables, I think. It's not even worth asking him about. He's looking out the window, and I sneak a glance at him. I take in the quarter profile he's offering me: the left jawline, the tip of his nose, the young, strong neck.... He turns suddenly to face me, and I glance away.

We travel down the highway for a long time without saying anything. After a while, Billy slouches down into his seat and closes his eyes. He starts snoring lightly. I look at him again. He's a handsome kid, his face boyish but just beginning to take on the shape of a man's. His mouth, half open now, is wide and sensual. My eyes slide down his tight, muscular torso and settle on the bulge beneath the crotch of his tattered jeans. I glance back at his face again, and see his eyes staring back, fixing me with a sharp, knowing look. Neither of us says anything as I direct my eyes back to the road.

Traffic comes to a dead halt just outside of Elk Grove. The highway's a fuckin' parking lot, nothing but cars, bumper to bumper, for as far as the eye can see. I turn on the radio and find a traffic report, which tells us that there's a five-car pile-up just north of Stockton that has traffic backed up for twenty miles. After two hours, we creep no further than half a mile. "Screw this," I say. "I'm going to get a motel room, and finish this trip tomorrow." Billy says nothing.

We inch up to the next exit and pull off the highway. There's a Holiday Inn just down the road, and I pull into the parking lot. The sun is beginning to set, and the shadows from the motel buildings fall across the asphalt paving. I turn off the ignition and turn towards Billy. "Okay, Billy," I say. "This is where we part company."

Billy just looks at me. "Can I sleep in the back of your car?"

"I don't think that's a good idea," I say. "I'm sorry." Billy doesn't say anything. I don't bother asking if he's got money for a room. "You need to get out, now, Billy," I say, putting an edge to my voice. Billy still doesn't say anything. "Billy..." I say.

Billy turns to me. "I got nowhere to go, man," he says.

I give Billy a long, level look. "All right," I finally say. "Just don't scuff up the upholstery with your shoes, okay?"

"Sure," Billy says. "No problem."

I check in and secure a room. I grab dinner in the motel restaurant, deliberately pushing Billy out of my mind. As I walk back to my room, I notice how cold the night has gotten.

Once inside, I stretch out on the double bed and turn on the TV. After about an hour of this, I turn it off. *Fuck*, I think savagely. I put on my coat and walk out to the parking lot. There's a pole fixture near by, and by its light I can see Billy curled up in the back seat.

I open the door, and Billy raises his head and looks at me. "Okay," I snap. "There's a couch in my room. You can sleep there. Or the floor, if you prefer."

Billy's face is in shadow, so I can't see his expression. "Just let me get my duffel bag," he says.

Inside, the first thing Billy does is head for the bathroom. "I'm going to take a shower, okay?" he says.

"Fine," I say. He's probably long overdue. God knows when he's last slept in an actual room with a bath.

I lie back in my bed and go back to watching the television, half-listening to the hiss of the shower. After a few minutes, Billy comes out, a towel wrapped around his waist. He sits in a chair that faces the bed, grinning. "I fuckin' needed that," he says.

I grunt something, trying not to stare at how the muscles of his torso are cut, the stomach lean and chiseled. I turn my attention back to the television, but I keep sneaking glances in Billy's direction. Billy returns my stare calmly. Each time I look at him, his legs are spread a little wider, until I finally get to see that he's got half a hard-on, flopped against his thigh. My dick is straining against the fabric of my slacks like there's hell to pay.

I give Billy a hard stare. He smiles. His dick is fully stiff now. "Look," I say. "You don't have to do this. I wasn't attaching any strings when I said you could sleep here."

Billy undoes his towel and lets it fall beside him. He's slouching in the chair, and his stiff dick lolls lazily against his belly. It's a beauty, fat and veined, the head a red, shiny knob. He twitches it, and gives me a sly look to gauge my reaction. "I'm not doing anything I don't want to," he says. His balls hang heavily between his legs, furred by a dusting of fine, dark hairs. I imagine them slapping against my chin as he fucks my mouth.

"Christ," I mutter. I climb out of the bed and bury my face in his red, wrinkled sac, tonguing it, inhaling deeply. In spite of Billy's shower, his balls have a faint, musky scent to them. I open my mouth and suck them inside, rolling my tongue over them. "Yeah," Billy murmurs. "That's right." I look up and lock eyes with him, his ballsac still in my mouth. Billy's mouth curls up into a slow grin. "Why don't you get naked, Al?" he says.

"Yeah," I say, standing up. "Good idea." I unbutton my shirt while Billy unbuckles my belt and pulls my zipper down. My slacks slither down to my ankles, and with a quick yank Billy tugs down my boxers. My dick springs up and sways heavily from side to side.

Billy looks up at me, grinning. "Jesus, Al," he says. "What a big dick you have!"

"Who the fuck are you?" I ask. "Little Red Riding Hood?" Billy laughs. I pull him to his feet, and we kiss, our bodies squirming together, flesh on flesh. Billy's tongue snakes into my mouth as he grinds his hips against me. I wrap my arms around him in a bear hug and topple us onto the bed.

We wrestle on top of the bedspread, our mouths fused together. "Scoot up my chest," I say, "and drop those balls in my mouth."

"Sure, Al," Billy says. He straddles my torso, his dick and balls looming above my face. I crane my neck and start washing his low-hangers with my tongue. I suck the meaty, red pouch into my mouth, and reach up and tweak Billy's nipples.

"Yeah, that's right," Billy breathes. "Squeeze them hard." I lock my gaze with Billy's as I roll my tongue around his balls and give his nipples an extra twist. Billy's eyes burn into mine with the look of a man with a serious nut to bust. He rubs his cock over my face, smearing my cheeks with pre-cum, and then shifts his position and pokes the fleshy knob against my lips. I open my mouth, and Billy slides his cock full in until his balls are pressing against my chin and my nose is buried in his crinkly pubes. He holds that position for a few beats. "You like that, Al?" he croons. "You like having your mouth stuffed with dick?"

I grunt my assent. Billy begins pumping his hips, fucking my face with slow, measured thrusts. He reaches behind and wraps his hand around my dick. "You got such a nice, fat dick, Al," he says. "I'm just going to have to suck it for a while." He pivots around. I feel his mouth slide down my shaft, and I groan appreciatively, my mouth still filled with his dick. We fuck face and suck dick, our bodies pressed tightly together. I slide my hand down Billy's back, across the smooth, tight mound of his ass, and into his asscrack. I find his asshole and massage it. Billy gives a muffled groan, and I push in, working my finger up his chute knuckle by knuckle.

Billy takes my dick out of his mouth. "Jesus," he groans.

"You want me to stop?" I ask.

"Fuck, no!" he says.

I slide my finger in and out of his hole. Billy's got a spit-slicked hand wrapped around my dick and is jacking me with quick, urgent strokes.

I add a second finger to my first, and Billy squirms. "You like that, baby?" I grunt.

"I'd like it better if it was your dick," he says. I hesitate. "I have a condom in my back pocket," Billy says, reading my thoughts. He jumps out of bed, picks up his jeans, and fishes out the condom and a small bottle of lube. "Here," he says, tossing it to me.

I toss the condom back. "You do the honors," I say.

Billy gives my dick a few last sucks and then rolls the condom down my shaft, greasing it liberally. He rolls over onto his belly.

"No," I say. "Turn around. I like to look into a man's eyes when I shove my dick up his ass."

"Sure, Al," Billy says, grinning. "No problem." He flips onto his back, I seize his calves and wrap his legs around my torso. I probe against his asscrack and pop the head of my dick in his hole. "Fuck, yeah!" Billy groans. I thrust my dick full up his ass, pumping my hips, slowly at first, my cockshaft sliding out of Billy's ass to the very tip and then plunging full in again. I pick up speed, pumping my hips faster now, and Billy pushes up to meet me, squeezing his ass muscles tight, clamping down on my cock with a velvet grip. I bend down, and we kiss, lots of tongue and squirming flesh on flesh. I wrap a lube-smeared hand around Billy's dick and jack him off as I thrust in and out of his ass.

Billy closes his eyes and pushes his head against the pillow, arching his back up to meet me thrust for thrust. He opens them again, and I pin him down with my gaze as I skewer his ass with a series of quick, deep strokes. Our bodies are slippery with sweat, and they come together in wet, slapping sounds. I twist Billy's nipples. Billy reaches behind and pulls hard on my balls.

"Yeah," I snarl. "That's right. Give my balls a good tug." I can feel the orgasm rising up inside, ratcheting to the trigger point. Billy gives my balls another tug just as I plunge deep into his ass, and that's all it takes to push me over the edge. I groan loudly, thrusting deep into Billy, my load pulsing out into the condom up Billy's ass.

I start jacking Billy faster, and just when my dick gives its last throb he cries out and arches his back. His spunk squirts out and splatters against his belly. I quickly bend down and take his dick in my mouth, catching the last of his load as it pulses out. I give Billy's dick a few good sucks, and then fall on the bed beside him. I slip my arm under Billy and pull him toward me, giving him a lingering kiss. "Goodnight, baby," I say.

Billy smiles. "G'night."

When I wake up the next morning, Billy's not in bed. I think that he might be in the bathroom until I notice that his clothes are no longer strewn on the floor. Then I notice that his duffel bag is gone and that my pants, which had been lying at the foot of the bed last night, are now on the floor by the door. My belly clenches. I leap out of bed and grab my pants, praying that I'm jumping to conclusions. A quick check reveals that my wallet and car keys are missing. "GODDAMN, FUCK, SHIT, PISS!" I snarl, slamming my fist against the wall. I walk the length of the room and then come back and slam the wall a few more times.

Out in the parking lot, I stare at the empty space where my car had been. Rage slams into me like a gale-force wind—pure, blind rage like I've never felt before. "BILLY, YOU MOTHER-FUCKER!" I scream. I stand in the middle of the lot, panting.

After a few minutes I calm down enough to weigh my options. The whole day stretches out ahead of me like some field of shit I'm going to have to slog through: getting hold of the local police, calling the credit card companies, somehow arranging to get back home…. It's all just too fuckin' much. *What the fuck possessed you to pick that little hoodlum up?* I think furiously. *Everything was going fine until then.* As I walk across the parking lot to the motel lobby, I think that that's one thing that punk and I had in common. Neither one of us knew when to quit while we were ahead.

The Thanks You Get

Simon Sheppard

"Never make a neurotic your footslave." He pulls the rope tighter around my balls.

"Ouch!" I yelp. "That hurts!"

"It's *supposed* to hurt," Sir growls.

"Not like that. You pinched my skin." I try—and I think succeed—to maintain a tone of respect.

"So I took the guy to this play party." Sir is fiddling with my scrotum. "All around, guys were fisting, whipping, moaning, barking orders like they were in some Falcon video."

"Saying stuff like 'Suck that dick'?"

"Yeah, 'Suck that dick.' " He readjusts the rope, like the nice guy he is. To look at him—at the photo of himself he sent over the Internet, scowling in full leathers, brandishing a pair of handcuffs—you'd never guess he worked as a dresser at the opera. Really, you wouldn't.

I sigh, the way happy bottoms do. "Mmm. That feels better." A pleasant, familiar ache spreads through the base of my belly.

"And he was just lying there in hog heaven, with my

sneaker over his face," he continues. "Not my boot, see, but my old black leather hightop. Because he just loved to sniff dirty sneakers."

"And because you're a very good Sir, Sir."

He smiles. "And even when I was standing on his chest and spitting on him, the scene seemed so damn low-key. Other guys were walking by, guys in straitjackets, guys with needles through their flesh, and they were looking at *us* like we're perverts. Which we were, of course. But not in the generally approved SM way."

I smile back, in a way that I hope conveys that I'm laughing with him, not at him. He has my dick pretty well tied up now, balls stretched and separated, cock confined so the head is darkish purple and bulging. He reaches over and fumbles in his toy bag for a second, in that slightly incompetent way I find so charming. When his gloved hand emerges, it brings with it his favorite set of titclamps.

"And he was enjoying himself?" I gasp as one of the clamps chomps into my almost-pencil-eraser nipple.

"I sure guess he did. He sighed and moaned. His dick never did get fully hard—he had a cute one with a P.A.—but soft dicks are not necessarily a bad sign."

"Gotcha." Clearly, foot worship scenes are not precisely about dicks, in any case.

"Now raise your hands above your head."

"Yes, Sir." He snaps the restraints around my wrists onto a chain hanging from a ceiling beam. I'm gratifyingly stretched out and vulnerable.

"Could I possibly have been any nicer to him?"

"No, Sir." *Not unless you beat the shit out of him,* I think.

"He wasn't into pain at all," Sir says, as though he can read my mind. "Unfortunately." The back of his leather-clad right hand smacks my pec. My cock throbs against the rope that tightly encircles it. Like any submissive worth his salt, I figure I know how to get what I want.

"Thank you, Sir." Another slap, coming from the other direction. My body tenses, then relaxes.

"I mean, we'd only played once before. I took him to the play party, introduced him around...." His handsome brow furrows.

"Was he good-looking, Sir?" *As good-looking as me?*

"Yeah, very nice face. Good body, not gym-toned, but trim. Just my type. Like you." His chest-slapping has become rhythmic. Like a waltz. One-two-three-pause. One-two-three-pause. Positively Viennese. Or maybe like Musetta's Waltz from Act 2 of *La Bohème*. But I digress....

"Thank you, Sir."

"Only he had self-image problems, see? Good-looking boy like him didn't deserve to have self-image problems. Made me want to...."

"To slap him, Sir?" I offer helpfully.

"Yeah, only he wasn't into it, so I couldn't. Goddamn 'safe, sane, and consensual.' "

"Well, some of us are into it. Sir. Being slapped, I mean."

I mean it as a compliment, but maybe he hears it as a demand—sometimes tops can be so touchy. He scowls, stops working my now-fiery chest, and reaches down to my well-tied balls.

"Aaagghh!"

He pulls harder.

"AAAGGHH! THANK YOU, SIR!"

"Only problem is, between the blindfold and the sneaker over his face, sometimes I wasn't sure that he wasn't getting bored."

"That shouldn't matter, Sir. You're the top."

He doesn't say anything, just stares deep into my eyes. Through me.

"Then this very cute boy I'd seen around came over, while

I was standing on my slave. The boy looked in my eyes for permission, then went down on my dick."

"Did you have trouble keeping your balance, Sir?" Which is cheeky, I know. If we hadn't already played together so often, I never would say it. I swear. He puts his hands on my hips and spins me around, facing away from him.

"This cute new boy seemed like he'd be a lot of fun, but like I said, the footslave was real insecure. When we'd first negotiated, he'd told me he didn't enjoy parties because he was always afraid he'd be left for someone else. So after a minute, I pulled the boy off my dick and whispered to him, 'Not now. I'll get to you later.' Boy smiled—and oh God, he was cute—and said, 'I'll be here.' "

All this stuff about how cute the other boy looked is starting to make *me* feel insecure. "Please, Sir..." I begin.

Sir's gloved hand comes down on my butt. Not too hard, but hard enough to smart.

"Thank you, Sir."

"So the next time I checked in with the footslave, he said he thought he'd had enough. I had him kiss and suck my feet a little while longer, then we got dressed and left. On the way out of the dungeon, the cute boy and I winked at each other." Sir's starting to really spank me now, each practiced blow of his hand sending waves of peculiar pleasure coursing through my body.

"I'd decided to walk the footslave to the streetcar line, so he wouldn't think I didn't like him or something. On the way, he was talking nonstop about his therapist. His therapist! How he didn't think of himself as attractive. Meanwhile, I was thinking how good he looked with my toes stuffed in his pretty mouth. I was wishing they were still in there."

I'll bet, I think. But the spanking is making thinking a chore. Fuck, Sir's blows are beginning to *hurt.*

"At the streetcar stop, we arranged to have coffee. Not the

next day, but the day after that. Monday. Just to talk things over."

"To debrief?"

"Debrief, yeah. Plus, I wanted to see him again, neuroses and all." Suddenly, I'm wondering what he really thinks of me. I mean, does he talk to other bottomboys about *me?*

He reaches around me to take his best flogger from the hook on the wall.

"By the time I got back to the party, the cute boy was gone. Didn't wait around, after all." In my mind's eye, I can see Sir standing behind me, flogger in one leather-gloved hand, the other hand stroking the thick bullhide tails.

"So I called the footslave at work Monday morning, as arranged. He wasn't at his desk. I left a voicemail." The flogger whizzes through the air and lands with a thud on my shoulder. It feels great. I start wallowing in that familiar, dark place that Sir takes me to so well. It's that feeling, and not the comp tickets to the opera's dress rehearsals, that keeps me coming back to him. And this opera season has been lousy, anyway.

"Thank you, Sir."

"But he didn't get back to me. Finally, at four-thirty, I called him again, just to find out what's what. 'Sorry,' he said, 'it's been real busy here at work.' Which I could understand." The blows to my shoulders are harder and more frequent now. I do wish Sir would stop talking. "But then he told me about this date he'd had the night before. Some Latin bear he met at a bar. How wonderful the sex was. How great the guy was." I'm trying to pay attention. *Please shut up, Sir,* I think, something I daren't ever say. But he doesn't. Shut up. "I mean, I'd only known this footslave for, what, five days?" I try to concentrate, because this is Sir talking and what's important to him is supposed to be important to me. *Is.* It *is* important to me. Still.... "So wasn't that sort of emotional confidence a bit premature? I mean, thanks for sharing. I knew he had self-esteem problems, but I'm not without...."

I've done it. I've managed to sneak off to my own little bottom space. For a while, phrases float through my brain: "...didn't show up...stood me up...ungrateful...I'm not going to compete...to compete...." And then Sir's voice becomes white noise, comforting white noise. Ahhh.

Finally, some timeless span of time later, the flogging stops. I struggle back to the surface as Sir undoes my shackles, holds me in his arms, strokes my face. My back hurts, a raw, wonderful pain. He smiles at me. My Sir—handsome, bearded, beaming. He knows he's done a good job; the sight of me confirms it. I'm sure that I'm glowing. "Hey, I'm sorry for going on about that footslave. Sorry to vent. It's just that...."

Never make a neurotic your footslave? I think. *Well, how about "Never make a neurotic...."*

But I don't finish the thought. I don't let myself say it, not even to myself. I wouldn't dare. I just smile right back. And when there's an appropriate pause, I say, "Thank you, Sir."

Wrestler for Hire
Greg Herren

I can't believe I'm doing this, I thought for maybe the thousandth time, lighting another cigarette and pacing.

I know I shouldn't be smoking—usually when I'm about to wrestle I keep my bad habit a secret. I don't tell my opponent I smoke; I rinse my mouth several times with mouthwash and gobble breath mints as if they were M&M's. Intellectually, I know I'm not fooling anyone—you can't get years of smoke stink out of your breath, off your clothes, and out of your hair in just a couple of minutes with Scope and Tic-Tacs—but no one has ever said anything. Maybe they're just being polite—maybe they just want to wrestle so bad they don't care—maybe that's why some of them won't ever wrestle me a second time. Fuck if I know. There's no point trying to figure out people's motivations. If they don't want to wrestle me again, I just blow it off and shrug. Hell, there's guys *I* won't wrestle a second time.

Manhattan is full of wrestlers—all the contact sites have pages and pages of Manhattan wrestlers, many of them with stunning bodies and into the same kind of wrestling I am. But

I'm here on business for a few days, and my time is limited. I'm meeting one of my publishing buddies for drinks downstairs in a couple of hours, and this is the only open window of time for a match. None of the guys I'd emailed or who friends had recommended I get in touch with could make it at this time, which sucked. I'd hoped to get a match in while in New York.

One guy told me after we'd wrestled that sometimes, when he was in the mood, he picked up a street hustler and paid him fifty bucks to wrestle for an hour. I'd been shocked— the thought of paying someone to wrestle when they were plenty of guys who'd do it for free didn't make sense to me. Although I'd gone months at a time without wrestling— sometimes I could coax a bar pickup into wrestling around, but while they liked it and got into it, they didn't really know what they were doing and it wasn't that much fun. Oh, sure, my cock had gotten hard and the sex was always intense, but it wasn't what I really wanted.

After my lunch meeting, I'd come back to the hotel, the escort thought going through my mind. I'd never hired one, and I was nervous. But I'd picked up a gay bar rag with an escort section in the back and started paging through it in my room. The ad jumped out at me.

WRESTLER FOR HIRE. *You like to wrestle? Then I'm the stud for you. 5'9, 200 pounds of solid muscle; 31 waist, 50 chest, 20 arms, 28 quads. Out only. Chase.*

The picture of a bare torso made my mouth water. His body was smooth, tanned, the muscles huge and defined. My hand had trembled as I dialed the number. He'd answered on the second ring. "This is Chase." His voice was deep, masculine. My cock stirred.

"Um, hi, Chase, my name is Greg, and I was wondering if you had any time available this afternoon?"

"Well, yeah, about four. Does that work for you? How long?"

"Two hours?"

"Okay, I charge two hundred per hour, cash only. That a problem?"

There was an ATM in the lobby of the hotel. "No, not a problem."

"I need to tell you up front I don't do anything anal. We can do oral, that's fine, but I save the anal stuff for my lover." He laughed. "You like to wrestle, Greg?"

"Yeah, I do." I gave him the address and room number.

And now it was five minutes to four, the four hundred dollars in crisp new $20 bills was sitting on the nightstand, and I was nervous as hell. I took another swig of water. I sat back on the bed. I was wearing a black T-shirt and sweatpants. I had a thong on under the sweats, but didn't know the protocol. I jumped at a knock on the door.

A tank of a man stood there, a big grin on his face. He was five nine, for sure, a few inches shorter than me, but that was the only way he was smaller. He wore a white string tank top that perfectly showed off the heavily veined muscles in his shoulders and arms. The deep cleavage between his massive pecs disappeared beneath the white cloth, but a tanned, half-dollar-sized nipple peeked out on the left side. His baggy black nylon sweatpants didn't hide the size and power of his mighty legs. A gym bag was slung over his left arm. His black hair was buzzed short, Marine-style, and his green eyes stood out brightly against the dark tan of his skin. "Greg? I'm Chase." He stuck out his hand and I shook it.

"Um, come in." I stepped aside and let him pass, looking at the round mound of hard ass under the nylon.

"Oh, thank God, you smoke! Mind if I have one?" he asked, kicking off his shoes and sitting down in the chair next to the nightstand. He rummaged around in one of the side pockets of his bag, producing a rumpled pack of

Marlboro Lights and a lighter. "I haven't been able to have one for hours."

"Go ahead," I said, bemused. The last thing I expected was a muscle god to want a cigarette.

He lit one with obvious pleasure and blew the smoke across the room. "Man, that's nice."

I lit one and sat on the bed. "Your body is gorgeous," I blurted, a complete dork.

"Thanks!" He smiled, a genuine smile that lit up his eyes. "You've got a pretty nice one, too."

"Yeah, right," I shrugged. Next to him I looked like I'd never lifted a weight in my life. But then, he was getting paid to please me, right?

"I mean it." He flicked ash. "Take your shirt off."

I obliged self-consciously, aware of the love handles no amount of cardio seemed to get rid of, the little roll at my navel. He whistled. "That's nice, man."

"I could be leaner."

He stubbed the cigarette out in the ashtray and placed one of his big hands on my leg. I jumped a bit, and he laughed. "Relax, man, I'm not going to bite you. We're gonna have some fun, right?"

I nodded.

He stood and pulled the miniscule tank top over his head, folded it, and put it on the floor next to his gym bag. I stared. The cuts in his stomach were deep enough for me to stick an entire finger inside. His torso was shaved completely smooth, and there was no hair under his arms. His armpits were really white. He gestured to me. "Come here."

I walked toward him. "Jump up on me and wrap your legs around my waist."

"Okay." I did, and he put his arms around my back and pulled me in close. His skin was warm and smooth against mine, and I felt my dick growing. His skin was also surprisingly soft over steel-like muscles. He carried me to the bed and lay me down gently, then stood and popped his arms up, and flexed. Huge veins snaked along his forearms, across his biceps, and in his shoulders. "Damn," I breathed out.

He grinned, and slid his hands inside his sweatpants, then inched them down. All he had on was a black thong. His pubic hair had been waxed so none showed around the Lycra hugging the big hanging package. He had a bikini tan-line that showed stark white, like his armpits, against the deep tan. "I wasn't sure what you wanted me to wear," he said. "I have other things in my bag."

"That's fine," I said, my heart racing.

He turned around and showed his beautiful muscled ass. The thong was just a couple of strings running above the top of each perfectly molded cheek, then a tiny triangle just above the deep canyon between them. He bent over and touched his toes, making his ass flex and curve.

I almost came right then.

He turned back around and grinned at me. He started pulling my sweats down. I lifted my hips to help, embarrassed at how my body looked in my white thong. "Nice legs," he whistled. "You have to promise to head scissor me at some point. I fucking *love* that."

"Okay."

He jumped on the bed, which bounced, and lay beside me, on his side, resting his head in his hand, the bicep bulging. "What you into, Greg? Sub? Pro? Jobber/heel? Give/take? Just trading holds?" He put his top leg over mine. It was heavy. His free hand began tracing around my left nipple.

"I like it all," I said, hearing my heart beating in my ears. "I usually leave it up to my opponent."

"Dude, you're paying—you decide." He rolled over on top of me, our crotches against each other. His dick was hard, too. He grabbed my arms and held them down over my head, making my back arch up just a little bit. He bent his head and started flicking his tongue over my neck. My body started to tremble. He grinned. "Why don't we just roll around a bit and see what we feel like?"

I swallowed. "Sure." I actually liked what he was doing, but didn't say anything. I wanted to see what he would do next.

He let go of my arms and rolled off me, getting up on his knees. I sat and admired the beauty of his body. He settled on his haunches and grinned at me until I finally got up on my knees. "Flex your arms," he ordered.

I did, feeling a little silly. Mine looked like pipe cleaners next to his. He whistled, and grabbed each bicep with one of his hands and squeezed. "Nice, man." He let go and traced an index finger from the base of my throat down between my pecs to my navel.

"Can I—" I swallowed. "Can I put you in a full nelson?"

"Thought you'd never ask." He turned so his back was to me. I slid my arms under his armpits and locked my fingers behind his neck and pressed down, moving closer so my crotch was right against his boulder butt, my hard cock between the cheeks. He groaned and struggled against the hold, so I applied more pressure to hold him in it. He began flexing his buttcheeks, so my dick was getting a kid of massage.

Incredible.

"Oh man," he breathed, "that's nice. A little tighter, do you mind?"

I squeezed and he let out a long moan.

"Yeaaaaaaaaaaaaahhhhhh...."

I fell backward, pulling him so he landed on top of me. I straddled his waist and locked my ankles, squeezing hard.

"Oh, yeah, man, that's hot...fuck yeah...torture me, man...I can take it!"

I squeezed my legs together with every bit of strength I

could muster, and he groaned, his breath coming faster and shorter as I pushed his head down further, pressuring his neck with my arms, until finally I couldn't squeeze anymore and relaxed.

"Fuck!" he said, rubbing his back against me. "You're good, man."

I squeezed again and he cried out, fighting against it, until after a few seconds more he said, "Okay, man, okay! I give, stud!"

I let go and he rolled onto his stomach. He grinned, shaking his head. "You know what you're doing, man. Fucking hot! So many of these people who hire me don't, you know?"

"Really?"

He shrugged. "Most of 'em don't really wrestle—it's just a fantasy for them, and sadly, many of them aren't in very good shape. They don't know how to put on holds, so I have to pretend." He rolled onto his back. "Sit on my chest and work my abs over."

"Okay." I climbed on his massive chest, enjoying the feel of his hard pecs under my ass, and punched him lightly in the stomach.

"Yeah, nice. You can go harder."

My punches landed harder and faster. With each one his body reared, reacting, and he moaned. The head of his cock jutted from his thong. I kept punching, harder and faster, until he tapped my back. "Break, man, break!" I looked over my shoulder at him. "That's hot, guy, I fucking love this! Your back looks so fucking hot up there." He traced a finger down my spine and I trembled. "You want me to do something to you?"

"Scissor me," I said, falling to the bed. "Around the waist."

"A man after my own heart," he said, sliding his legs

around me. He squeezed, not hard, just enough for me to feel the power in his legs.

"Yeah." I grinned. "Really give it to me, man."

He rose up on his hands and flexed his ass, his legs powering together. The breath was crushed out of me, blood rushed to my head, but I didn't give in, though spots were appearing before my eyes…it felt so fucking incredible, those massive legs around me, his balls flopping against my side. I felt like I could die right then and there, looking at his rippled stomach and strong pecs.

He let up and whistled, "Damn, you can take it."

I gulped in a breath, my vision clearing. "Feels good, stud."

He squeezed again, but this time I couldn't hold out, couldn't resist. I smacked his legs, and he immediately let go, and I rolled out, gasping for air. I reached for the bottled water on the nightstand.

"You okay?" he asked, concern in his voice. "I don't want to hurt you."

The water felt good and I gulped down another swallow. "Fuck no, man, that was fucking hot!"

He smiled. "I'd love to get in a ring with you sometime. A friend of mine has one on the Upper East Side."

"Yeah." I reached over and tweaked his right nipple. "That would be fun…but I don't have time on this trip."

"Oh." He reached over and rubbed my dick. "You wanna lose these thongs?"

I grabbed the strap of his with my teeth and pulled it down. He laughed as his cock sprang out and slapped against his lower abdomen. I kept his thong tight between my teeth until it was down around his ankles, then used my hands to pull it off his feet.

"My turn." And he did the same thing, his hot breath on my legs as he worked the thong down. He grabbed my ankles and pulled me onto my back, and stood, holding my legs apart. Before I could wonder what he was going to do, he started running his tongue up the inside of my left calf and my entire body went rigid. His tongue slid further and further up, until he was licking my inner thigh. I closed my eyes and moaned. *My God.* No one had ever done that to me. Fucking amazing. And then his tongue was licking my balls and then the underside of my cock and then lapping the head.

I grabbed his shoulders, kneading the hard muscle, digging my fingers in. The muscle was tight and hard, full of knots. I started working one of the knots out.

He moaned, letting my cock go. "Oh man, that feels great! Don't stop!"

I swung out from under him and straddled his back. He dropped his head and I slid my thumbs down the muscle along his spine, digging in deep. He moaned, his ass flexing and unflexing, his legs swinging at the knees and slapping against the bed. When my thumbs reached the curve of his ass, I hesitated. *Nothing anal,* he'd said.

Instead, I sat on the small of his back and grabbed both of his arms, swinging them up and back. The muscles of his back jumped out in relief. "ooooooHHHH!" he grunted, his skin flushing as he fought to bring his arms back down. I kept applying pressure, struggling against his incredible strength. A bead of sweat rolled off my nose and dropped, joining the sweat slicking his back, as he strained. "Fuck you, man!" he half-shouted. "I'll never give!"

I drove my knee into his side.

"NO WAY!"

I kneed him again, and his body convulsed.

"Okay, man, fuck you. I give, man!"

I let his arms drop and sat on his back again. He was breathing hard, and his back was shimmering with sweat in the late afternoon sunlight. I wiped sweat off my forehead and leaned down to kiss the back of his neck.

He rolled me over onto my back and slid on top, his cock against my stomach. He grabbed my arms and forced them over my head again, putting his weight against them. He smiled into my face. His own was wet with sweat. "Nice sneak attack, stud." He nuzzled my right armpit and licked it.

Oh, wow. I tried to arch up, but he was too strong, holding me helpless as he kissed the sensitive skin there, and then nibbled it. My cock strained, my body strained, sweat tricked down all over my body. I had to get up, I had to get his mouth off me, it was too much, it was too much, if he didn't stop I was going to come, I couldn't believe how fucking amazing it was, how it felt—

And then he stopped.

I lay panting. "Jesus."

"Pretty intense, huh?" He didn't release my arms. I didn't mind. I liked lying there with his hard, heavy body on mine, completely in his power. Then he got off the bed and stood there looking at me, then slid one hand under my neck and the other under my lower back and he was picking me up, *my God, how fucking strong is he?* I marveled as he pressed me up and over his head until I was lying stretched over his left shoulder, one of his hands around my neck and the other under my balls, balancing me.

The stretch on my back felt good. My back is limber.

"Doesn't that hurt?" he asked, amazed.

"I was a gymnast," I gasped.

"Damn, I need to get you in a ring," he said, bending his knees then straightening them so that I bounced on his shoulder, my back arching further with every bounce, and he kept going until the pain started, and I shouted, "Okay! Okay, I give!"

He flipped me neatly onto the bed, where I bounced again before settling in.

"How was that?"

"Fucking hot," I said, trying to catch my breath. "No one's ever done that to me."

He stood looking down at me, until I sat up and got off the bed. I grabbed his head into a side headlock and dragged it down to my hip, turning him until I could flip him over onto his back on the bed, which groaned.

I drove down on him, squeezing and flexing my arm as much as I could. His face started to redden, but he struggled, trying to break the hold with his own arms, but somehow I found the strength to hold him off, until he tapped my arm. "Okay!" he squealed. "Okay! Okay! Okay!"

I let go and moved away, but not fast enough. He grabbed my shoulders and dragged me toward him, until our faces were inches apart, and then he pressed his lips against mine. I opened my mouth to take his tongue, and sucked. He moaned, and I rolled on top of him, my cock rubbing his. His pelvis started thrusting, and I matched the motion, our cocks stroking each other. I moved my mouth down his throat, tracing his Adam's apple with my tongue, sucked the base of his throat, then moved down to his pecs. I flicked my tongue over his right nipple while pinching the left. I grabbed his cock with my free hand, squeezing it tightly.

"Oh, you fucking stud, yeah, that's the way, man, that feels good." He kept up a steady stream of talk while I worked his nipples over with my tongue, then worked on his navel. His back arched, and I went back to his nipples, pinching both hard.

He swung his legs around my head, resting them on my shoulders as I took his cock in my mouth. As I worked it, his legs squeezed, just enough pressure against my temples to know they were there, not hard enough to hurt. I ran my hands up and down his flexed quads while I suckled his cock. *Awesome.*

He settled his hands on my head. "Dude, you've gotta stop or I'm gonna come, and I don't wanna come yet."

I pulled back from his cock and looked up at the gleaming torso and the beautiful face smiling at me.

"I want you to fuck me," he said. "I want you to come inside me."

"I thought you said no anal."

He pulled me alongside him and embraced me. "That's a rule I have to start with, until I meet the guy and know what he's like. I don't let just anyone fuck me—but you've gotten me so fucking hot I have to have it."

"What about your boyfriend?"

He shrugged. "I don't have a boyfriend. That's just my excuse."

"I can't believe you don't have a boyfriend!" I ran my hand down his torso, and he shivered.

"Just unlucky that way. Never met anyone I wanted to be involved with—and besides, he'd have to wrestle." He grinned. "That makes it a little harder, you know." He pointed to the wedding ring on my left hand. "You're married?"

"To a man. We've been together nine years."

"Does he wrestle?"

I shook my head. "No."

"Does he know you do?"

"Yeah, and he doesn't mind." I shrugged. "There's things he's interested in that don't interest me, so we kind of agreed to allow each other the latitude to explore."

"Most guys aren't that cool," he said, stroking my inner thigh. "Why couldn't I have met you when you were single?"

"I would have never dared to talk to someone like you when I was single."

He licked my neck. "That's silly. Everyone is so afraid of guys like me, like they won't measure up or something.

Everyone is attracted to something different, you know? I really don't like guys who are built like me." He grinned. "Your body, on the other hand...." He grabbed my dick. "And this cock! Hell, man, I've gotta have that inside me. You sure you want to?"

"Hell, yeah."

He walked over to his bag, pulled out a condom and a bottle of lube, tore the package open with his teeth, then gently slid it over my aching cock, squirting lube until it was nice and wet. He squirted more into his hand, reached back, and lubed his ass.

He lay on the bed, legs apart. "Come fuck me, stud."

I knelt between his legs, and he spread them further, his eyes open and staring up at me. I grabbed my dick and guided it between his massive asscheeks till I found the tight opening, and pushed gently. He moaned, then relaxed, and I slid my cock in about halfway before meeting resistance. He was growling, a low sound that only eased when he needed to breathe. I slid my cock slowly in and out, not forcing it all the way. *Let him get warmed up and turned on some more, and then I'll try,* I figured. Besides, it felt good.

His eyes closed, and I started lightly punching his stomach as I slid in and out, and he started stroking his own cock.

"Yeah, that's nice, you can punch harder."

I started slamming my fists into his abs when I moved my cock out, letting him breathe as I went back in, and then, just as I thought, just as his legs got slick with sweat, the resistance gave and I plunged all the way in. His entire body bucked, his back arching, and his eyes flew open.

"Oh you fucking stud, fuck me, fuck me, FUCK ME!!!"

I slammed my fists into his gut with greater power as I slammed my cock deeper inside, and he groaned and moaned and then he shot a load, cum spitting out of his cock's slit, his body jerking, and a crying out with each shot. I stayed deep inside as he came, until he was finished, until his body relaxed, then I slid out. I peeled the condom off and started stroking my own cock.

"You didn't come?" he asked, his eyes half shut. I shook my head. "What do you want me to do to help you?"

"Scissor my head," I said, lying down. He swung his big legs around my head so that I was staring at his beautiful ass, and started squeezing. It didn't take long—the feel of his legs and the sight of his ass had me shooting in maybe six strokes.

He let go of my head, and I got up and walked into the bathroom to grab a towel. I wiped the cum off, then offered it to him. "You wanna shower?"

He shook his head. "Nah, I need to get running." He wiped himself down and then gave me a strong hug and a wet kiss. "Thanks, man, that was fucking awesome."

I walked to the nightstand while he dressed and counted the money out. "Here you go, Chase."

He looked at me, then at the money. "Nah. Keep it."

"You sure?"

"I enjoyed myself too much to take money." He reached into his bag and handed me a business card with his name, a body shot, his phone number and email address on it. "Next time you're in town, give me a call. We'll go to my friend's ring."

I got out one of my cards and handed it to him. "If you ever get to New Orleans—"

"You're from New Orleans?" A big grin split his face.

"Yeah. Why?"

He started to laugh. "I'm from Baton Rouge. I get down there, I don't know, four or five times a year."

I laughed. "Well, you'd better fucking call me then!"

He kissed me again, long and hard and slow. "Count on it, stud."

The door shut behind him and I lay back down on the bed. I had about an hour before I had to meet my friends. The bed sheets were damp from his sweat. I buried my face in them, to drink in his smell. I lit a cigarette and blew smoke at the ceiling.

Well, I definitely have something to look forward to the next time I come to Manhattan, I thought. *Chase, in a ring? Man, oh man.*

And I wondered when I could arrange another trip.

This Little Piggy
Jim Gladstone

When I think of summer, I see an innocent boy of ten. He strolls along a path in the woods of Vermont. There is a reed between his teeth, releasing the essence of sweet green onto his tongue. The other end bobs jauntily in the air, eight inches from his face.

He is carefree, barefoot. His toes kick up at sunny sky. He is my icon. He comes to mind each year, about the same time the Coppertone billboards rise along the roadsides with that sprightly tyke, that bottom-tugging puppy.

When I think of summer, my mind overheats, drenched in other notions. Other lotions.

Let me be your squeeze bottle icon.

Let me tell you about Indian Camp.

All these years later, let me scribble one more postcard home to Daddy.

Help me.

Share my crayons.

Pick one. Stick it in the box hole and twist.

Sharpen my colors.

Grape Green. August Tan. Cream.

Draw a full circle around the boy on the path.

Start at the reed and move to the brainpan. Press your tip to his head and tousle his sun-streaked curls. Then curve down behind his back. Be careful not to get too close. Don't dare touch the jut of his bum. (You could get into trouble, you know.)

Come round to his rear heel now. Get right beneath it. Perfectly traverse the arch, and ride up on the big toe of his forward foot. Momentum's with you now. Your shining trail presses hard, swings up, and makes the perfect connection, a shooting arc from his upthrust toe to the bobbing tip of his straw.

Put the pressure on as you complete this circumscription. Bear down on his crazy head.

Make my bottle-top explode.

Indian Camp was an all-boys affair.

Our bunk was called Navajo. Carl, our dense, gorgeous seventeen-year-old counselor—as well as the chief swim instructor—was more upstanding and less intelligent than the camp's other young employees. As a result, we kids in Carl's bunk bore the brunt of the rest of the staffers' disdain (which was only aggravated by the jealousy-inducing fact that Carl had a girlfriend in nearby Montpelier).

"Nava-Homos," the other counselors deemed us, and whenever Carl had his night off and went rutting, they waited for their own charges to fall asleep, then snuck in to torment us.

Flashlights—held inches from our eyes—blasted us awake, as these boys with hairy arms and attempted goatees loudly threatened us with candy confiscation, revocation of movie privileges, and banishment from cookout night should we ever speak a word of these necessary trials.

"Do I hear whining?" taunted Animal Caruso one Saturday evening as we lined up along the foot of our bunk beds. "Did one of you piglets just *whine?*"

"Nah," Jerry Storch replied, producing a brown paper bag from behind his back. "I think I heard one of the little girls say she wanted to *drink* some wine."

At that point, scrawny Brady Brennan, the smallest boy in our bunk, really did begin to whimper.

"N-n-no! Please, guys. I can't. I really can't."

"Can't what?" grunted the Animal.

"I can't drink wine!" Brady was terrified, begging. "Our Dad went away. Mom said it's 'cause he's alkolic. We don't even have a real father now. Please don't make me drink wine."

"Awwww, I understand," purred Jerry. "That really would be going too far, don't you think, An-man?"

Animal nodded and feigned wiping a tear from his eye.

"Why don't we give him some lemonade instead," he said, gesturing to Curtis Slova, the third and bulkiest of their band. Curt bent down, grabbed Brady by the ankles, and swung him head over heels, sweeping the floorboards with his hair.

"March!" Jerry commanded the other five of us campers. We followed Curtis and dangling, red-faced Brady into the bathroom. Animal was taking a piss.

"I'm gonna drown!" screamed Brady as his head descended into the flushing maelstrom. The floor around the toilet was splashed with coughed-up water. As sorry as I knew I should feel for Brady, I couldn't pull my eyes from his upside-down toes, writhing wildly, as if they wanted to braid themselves together.

"Alrighty then," asked Jerry, releasing Brady, who scurried to cower on his upper bunk, "does anyone else have a problem with wine?"

As it turned out, Jerry's brown bag contained not a bottle, but a huge bunch of grapes.

"File outside, Homos!" called Curtis. "Time to make some wine."

Out front, we shivered silently in our sleeping briefs, illuminated by two lanterns that Jerry had propped on the cabin steps.

"Now," whispered Animal, "in my grandmother Caruso's village in Sicily, they made wine the old-fashioned way, like we're going to. But before the work began, there was a town festival, with fun and games for the *bambinos*. So that's how we're going to start, too, piglets, with a traditional vineyard relay."

The camp path was alternately rocky and muddy. The prospect of running barefoot was uninviting.

"Pull down your panties, girls," said Animal. "Put 'em around your ankles." Anyone who hesitated got a poke in the back from Curtis, who stood behind us, wielding a broomstick.

"Now." Animal plucked one green grape from the bunch, displayed it between thumb and forefinger, and then handed it off to Jerry. "Let me show you young cunts how this is done in the Old Country. C'mere, Finegold."

David Finegold shuffled over. The empty pouch of his Jockeys dragged in the dirt between his feet.

"About face!" ordered Animal.

Finegold's face crawled with fear. His bony rib cage swelled and retracted in an involuntary wave as he felt Animal's lacrosse-calloused hands take hold of his buttocks. Animal's fingers reached wide to brace Finegold's hipbones. His thumbs pressed into the soft white mounds and spread the cheeks open, like the pages of a handbook on humiliation.

Responding to Animal's nod, Jerry stepped forward and reached down along the small of Finegold's back, the grape pinched in his fingers.

"Ri-i-i-ght there," whispered Animal and he released

Finegold's ass and Jerry drew back his empty hand.

Animal set his palms on our bunkmate's shoulders and turned him back around, butt toward the rest of us. He shined his flashlight directly on Finegold's ass; we could see a spot of pale green, shining deep within the cleft.

Curtis had placed a large metal bucket some twenty yards down the path, and now, following Animal's instructions as the rest of us squirmed in embarrassment, Finegold waddled toward it, his underpants soaking up muddy water from the puddles.

"Oooowww!" He cried as he stepped on a jagged stone, almost losing his balance in the pain.

"Don't let it drop!" snapped Animal. "Else you'll eat it right now and start all over."

It seemed to take forever for us to pick that pendulous bunch of grapes down to the twigs. A dozen times each, the five of us bent over, clenched a tender ovoid, then made our ungainly way down the path, squatting astride the bucket to release the newly bruised fruit.

"I hope your mommies taught you how to wipe properly," Curtis cracked as Finegold deposited his final grape, " 'cause this is supposed to be *white* wine."

Jerry howled at that one.

I was relieved that Animal ordered us to "get your bloomers on, ladies!" before issuing his next command. White briefs helped obscure my most unladylike reaction to the slippery, sluicing sounds of my bunkmates' feet as they stepped into the bucket and worked their toes into the pile of glistening green. It was as if I had supersonic ears, like the bats we'd learned about in nature club, able to zone out unimportant sounds and keep focused on target. So while I'm sure Finegold and company cried "Gross!" and "Disgusting!" and "Vomitrocious!" (our favorite new word that summer), I didn't hear them.

What I heard, amplified and converted to a sort of internalized surround-sound, was the fleshy underbubble of a pinky toe wetly pressing a grape skin until it popped and released its pulpy guts. I heard the slow squoosh of pulverized fruit, squeezing up over knuckles, then sliding back through sticky interstices, dripping off toe-webs and leaving a sediment of must under nails.

Finally, it was my turn to step in. My heartbeat grew faster. Tiny sunbleached hairs quivered along my arms. Interlacing my fingers, I made a mask over my face to hide my ecstatic grin, my back-rolling eyes, the dart of an uncontrollable tongue poking out to lick my lips. I hunched over to obscure the solid throb below my waistband, and through the gaps in my mask, I watched a sole touch down upon the warming ooze, and then felt myself slip under. I angled my left foot in, slowly, toes first, so the gaps were crammed full, then ball, arch, and heel. I shifted my weight in a juicy, rocking motion.

From below rose the fruit-drenched perfume of dirty feet and tight-squeezed cheeks...I felt oil and tongues and creamy spit, ankle deep...I heard suction, wetness, and the sweet slimy snap of toes, crawling on each other for mutual pleasure...I wanted to drink that wine...to dive in...to swim....

"It's Carl!" Animal hissed to his cronies, spotting a flashlight moving in our direction from far down the path. He yanked me out of the bucket and kicked it under the cabin, spilling, as they rushed us all inside.

"You're fucking lucky," Curtis snarled as we jumped into bed. "You missed out on the homemade refreshments."

"Are you okay?" Brady whispered to me from under his blanket.

"Yeah, they're okay, you little pansy." Animal flipped out the corkscrew of his Swiss Army Knife and twisted it menacingly in the air. "And you'll all *stay* okay if you keep your traps shut. Got it?"

"We were just having some fun, right, piggies?" sneered Jerry.

I nodded along with the rest of my bunk as the three of them climbed out the rear window, then popped the screen back into place just as Carl stepped in through the front door, being careful to make as little noise as possible.

As I did each night, I lay on the bottom bunk below Carl's bed, watching his shorts and underpants come down, his striped tube socks come rolling off. He always lifted his nuts with one hand and sprinkled baby powder underneath with the other just before pulling himself up top, making the springs squeak above me. I would drift off in the trailing cloud of talcum and ballsweat and damp Adidas.

Carl was so good. He never tortured us like the others. He had white, white teeth, smooth, smooth skin, and lank, ash-blond hair like the boys on *Flipper* reruns. When he stood on the lake dock with a whistle in his lips, the palms of his hands and the bottoms of his feet were rosy-white accents to his flawless tan. Other than the secret sub-Speedo zone I got to see each night, the rest of his body was the same milky-brown as the Kraft caramels he'd give us whenever we swept the cabin.

Sometimes, I would sweep three or four times a day. Carl would sit there smoothing Blistex onto his thick maroon lips. "Such a *clean* kid," he would say, chuckling as he tossed me another cellophane-wrapped cube. "You've figured out how to turn a broom into a candy cane!"

What Carl didn't know was that, on some of his nights off, Animal and the gang would use this very same broom to give us Witchy-Wedgies, folding the waistbands of our briefs back over the broomstick, then jamming it upward until our feet were about to lift off the ground. You could hear the elastic beginning to tear from the cotton, and feel the burn of bunched fabric cutting into your butthole and balls. On laundry day, my bunkmates and I never teased each other about skidmarks.

Wednesdays, because I had private tennis lessons, I got to skip late-session archery with my bunkmates. I ran back to the cabin at the end of afternoon assembly. For a half-hour, before grabbing my racket and heading up to the courts, I was free to read my comic books and to write postcards with the sixty-four-color crayon set my parents had sent me. I would also get to see Carl, just off swim duty, coming back to the bunk to peel off his vibrant second skin.

Dear Mom and Dad, I would write, transfixed by the pounding water of Carl's shower in the background. *Camp is great! All of the counselors are fun. Carl—my bunk coun-selor—is kind of shy, but he's really cool too. Can you send the new* MAD Super-Special *and some of this stuff called Blistex, for chapped lips?*

My postcards were fantastic Technicolor creations, alter-nating lines of text in Peach and Flesh and Cornflower Blue.

After showering, Carl would lie on his bedspread, face down with just a folded towel draped over his butt. He would read a fat gold paperback called *Nicholas and Alexandra.* It looked hard and serious, but Animal said he thought there was a part in there about some Russian queen who liked to do it with a horse, so maybe it wasn't boring. The third Wednesday of camp—I guess he realized I was a cool kid by then—Carl asked me if I wanted three extra caramels to give him a backrub before I took off for tennis.

"I can skip lessons today if you need a long one!"

"Nah," he said with a laugh. "I'm not getting into trouble with the coach!"

My balls tingled as I sat on the back of his thighs, kneading his back and shoulder blades. Carl just lay there, oblivious to me, caught up in the adventures of Nicky and Alex. I thought maybe I wasn't pressing hard enough, so I stretched my legs back and dug the heels of my palms into his shoulders, the whole weight of my body on my hands, like I was about to do push-ups into his ass towel.

I kept thinking he should make some noise, or roll over and run his tongue across his teeth like the Pearl Drops lady on TV, but nope.

"Is this good?" I asked him in a whispery voice. "Do you like it this way?"

"It's fine," he said. "But please, I'm reading. Shut up if you want your caramels."

In the *Penthouse* that Jerry kept hidden under his mattress, I'd read an article called "The Art of Sensuous Massage"; I tried to do the Swedish Knuckle Wave on Carl.

"Hey...hey...cut it out, that tickles!" he complained.

After ten minutes, he said I'd better go to tennis and that I could help myself to three caramels. The bag was tucked under his sock pile.

The next Wednesday, I was perfectly silent as I gave Carl his rub. Again, he read and ignored me. I would have been totally bored if I wasn't thinking of the surprise I had planned. My little pretzel stick of a boner poked up against my shorts. There were two techniques from the massage article that I was particularly interested in trying out. I sprung the first on Carl just after I hopped down from his bed; he told me I could have four caramels because I did a better job this time, but instead of going over to his socks, I reached down, grabbed a bottle I'd set on my mattress, and squeezed my hands full of suntan lotion.

Then, without a word, I stood on the metal bucket, which I'd upturned on the floor. I stared directly into Carl's size eleven soles, which dangled over the bar at the end of his bed. I slapped hold of them with my cream-coated palms, gripping them around the arches, like vertical dumbbells.

"Yow! What are you doing?" yelped my horizontal dumb-bell.

"Just let me! I read it in a magazine. It's foot therapy."

"Tickle me and you start losing candy!" he threatened.

"It's not tickling," I breathed. "I promise."

My thumbs dug over the sand dunes of this new terrain, pressing into muscle and tendon, vibrating in circles against dense packets of deeply buried nerve. I greased my fingers and laced them between Carl's toes, sliding them back and forth, popping the webs like harp strings.

His back torqued, serpentine, and just over the mimick-ing horizon of Carl's heels, I saw the towel start to crawl up the twin curves of his ass. I swallowed a mouthful of my own drool. There was a dull thud as *Nicholas and Alexandra* plummeted to the floor at the head of our bed.

"Whoa! Whoa! Stop!" cried Carl, flipping over and yank-ing his legs free. He curled bent-kneed on his bunk, half trembling. "That's enough! You've got to go to tennis now."

During the final ten days of camp, there were a lot of one-on-one canoe trips. Animal Caruso took me out to Deer Island and showed me the cave.

"Dude?" he said. "You're not gonna tell, are you?"

"Tell what?" I asked.

"All the stuff Jer and Curtis and I did with the Navajos this summer."

"It was just fun," I said. "No biggie, right?"

Animal laughed, kind of surprised. "Right. No biggie."

I affectionately squeezed his crotch through his denim shorts, and scrambled down the hill. "Right!" I laughed. "No biggie *there* for sure!"

"You're fucked up, man," said Animal, when he caught up with me, his face twisting in genuine revulsion. "But here's ten bucks from me and the guys anyway. We need our jobs again next summer, if you know what I mean."

I skipped my final tennis lesson for the Needles of Ecstasy.

Since that second backrub, Carl had hightailed it out of the bunk after showering each Wednesday afternoon, telling me to sweep and take four caramels if I wanted. But this was my last chance.

"No, Carl!" I snapped as he started to leave. "I think you want a backrub."

"No thanks, man. I'm cool. Help yourself to candy if you want." He flashed his dimwit grin, all those sexy Chiclet teeth wasted on such a straightedge dorkus.

"Come on, Carl. Just hop up on your bed. You know you liked it."

"Nah, bud. Gotta run."

"Hey Carl," I hissed. "What if I tell?"

I almost didn't let him have the towel.

"C'mo-o-on, ple-e-e-ase," he'd squealed, like pussy little Brady, begging to keep it.

He was flustered and blushing and I knew he'd lose it anyhow.

I grabbed the underpants he'd dropped on the floor and pulled them over my head to make a mask.

"Did you ever see *Friday the 13th*?" I asked. "Well, now you're you, and I'm Jason."

I treated myself to something sweeter than caramel; the winey ferment of his raw teenage feet. I poked my face through a leg hole of his crotch-smelly BVDs and pressed my nose and mouth against each sole for five deep breaths. Each exhalation drove him to writhe and whimper. Then I drizzled cool coconut lotion over his heels, letting it run down to his toes in shiver-inducing rivulets.

"Oh stop oh stop oh stop," he squeaked as his ass bucked.

The towel slid off and fell to the ground. Then, like a snake, I wove my tongue between his toes.

"Oh oh oh."

"You love that, don't you?" I growled, hearing Jerry's voice emerge within my own. "Piggy, piggy, piggy!"

There were no words coming out of Carl any more. Just muffled noises as he buried his shamed face in his pillow. I gave him the cream rub for a good ten minutes, smelling the heat that rose off his asscheeks, spying the golden hair on his balls every time his pelvis arched. When I let go of his feet, they were flexing and unflexing involuntarily, like hooked fish on a line.

"Jesus Christ!" he shouted as he sat up, about to spring down from the bed. "Are you satisfied, you little pervert?"

"Back down!" I growled, stepping over to the corner of the bunk and heading back to the bed, broom in my grip.

"No fucking way!"

"I'll tell! I'll tell! I'll tell!" I cackled.

"So?" shouted Carl. "In prison I'd at least have a chance to fight this shit off!"

"It's not what you think, Carl." I thrust the broom toward him, letting him catch hold of the handle. "I haven't done anything to hurt you yet, have I? Now lay down, counselor."

He did as I said. I ran my hands down the length of the broomstick beside him, then plucked out two tawny straws.

The view was excellent from eight inches back, all the clenching of buttocks, all the gooseflesh rising on thighs. I pinched one end of each straw between a thumb and forefinger, and then, barely touching the opposite tips to his feet, I drew long, slow, excruciating lines. Carl whelped, and groaned, and gurgled staccato symphonies. I traced the silk-smooth skin along his insteps, turning the merger of white flesh and tan line into a full-body network of electrical nerves. Each toe pad, in turn, was poked and circled, every exposed millimeter of sole most unlovingly and pointedly caressed.

And in the end, as Carl reached ceilingward with his perfect asscheeks and thrust a greedy hand down to his own proud whiskbroom, I thought of writing home to share one last wonderful summer memory. Carl screamed and squirted as I invisibly signed my name upon his feet.

Kindled by Vowels
(An Epistolary Seduction)
Ian Philips and Greg Wharton

1. Nearer My Greg to Thee

I lie.

We both do.

I, naked, in San Francisco. Waiting for your call.

You, naked, there. In Chicago. Dialing the numbers hurriedly.

I shudder as the phone—as thick and hard as Bakelite, as red as Fiestaware—rings. It is an old phone, loudly rattling its metallic phlegm.

"Hello?"

"Hello," you coo. Your voice is deep and sonorous. My marrow liquefies. My bones melt as if they were sculpted of butter.

What a priceless lubricant the sound of your voice has become. My sweet aural sop. Confirmation that you do exist. Evocation of the very body that—because of only a week's worth of hours together since this year began—I am slowly, unbearably forgetting as days accumulate into months apart.

That, and your daily emails.

I read of your body weeks before you ever sent me a photo, months before I finally stripped away the last barriers between us on the way from my kitchen to the bedroom.

Ours was an epistolary seduction. An incendiary flirtation, kindled by each dry, brittle consonant and every oily vowel.

Dangerous Liaisons penned by two middle-aged queer men. One as terse as the other is verbose. One with a fondness for the violence, born both of nature and of artifice, that flowers so well in the Midwest. Tornadoes spun of cotton candy and blood. The other dreaming of being made a word in an 18th-century novel or a note in a baroque opera. Consumed by seething festoons of trills, of participial phrases.

One with a husband. One without.

Both now with a paramour.

You and I.

Two professional writers pitching woo through an endless stream of ghostly print in cyber–*billets-doux*.

Love among the fiber-optic cables.

And now, every Monday, while your husband sits unaware at work, in the hour and a half before I go to sit mindlessly myself at a desk, we telegraph—in a series of gasps and grunts and *oh, god*'s—our newest desires for what we shall do, one unto the other, the next time we can swap skin cells and spit and sperm.

"Are you naked?"

I hear your well-lubed fist sucking on your dick. It is a loud and constant sound. Like the sea.

"Yes," I say, half-present. I am imagining your porn-star dick.

It is the kind that, as it grows, droops. Hangs heavy from the weight of the blood now widening the middle of your river of flesh, tributaries of veins swirling off, before tapering to the small, swollen pink dam that is your cockhead.

Without setting eyes on you, I know it is once again broken, leaking—like our love—immoderately, and will inevitably burst.

"Are you hard?" you ask more breathlessly.

"Yes." And I describe the rigid crook of my cock that has delighted you every time I have thrust it—in word or in deed—into your mouth or hole.

"I wish I had my mouth around your dick right now."

"I do too. I wish I had your head between my hands so I could pull it down onto my fat cock. Shove it all the way into the back of your mouth."

You moan. You are flushed—with memory and more blood filling your swollen dick.

"Yes," you say when you remember to breathe. "Oh, god, my dick is so hard. I don't know what you've done to me but it's bigger than it's ever been."

I imagine it, red and engorged, twitching. My Sears Tower, I've called it. And it is a marvel. A wonder of flesh that stands alone and several thousand miles from me.

But the sound of you is here. In this room. The earpiece of the phone is cupped against my ear like your hands. It cradles your absent mouth. But I feel your breath. I feel the lips and tongue and teeth that shape it and push it toward me. It is as if you are beside me, whispering as we spoon.

"What are you doing?" I know but I want to hear you tell me.

"Jerking my dick."

"Good boy. I wish I were there to watch. Let me hear you twist your tit. Go on. Pull it."

"Okay," you purr. And then your mouth buzzes with a swarm of consonants that stream out of your mouth as honey-coated *mmm*s.

Mmm. This is the most frequent call and response in our emails. This is the succinct written testament to the vibrations that hum throughout either of our bodies whenever we communicate. However we communicate.

"Harder," I encourage—I demand. "I wish I could be there to bite it. Chew on it. Remember how I chewed on your whole pec."

Now come the sweet vowels. Long *o*'s and short *u*'s.

"Take that hand and suck on your finger."

The receiver bangs against your jaw and shoulder as you make way for your hand. There is slurping. There is smacking. There is humming. I am happy.

"Rub it over your hole."

"Oh, yes," you throatily agree.

"Now push it in."

Staccato breaths tap against the mouthpiece.

"How's it feel?"

"It's never the same as yours."

No, I think—sad for us both.

"Stick it in deeper. And wriggle it around like I do."

You oblige, warming quickly to the request, but it is I who am rewarded.

"Anything," you sigh in response to a question I have not asked. "You can have me do anything. What do you want me to do?"

"I want you to crawl through the phone," I say without thinking.

You laugh. Either at my breaking of character or at a more private joke between you and your finger.

"What do you want to *hear* me do, babe?" you say.

"I want you to slide that butt plug of yours into *my* hole." I swear I can hear you grin. "And I want you to talk me through it. All of it."

"Yes, Sire."

I smile at your nod to my Jacobean fantasies—games we play whenever we are skin-to-skin.

I listen to you move loudly about your bedroom. At last, you speak, winded more from excitement than exertion. You tell me you how you are sitting on your bed, your knees spread and your ass arched, one hand prying a round cheek from the sleepy embrace of its twin, the other pushing in the tip—you groan enticingly—and then the shaft—you grunt out a long, maddeningly arousing string of "unnh"s—and finally the base.

We both *oh, god* appreciatively. I hear the loud tides of you pulling feverishly on your dick and I stroke mine all the faster and tell you so. You are inspired to get off the bed and stand up, thus wedging the plug into a new and more sweet-burning position.

I have never heard you make such a sound—any man make such a sound—the raw, yet stylized last gasp of one of Michelangelo's dying stone slaves.

I have never wanted you more.

I have never felt farther from you.

"Take it...."

"What?" you say as your mind staggers up your spine from your asshole.

"Take it. Take the plug and fuck your hole with it."

You moan something that sounds like "Okay."

And this is what sends us both over orgasm's edge. You: the sensations that I graphically attribute to my phantom limb. Me: your rapid, rabid pants and hissed whispers of "fuck me, fuck me, fuck me."

I shoot. My cum slides out in time with my spurting breaths. You explode. Howl. As if your cum had crystallized into diamonds that tear and bleed you as you spill a king's ransom onto your bed.

I press the phone to my ear, smiling. It will ring with the sound of you all day. And my dick will thrum from your imagined touch. And your hole will quaver around the butt plug until I write you later to give you permission to remove it.

We gasp our way back to breathing. When we can speak, we talk over the other. To thank you, to thank me for the pleasure of the last hour's lustful riposte and release. You piss and I stop to listen to the water rumbling in the bowl. You have already begun to move about the house. You can only lie still if I am truly there and holding you.

As you inhale on a cigarette I have yet to hear you light in any of our calls, we chatter about the day before us. The errands to run. The chores to be done. The words to be strung into sentences, into paragraphs, into stories to sell. Like this one.

Then we come, at last, to the true little death.

"Good-bye," you say quietly.

"Good-bye," I echo.

We hang up.

And, until our next telephonic tryst, we will lie.

Here and there.

Lie in wait.

You and I.

Lie.

And wait.

2. Husband, Sire, It

At thirty-nine, who would have suspected that I would find sexual bliss? Hasn't it always been a much-repeated fact that a man reaches his sexual prime at seventeen? How horrible to be just at the beginning of something as wonderful as sexual activity, knowing that it will go downhill from there. At seventeen, I was certainly active, but the pleasure then—in fact the pleasures I have enjoyed my entire life—are nothing compared to what I have now. I have found IT.

The IT has come after a long-distance courtship via email

with SIRE, a writer I've admired for years. Our friendship grew over months of writing, secrets shared, desires confessed, pictures taken and attached. And then I took a trip to be with SIRE. And I found IT.

I live with HUSBAND.

The dried rose lies on his bedside table, perched on a pile of books. A single rose, now lacking most of its color and scent, but not the meaning. This rose was a small gift—a sur-prise—from me while SIRE was on a reading tour. He was in Vancouver, so far away, and I was home in Chicago wishing I could be with him. I had a friend who lives there deliver it at the reading, with a whispered message, "To SIRE from your boy," knowing that hearing those words would be as precious a gift to him as any I could offer.

The pressure builds with every day.

I jog. I play tennis. I work out. Nothing helps. I think of him every minute as I sweat and sweat and sweat, trying hard to feel release. Nothing helps. I will see him again in a month.

I live with HUSBAND.

It is my first night with SIRE. I am naked, standing alert and aware—at attention—waiting for the games to begin as he lights candles around his bedroom.

He shows me the way he expects me to always position myself when starting a night of play between SIRE and boy. He then inspects me, whispering firm yet loving descriptions of what he sees and feels. We discuss my "safeword" and what it means, and when—if ever—I should use it. I am shown all the toys he might use to either please or discipline me—dildos, clamps, restraints, rope, his new riding crop, soft floggers, not-so-soft whips, a cane. The cane, he says, will never be used on my soft beautiful skin; he doesn't wish to cause that kind of pain, to scar me in that way.

Whispering softly in my ear, he asks what I want. When he speaks this way during play, he sounds very much like an 18th-century Lord, much like one of the characters he has created. "What do you want, boy?" Partly from this reverie of his, of my being one of his lordly characters, and partly because I am excited to be here, I smile and stifle a giggle. I tell him only to please himself, whatever SIRE desires. The smile is returned.

The pressure builds with every day.

I hear pop songs from open car windows and take the melodies of love to heart, make them my own. Feel them as if written for me. I am falling in love with SIRE. I will see him again in three weeks.

I live with HUSBAND.

When I take the position he expects—on all fours, knees spaced far apart, ass spread wide, my mouth and tongue cleaning his boot—I know that I have found IT. I clean his right boot with complete attention until I am told that I have done a good job, and start on his left. I lick every inch of his jeans, spending extra time at his crotch, licking until my tongue is dry and scratchy and his crotch is completely wet. As instructed, I undress him slowly, enjoying every inch of skin I bare as if I hadn't spent the entire weekend already getting to know it.

I take SIRE's cock in my mouth. I am suddenly hungry to make him come. I worship his hardness with undying focus, spending time with his balls all the way up to the wonderfully wide piss slit that I lap at heartily, eager to get as much of my tongue inside as I can. I fuck him hard with my mouth, the intent simple: to pleasure him, to feel him buck against me and fill my mouth with his cum. I am almost there; I know this from the way his thickness is building, his balls pulling up tight, his legs slightly shaking. He instructs me to stop and firmly pulls my mouth from his cock, leaving a trail of his pre-cum and my spit down my chin.

The pressure builds with every day.

I masturbate several times daily to release it. It doesn't help. I work all night—editing and writing—and I smoke more and more, hoping to feel the release. But it doesn't help.

The pressure is much deeper; a scar is now forming in my heart. A permanent tattoo, more permanent than the marks he leaves when we play, that mark me as his, as belonging to SIRE. I will see him again in two weeks.

I live with HUSBAND.

Slowly, methodically, he wraps my body. And I am more than a little afraid—no, nervous. He wraps me in Saran Wrap, like a mummy, until I cannot move. My entire body, except for feet and head, are completely secured. It is a test of my trust. And I do trust him. I trust SIRE. The fear is real, but I am relaxing into it. I love and trust this man more than anyone ever in my life. He tilts me back and lifts me onto his bed, positioning me on my back like a lab specimen that he will now test. And I am so hard. And my skin is so alive.

He brings out his riding crop, the one he said he kept only for show and that I might never feel, the one that I knew instantly I wanted him to use. He brings it to my lips and I kiss it, the sensation causing me to shiver.

With scissors he slowly cuts circles around my nipples, and the air hitting them is almost enough to make me cum. My cock pushes and thumps against my second skin. But this wonderful sensation is nothing compared to what I feel when he starts snapping the crop down in quick sharp slaps on first one then the other nipple. IT.

After a few—ten, twenty, sixty?—minutes, he flips me over, carefully. The fear rises again, but his voice is soothing, calm, hypnotic. He cuts another patch of the Saran Wrap away. I think I will black out as I feel his breath on my asshole. I writhe trying to bend my ass up, without much success, and finally just bite down on the bedcover, screaming as I feel the first finger touch, then probe. IT.

Eventually, the Saran Wrap skin stretches and pulls apart at spots. My body's writhing and bucking has been too much. At first, I resisted the urges to let go—afraid he would not be pleased if I enjoyed it too much—but these fears were put to rest when he said he wanted me to receive pleasure, that it is his reward. It is not just for him. It is for me.

The wrapping is slowly cut off and the shock of the cold air paralyzes me. Not what I expected after being so totally restrained, finally free but unable to move. He pulls me to him and I am held tightly and kissed fiercely on my lips, cheeks, and eyelids. I cry and tell SIRE that I love him.

The pressure builds with every day.

How do I tell my partner of eighteen years that I love another? How do I tell HUSBAND that I have found something that he can't offer...and that I need to do this, that...that I love him, but that I need to do this.... How can I tell my best friend this without breaking his heart, his spirit?

I will see SIRE next week.

We exchange rings and vows. SIRE and boy. The rings are to be worn when we play. The vows are to be together, forever.

He gives me a present. He lifts each leg and fits my new leather restraints on each ankle. I gladly offer each arm so he can do the same, and I am then tied to each corner of his bed—face down.

The dried rose lies on his bedside table, perched on a pile of books. A single rose, now lacking most of its color and scent, but not the meaning. This rose was a small gift—a surprise—from me while SIRE was on a reading tour. He was in Vancouver, so far away, and I was at home in Chicago wishing I could be with him. I had a friend who lives there deliver it at the reading, with a whispered message, "To SIRE from your boy," knowing that hearing those words would be as precious a gift to him as any I could offer.

It is late and I've lost all track of time. When I realize that he has spent four hours on me, I tell SIRE what I experienced—that IT was better than any orgasm. That every time I felt the bite of his whip on my back and shoulders, or of his teeth on my ass and legs, IT intensified. That the sensations I felt while being restrained, having my ass worked over by his mouth and experienced fingers, then by a butt plug and a dildo, and finally by his fat cock, was one very long intense orgasm that was not focused just in my cock and balls, but my entire body and very soul. Pure pleasure. Bliss.

I cancel my flight home to HUSBAND. The pressure is gone. In its place is IT.

Old Haunts
Jay Neal

You could say my problems began when I was born. I was always a chubby child. I didn't overeat, I didn't under-exercise, I was just husky-prone. My father cajoled, my mother despaired, but there was nothing I could do about it. Not that I tried all that hard.

Then when I was eleven, things got worse. Puberty set in and I sprouted hair all over my body. Lots of hair—really, an overabundance of hair, even considering my generous surface area. By high school I was pretty well covered and had been shaving every day for several years.

Of all the time-wasting courses I had to take in high school, gym class was my least favorite, which I've come to regret. The locker room was not the carefree masculine haven for me that it should have been. True, there were lots of naked boys to look at, including Matt, the other guy with body hair, a dark tuft on the chest in his case. Matt was revered as an ultramasculine god. I was reviled as a gross, hairy fairy.

Maybe that's when my problems began. Fat, hairy, and homo was not a socially rewarding combination in the mid-'70s. Among the men I was attracted to, it was the clone era and very hard to get laid if one didn't fit the mold. I didn't even come close. I had no problem with the full, bushy moustache, or the butch, short-cropped hair, or the masculine, furry chest. In fact, I had too much of the masculine furry chest for most guys.

The problem was the T-shirt and the jeans. They just wouldn't fit right. My waist was nearly the same size as my chest, so the T-shirt did not taper down my body, let alone ripple across any rock-hard washboard abs. And given the size of my waist, my 501s never hugged my ass in an appropriately alluring fashion. I looked more clown than clone.

In a weak moment of celibate desperation, I decided that going to the gym was better than going without sex for the rest of my life. I discovered that with enough torture, even the most criminal waistline will submit. I pumped and pressed and curled and crunched and lunged and squatted until I no longer heard derisive giggles behind my ripped-deltoid back. I even started to enjoy group showers. Finally I had reached that pinnacle of self-worth and individuality: I looked just like everyone else.

Except for the body hair. All the weight training in the world couldn't help that. But as long as I pumped and sweated enough, it could be overlooked as a tragic congenital defect rather than a moral failing. I had finally pained and gained and achieved my goals. I got laid more often, but didn't feel that much happier.

Then I met Michael. I think that's when my problems really began. Michael was the answer to my worst nightmares, the ones that I mistook for dreams. Michael was your basic super faggot, whose mission was to save the world from the evil influences of bad decorating, bad hair, and bad taste in all things frivolous. I think he saw me as his greatest personal challenge.

All the lover-dearest warning signs were evident, but my body-conscious neuroses were flattered by his attentions. We started working out together, and then we started shopping together. We became lovers and moved in together. We tasted fine wines together, we prepared all-natural gourmet food together, and we accepted invitations to the most exclusive parties together.

We led a harrowingly A-gay lifestyle for eight years. For eight long, miserable, and tiring years, Michael supervised every moment of my life. He managed my eating, my sleeping, my clothing, my grooming, and my dull but tasteful sex life. He even tried to introduce me to the joys of body waxing for hair removal. I don't know why I drew the line there, but I'm forever grateful.

It all ended suddenly and ironically when Michael died in a freak electrolysis accident. Tragic. One moment he thought his life would end because of some stray hair on his shoulder, and the next moment it did. For weeks after, I tried to feel sad about his death and discover some redemptive meaning in our dysfunctional relationship. I never did. My predominant emotional state was giddiness.

I stopped going to the gym. I stopped ironing my underwear. I let my beard grow. I was once seen drinking beer from a can. Our friends drifted away, making disapproving noises about how I was letting myself go. I was letting myself go, but I wasn't going downhill. I was enjoying an incredible feeling of liberation, a kind of freedom that I had never known before. I didn't even worry all that much about finding sex.

After a while, though, I started craving some social interaction and, to be honest, the lack of sex did start to wear a little. Then I found bears. What a relief. I can't remember anymore who first introduced me to bears, but I think it was during a tournament at the bowling alley. It doesn't matter. I thought my problems were over. I was wrong.

Imagine how disapproving Michael would have been of my cavorting with bears. Guys who were big, going to seed instead of the gym. Guys who didn't shave, pluck, wax, or depilate, but were covered in hair and didn't feel ashamed about it. Imagine Michael, fatally overcome by apoplexy if he hadn't already been dead. I didn't have to imagine it.

One evening I was enjoying the company of a dump-truck-sized bear named Dwayne who followed me home from the bar. In college he'd been either a football tackle or a refrigerator. He wasn't the most scintillating conversationalist, but conversation wasn't part of our game plan. Dwayne retained a taste for tackling, so we got naked and started our bedroom scrimmage. After a few fumbles, several first downs, and a conversion, the time came to sack the quarterback and try for the final score of the game.

I rolled a latex pigskin onto my dick and slicked it with lube. Dwayne was ready for the defense, leaning across the foot of the bed, wiggling his ass at me. I was ready for my offense, taking aim with my dick on the hairy bull's-eye of his butthole. I pulled Dwayne's voluptuous asscheeks apart and was about to penetrate his end zone when I realized that we were not alone.

"David, you're not going to stick your dick into that hairy ass, are you? You never know where it's been."

It was Michael, the late, never-lamented Michael. He sprawled casually across the top of the bed, pursing his lips and scowling disdainfully at the top of Dwayne's crew cut. Michael was always a bit prissy that way, but I was in no mood to deal with his prissiness right then. Having my dead lover settling in to watch me fuck Dwayne was not my idea of a hot group scene.

I scowled right back. "What the fuck are you doing here?"

"Saving you from a breach of good taste that you will certainly regret in the morning."

"Well, fuck you, I am most definitely going to stick my dick in this hairy ass whether you like it or not."

Dwayne squirmed and moaned, "Oh, I like it. Fuck me! Fuck me now!"

Without thinking, I slapped Dwayne across the ass. "Be quiet, Dwayne. You're not helping."

"Oh, oh!" Dwayne yelped. "I'm a bad bear, such a bad bear. You'll have to spank me!"

Michael rolled his eyes and smirked. "I'm sure even you see now what I mean. Q.E.D."

"*Quod erat demonstrandum,* my ass! I really don't need this right now."

Dwayne pushed his ass back against me. "Quote rot my ass! I need it right now!"

"Shut up, Dwayne!" I made the mistake of slapping his ass again.

"I'll be quiet! Slap me harder, make me obey!"

Michael sniffed and hopped off the bed. He began his pacing routine and our relationship started to flash before my eyes.

"Perhaps," Michael said, "all those years with me really did nothing to raise your level of sophistication. I'm sure I don't regret all the sacrifices I made solely on your behalf, but do try to show a little self-respect by not fucking this Neanderthal."

I was losing it by then, both my temper and my erection. It wasn't only Michael, but our entire, horrible relationship that was coming back to haunt me.

"Fuck you!" I yelled at Michael. Dwayne wiggled his ass again. "I am going to fuck this Neanderthal's fat, hairy ass and enjoy it like I never enjoyed fucking your pathetic, melon-like bubble butt!"

Dwayne stopped wiggling his ass and turned to look at me, perplexed. "What's a Neanderthal? I don't know if I like that."

Michael stood with crossed arms and glowered. "Go

ahead then, ruin your life, but don't blame me for not trying to help."

I yelled, "Go! Just go! Get out of my life forever! You're dead! Stay dead!"

Poor Dwayne. Michael vanished instantly; Dwayne took a little longer. He got off the bed without making any sudden moves and watched me carefully while he put on his clothes. Finally dressed, he backed out of the bedroom, saying, "David, you've got some weird issues to deal with."

I felt really bad. Bad for Dwayne, of course. He is a sweet guy, even if he is a bit Neanderthal. But mostly I felt bad, as in ill. I had finally been getting my life back on course. Now my stomach was churning again at the thought that Michael might be back.

He was most decidedly there to stay. Not continuously, mind you. That's what was so insidious, so Michael. He would only appear whenever I was about to get off on naked-bear companionship. Apparently no one else could see him or hear him, and I thought I could simply ignore him and get on with getting it on, but it was impossible. He'd always appear just in time to keep me from coming, leaving me with a limp dick and lame apologies to my guest.

It wore me down, ruining my sleep, my appetite, and my sex life, not to mention my reputation. I'd go to the bar looking for some companionship, but my friends would avoid talking to me, let alone consider sex with me. Even newcomers managed to avoid my glances. That left only Joe, the bartender, my sole outlet for social intercourse.

It was a quiet night, at least around me. I was sitting at the bar, unsuccessfully trying to drown my sorrows in glass after glass of diet cola. Joe stood behind the bar, squeaking a glass with a towel.

"Joe," I said, "what am I going to do?"

"What's wrong? You're looking pretty pale, like you've

seen a ghost or something."

"I have. Literally. For weeks now."

"Ah, ghosts of relationships past."

"More like dead lover from hell." I poured out my entire story to him, and he poured out diet cola to me. When we'd both finally had enough, he reached over behind his cash register, pulled out a business card, and handed it to me.

"Well," he said, "I don't really believe in all this mumbo jumbo myself, but you might want to give it a try."

The card read:

Onslo Bigpaw
Bear Psychic & Spiritual Healer
"Why settle for a Medium
When you could have an Extra-Large"

I didn't believe in it myself, but what was there to lose?

"Thanks, Joe," I said as I gulped the last of my cola. "I think I will."

It was well after midnight when I got home, but people who deal with the afterlife and all that are mostly working after midnight, right? It seemed safe enough to call Mr. Bigpaw then. I couldn't wait any longer to be spiritually healed.

The person who answered the phone, his voice unusually low and gentle, merely said, "Good evening," but it was somehow reassuring.

I began: "Is this Mr. Bigpaw, bear psychic…?"

"…and spiritual healer," he said. "Yes, but please call me Onslo."

I began again: "Fine, Onslo. I got your card from…"

"…Joe at the bar. Yes, David, I know."

Spooky.

"So anyway, I have this problem…"

"…with manifestations of your dead but still disapproving

lover. Yes, I understand."

Spookier.

"So, do you think...?"

"...that I can help? Most certainly, but it will take a committed effort from both of us."

"How?" I asked. "Some sort of psychic therapy? Isn't it true that people who die traumatic deaths haunt us until their souls find rest?"

"Usually," Onslo explained, "but not in this case. Someone like Michael will never find rest, so that approach is rather pointless."

"Then what do we do?"

"Bear exorcism is the only answer."

"Bear exorcism?"

"In layman's terms, we gross him out so much that he'll never come back. It's a sort of aversion therapy."

He proceeded with the details. I was to meet him in three days' time at his place, at midnight, and bring along six of my most hirsute and trustworthy bear buddies. He suggested that we wear loose clothing and no underwear.

It took a lot of pleading but I finally got six guys to agree. The prohibition on underwear was the most convincing argument. I even enlisted Dwayne by telling him I was working out my weirdest issue. We met at the bar on the appointed night and fortified ourselves with several beers each. Minutes before midnight we left for Onslo Bigpaw's house.

We were met at the door by Onslo, himself a massive bear with a magnificent white beard. I had expected he'd be wearing a turban and cape and was disappointed that he was dressed in jeans and a flannel shirt. However, the room he led us to didn't disappoint. It was large, draped with exotic cloths, lit by candles, and dominated by an enormous circular table at which we were to sit. I ended up directly across from Onslo, with Dwayne at my right.

"What we undertake tonight," Onslo began, "is a very delicate operation that requires everyone's fullest cooperation. Please follow my instructions most attentively.

"First, we must conjure the troubled soul by focusing our bear energy. Join hands with your nearest neighbors to close the spiritual circle. Good. Now purge your mind of all thoughts except those of your most recent sexual encounters."

Onslo began to hum a low, mystical tone. From the looks on the guys' faces, there'd been some pretty good fucking going on lately. Dwayne had his eyes closed and was smiling, obviously not recalling our last evening together. For my part, I tried to imagine the fun I could have with Michael permanently dead.

Onslo stopped humming. "The gamma energy is increasing nicely. David, while we continue focusing, go to each man around the table, unbutton his shirt, run your hand through his chest hair, and caress his nipples while you kiss him."

From the way the guys squirmed, you could bet they had never expected a bear exorcism to be like this. I stood and began with Jack, to my left. I slowly undid the buttons that marched down his chest and over the mound of his belly, then felt my way back up through the black forest of fur that covered him. When I reached his nipples I planted my mouth on his mouth, kissing and pinching until his gamma energy was fully tuned in.

I made my way around the table. By the time I got to Dwayne, the gamma energy must have been filling the room. As I unbuttoned his shirt and started playing with his nipples, he kept whispering that he'd been such a bad bear. It doubled my pleasure to shut him up by kissing him.

That was enough to provoke Michael. He appeared, standing right behind Dwayne so I wouldn't miss him.

"David, I thought you'd given up this Neanderthal phase

you've been going through. I don't know how you can kiss a man with a beard. It chaps the lips."

I stopped kissing Dwayne to say, "Fuck you!" to Michael. Predictably, Dwayne begged me to fuck him.

I looked to Onslo for our next step. He raised a bushy white eyebrow and said, "Everyone, please stand." They all stood.

Onslo said, "Quickly now, remove all your clothing." We all stripped. Michael's face registered his distaste.

"David, these butts have never seen an exercise machine. And all that hair! It's very unattractive."

I didn't even raise my voice. "Michael, I find it exceedingly attractive. These men are beautiful. It makes me unbearably happy to lick their hairy bodies and bury my face in their hairy asses." Michael shuddered. Dwayne's response you can guess.

Onslo said, "Grasp the dick of the man to your right and stroke." We grasped and stroked. Michael gasped and nearly had a stroke.

"David, this is disgusting. You can't possibly be enjoying this!"

"Michael, look around. We're enjoying ourselves very much. I like Dwayne's dick. I like to stroke it."

Dwayne: "Uh-huh, stroke it."

"And I like his big, hairy belly. I like to stroke that too."

Dwayne: "Stroke it hard!"

Michael was nearly at peak disapproval now. "I gave you the best years of my life, trying to improve your life, and this is the thanks I get. Even with the rest of eternity it may be a hopeless task. And stop doing that to his dick. It's nauseating."

"And Michael, I like his big, hairy ass, and I want to fuck it, too!"

Dwayne: "Oh yeah, fuck me. Fuck me now!"

I threw Dwayne onto his back on the table. "I will, Dwayne. I will fuck you now like you've never been fucked!"

I stood, my dick poised at Dwayne's asshole.

Dwayne shouted, "Fuck me! Fuck me!"

Michael shouted, "Don't do it, David!"

Onslo shouted, "Everyone, fuck now!"

And fuck we did. Bears on the table, bears on the floor, bears fucking everywhere. My dick, for the first time since Michael's return, was rock hard and aching. I plunged it into Dwayne's willing asshole and fucked him as if my life depended on it, which it did.

Michael covered his face with his hands, and started shaking and groaning. I fucked Dwayne harder. Michael started to lose his shape, as if he was melting. I fucked Dwayne harder and deeper. Michael looked at me with terror in his eyes, his mouth open in a silent scream. I fucked Dwayne harder and deeper and faster.

The end was near. Suddenly I was at the edge of coming. Dwayne yelled something like "I'm ready! Shoot now!" And I did. I shot load after load after load. As I filled Dwayne's big hairy ass with cum, a horrible, screeching sound escaped from Michael and he burst into flames. Bright, intense flames that consumed him in seconds. Then he was gone. It was a great exit. Very Michael. Too bad no one else could see it.

I collapsed on top of Dwayne. He stroked my back and mumbled something comforting about how good it was for him. It was quiet in the room, except for the heavy breathing. It was calm, too. And peaceful. I felt relaxed.

Onslo looked at me over the shoulders of the bear sitting in his lap. "Congratulations, David. Freedom is yours."

I couldn't believe it. "That's it?" I asked.

"That's it," he said. "He's gone and you've come."

Freedom. For the first time in weeks—no, make that years—I felt happy. Deep down happy. Happy at last to be who I was, happy to be what I was, and free to love the men I loved. I had finally arrived.

The Strange Château of Dr. Kruge
Drew Gummerson

It is almost dark when we cycle up to the old hotel. Morgan chains our bikes together and we step through double doors that stand half open. It is colder within than without.

"Helloa!" shouts Morgan in a sunnily fake-Hawaiian voice. There is no answer and Morgan is about to shout again, making a cone of his hands around his mouth, when a cadaverous-looking woman appears from the shadows at the side of a loudly ticking grandfather clock. She takes a step toward us, and then recoils. Perhaps it is our smell or perhaps something else. I am not sure.

"We have a room booked," says Morgan. "Name of Gonad. Mr. and Mrs. Gonad."

The woman looks at us as if we are both equally guilty of Morgan's poor joke and huffs over to a large reception desk. There is a book open there. She wipes dust from it with the outer edge of her sleeve and runs a finger down to the single entry.

"A double room?" she says, fixing us with a milky gaze. The words sound more like a threat than a question.

"Is there a problem?" says Morgan.

"I don't want any trouble," says the woman. She reaches behind her and pushes a large key across the desk. "This is a family hotel."

"Then think of us as family," says Morgan. And he takes the key.

The room has a large four-poster bed in it, a carpet worn almost through to the boards, and a window that looks out onto the night sky and a gibbous moon.

Morgan takes a shower first and then me. After, as is our ritual, we compare our underpants.

We have been doing this for ten years, ever since we were fourteen. The first year it was an act of rebellion, an abnegation of parental authority: No, Mum, I will *not* wear clean underpants. Now it is something else, more than that. For me at least.

"I think I'm the winner," says Morgan. He traces a large yellow stain with the stubby end of his forefinger. "Look at the size of that."

"I'm sure you're cheating," I say.

"In what way?"

"It has to be incidental staining," I say. "That's the rules. That stain looks like you've wee'd deliberately."

"Sour grapes," says Morgan. "Anyway, three days to go. I'm going to wear mine backward tomorrow."

"Now that is cheating," I say.

"All's fair in love and war." Suddenly Morgan strides over to the window and looks out. He has a towel hung low around his waist, a back the shape of a triangle on a point. "Do you think there's any action here? I need a shag."

I look down at Morgan's underpants where he has left them on the bed. I'd read once of Japanese men buying used panties from teenage girls and placing them over their heads while they masturbated. Once, that had seemed disgusting. Things always do when they are not you.

"Well?" says Morgan.

"I doubt it," I say and I cast my arms about. "We're in the middle of nowhere here."

Just then there is a knock at the door. It opens and a young woman enters.

"Excuse me," she says. "Ma sent me up with these." The woman holds up a pile of pillowcases. She looks at Morgan. "And if there is anything else I can do...?"

"There is one thing," says Morgan and he juts out that chin of his like some 1940s movie star. "If you would be so kind as to help a young man out with a pressing problem under his towel."

The woman lets out a peal of laughter. It sounds like live lemons being slaughtered by a fruit shop owner. I know what that means. It is time for me to make myself scarce. Morgan has found his shag. He always does.

I find myself in a cavernous dining area and, being at a loss about what to do, I take a seat.

Like the rest of the hotel this room is cast in darkness and it is ten minutes before I notice another presence. It is a man. He is at a circular table set magnificently for eight and yet he sits alone.

As I am looking he catches my eye. He holds up his wine glass and nods slightly. My table being empty and therefore having nothing for me to hold up, I merely nod.

Suddenly there is a small explosion of noise to my left, like that of a vacuum emptying involuntarily. I twist my eyes from the man and see now that in the center of my table is a glass tube with a door in it. In the center of the tube is a bobbing Ping-Pong ball.

I look back at the man, there being no one else to blame for this phenomenon, and he smiles slightly and mimes for me to retrieve the ball from the glass tube. I do and, holding the ball up close to my eyes, I see some words scrawled haphazardly across it. "Come and join me," they say. Under the words I can just make out a signature. "Dr. Kruge," I think it reads.

I look at the ball and then the man. I have to make a decision.

I stand up from the table.

Dr. Kruge and I are pleasantly drunk, like two oysters left to soak in vermouth. We have eaten only cold toast with dripping but drunk glass after glass of fine champagne. Dr. Kruge has a small moustache that curls up at the end and he wears a cravat and a fine purple waistcoat made of worsted wool. He seems to be a man of the world.

I am at the point of telling him about Morgan and his underpants when he takes the lighted cigarette out of his mouth and says through a cloud of smoke, "I wonder if you might be able to help me. You see, I am building a collection of arses."

For a second I believe that I have heard wrong. Dr. Kruge perhaps said, "a collection of vases," and I imagine large, bulbous ones set peacefully around a manmade lake in the center of an ornamental garden.

"Male arses, for the most part," says Dr. Kruge. "I take plaster of paris casts. It doesn't involve any pain and would take an hour and a half max."

I put my hands flat on the tabletop as if I am about to push myself up.

"Of course, I would pay handsomely," says Dr. Kruge.

I hover, halfway off my seat.

"Two hundred and fifty pounds a pop. Look." Dr. Kruge reaches into a pocket in his waistcoat and pulls out a gold-edged card. "If you are interested, call me at this number. I'll be waiting for your call."

"We'll see," I say. I gather up the card and make my way out of the dining area.

The room is full of the smell of cum but there is no sign of the woman. Morgan's bare torso sticks out from under the duvet and his breathing indicates that he is asleep. I put out the light, take off my clothes, and climb into bed next to him. After a number of hours in which I imagine what Morgan's bum would look like in plaster of paris, I fall asleep, my erection jerking spasmodically in the anticipation of use that doesn't come.

In the morning I am woken by a strong, bitter smell under my nose. I cough sharply and curse Morgan. This is one of his favorite tricks. He wets his forefinger with saliva, inserts it up his arse, wiggles it about, and then holds it in front of my nose.

"You're awake, then," says Morgan.

"Fuck off!" I say, only half angrily. I never know how Morgan expects me to take his games.

"I'm going for a dump," says Morgan and gets out of bed and walks naked across the floor.

I stand outside the toilet door and shout through it about my meeting with Dr. Kruge.

"He SOUnds like a WEIrdo," grunts back Morgan and then I mention the money. Money has always been a desirable beast for Morgan. When we were fourteen he used to let Mr. Richards, the one-eyed art teacher, suck his cock for five pounds inside the Romanesque gazebo on the perimeter of the school grounds. I sometimes wonder if I am the only person in Middle England who has not had sex with Morgan. This perhaps is an exaggeration but that is how I feel.

One time on the Starship Enterprise ride at Margate's World of Adventure, Morgan sat between my legs five times in a row as we looped the loop at a terminal velocity. I thought my balls were going to explode and after we came off I had to masturbate surreptitiously in an oversized bucket of popcorn I had placed on my lap.

Sex, Morgan had said, would ruin our intimacy. I wasn't sure exactly what he meant, but like everything else that Morgan said it sounded true.

"Two HUNdred and FIFty pounds!" explodes Morgan from the toilet. "Does he want me to wash it first?"

Dr. Kruge's house is more of a château than a house. It stands on the top of a precipice like a playing card tossed languorously from a hustler's hand.

I knock on the door and it is answered immediately by a teenager wearing nothing but a cock ring. The cock ring has caused his penis to enlarge dramatically.

"Dr. Kruge," I say.

"I'm not," says the teenager and appears to be on the point of closing the door.

"No, we are here to see him," I say and then I see Dr. Kruge appearing at the end of a long corridor rather like a magician does at the beginning of a magic show.

"You've met Helmut," says Dr. Kruge. "Large penis but no brain, I am afraid. It is often the way in the male of the species." Dr. Kruge holds out his hand toward Morgan. "You must be Morgan," he says.

"Two hundred and fifty pounds for my arse," says Morgan.

"There may have been a slight misunderstanding," says Dr. Kruge.

"What do you mean?" says Morgan.

Dr. Kruge's left hand drifts nervously up to the right-hand side of his pointed moustache. He begins to twist the hairs around and around his index finger.

We have repaired to Dr. Kruge's study. "Repaired" is Dr. Kruge's word. Dr. Kruge is sitting on one side of a large mahogany table, Morgan and I on the other.

"I used to be a quite brilliant scientist in the Transvaal," says Dr. Kruge, continuing a story that began somewhere halfway up the stairs. "I was funded by the highest echelons of governmental bodies to do research into the reproductive nature of the common bumblebee." Dr. Kruge pauses and holds up his hand as if fearing interruption by either Morgan or me. "My studies were going well, spectacularly well I should say, when one day quite unexpectedly as a by-product of my research I discovered something quite remarkable." Dr. Kruge stops here. He stands and places his hand on a large ebony phallus. He turns to us and I know he is going to say something incredible. "The instrument I had developed to look into the sex lives of bees could, I found with a little tweaking, be used to look into a human and see their deepest, darkest sexual fantasies."

At this point Morgan makes a loud farting sound with his lips.

"My government, too, found the idea extraordinary," says Dr. Kruge. "Until I proved myself to be correct beyond the most intrusive cross-examination." Dr. Kruge raises his hands to the air like a conductor pointing out a firework display on a cloudy night in Johannesburg. "Imagine a country being run by a prime minister whose population knows he wants to clean a whore's buttocks with his tongue after she has evacuated into a bucket. Of course, I was made to flee. And now I carry out my experiments on a smaller scale."

"What exactly do these experiments involve?" says Morgan.

"You are a very hasty and presumptuous young man," says Dr. Kruge. "One should never interrupt a scientist."

"Just tell us," says Morgan.

Dr. Kruge sighs like a knight chased from a field by a lusty dragon. He starts at the beginning and tells us the course of the experiment from start to finish.

"I'll do it," says Morgan, "but on two conditions."

"Which are…?" says Dr. Kruge.

"That you pay up front in cash and that it is my friend who carries out the procedure."

"It's a deal," says Dr. Kruge.

Morgan and I are in a black-walled room lit brightly by a strip of spotlights. In the center of the room is an awkwardly designed chair with leather straps fastened to its four extremities.

Morgan turns to face me and then piece by piece he removes his clothes. I have seen Morgan naked many times but for some reason this feels like the first time. He has strong shoulders, a wide chest, hairy legs. His cock is large and hangs to the left of big balls in a drooping sac. Morgan always said he had his father's balls. I wasn't sure. I hadn't seen them. For a second Morgan's eyes lock on mine and then he turns and bends over the chair.

There are straps for each of his arms and legs. I fasten them tightly, pulling the leather through the buckle and fixing the metal prong securely in its hole. The design of the chair is such that Morgan is bent forward and his arse is sticking up in the air, roughly on a level with my waist.

There is a rubber tube on the floor at the center of the chair. I pick it up with one hand and with the other I take hold of Morgan's penis. It is the first time I have ever touched it. Gently I pull back the foreskin and I place the head of the tube, which opens like the mouth of a viper, over the end of the cock. Dr. Kruge said that sometimes the experiment causes the patient to pee. My own cock is hard in my underpants. Neither Morgan nor I say anything.

As Dr. Kruge has said, I find hot water in a porcelain bowl and next to it a men's razor. I take the bowl and the razor and place them behind Morgan and then I part the cheeks of his arse.

It seems strange to be looking so closely at those most intimate of places. The hair is thick on both sides and then there is a clearing around the sphincter. The skin here swirls like a frozen whirlpool. It seems to both prohibit and welcome entry at the same time. I take up the razor and start to shave.

The hair falls away easily, drifting to the floor and collecting on the surface of the bowl of hot water, and soon I am left with a clear, white surface. The sphincter seems to breathe in and out, or twitch. I want to thank Dr. Kruge for giving me this opportunity. I wonder what he will accept as a token of appreciation, and then I remember he is paying us for this and that I have a job to do.

Dr. Kruge's contraption is on a table by the far wall. It somewhat resembles a French baguette connected to a pair of binoculars by a pliable pink neon tube. I lift it, remarking on its weight, and heft it back to where Morgan's arse is waiting.

"This may hurt a little," I say.

"You won't tell anyone about this, will you?" says Morgan.

This is the guy who has fucked everyone in every position. Morgan once told me he pissed in a pint glass and played a game of cards with a Dutch prostitute to see who would drink it. This being Morgan, it was the winner who would drink it. He told everyone this, his mother included. She had laughed like a drain gurgling and said something about urine being sterile.

"Will you?" says Morgan. "Tell them the fantasy, I mean?"

"I won't say anything," I say. "I promise."

I rest the contraption by the leg of the chair for a second

and take out of my pocket the small jar of lubricant Dr. Kruge had given me. I open it and massage the contents into Morgan's arse with the tips of my fingers. I move them around and around the circle of his arsehole, and I want so much to push them inside, know this would make it easier for the larger object that is to come, but somehow I cannot do it yet.

I tell Morgan to brace himself and then place the strap of the binoculars over my head and put the end of the "baguette" against Morgan's sphincter.

The baguette is about six inches long and probably six inches in circumference. I put pressure against it, pushing into it with my waist. At first the sphincter resists, the head of the baguette merely bouncing against it; but then gradually the sphincter opens up.

I push the baguette in slightly, wait, and then push some more. Morgan groans softly and I hear a slight gargling from the tube attached to his penis.

Gradually, bit by bit, the whole length disappears and I am in.

My best friend at school had been Rosie Diamond. I thought I was in love with her. I was fifteen. I showed her my penis and she showed me her breasts and let me touch them. Then I introduced her to Morgan.

"It's love," she said.

"Look at these," said Morgan.

He had taken pictures of them together with his parents' Instamatic camera. He standing up, Rosie Diamond on her knees.

"Can I keep this one?" I had asked. It was the cum shot. Morgan had caught his sperm in midair flying toward Rosie Diamond's mouth.

"If you like," said Morgan.

Alone in my room at night I would often look at the picture. Sometimes I would imagine that I was Rosie Diamond, sometimes Morgan. I was never me.

I take up the binoculars and place them against my eyes. I do as Dr. Kruge said. I adjust the focus by rotating a small dial between the eyepieces. For a second all is fuzzy discordant images: a severed breast, an arsehole smiling, a penis swelling from flaccid to erect. Then the image sharpens.

This is Morgan's fantasy.

A bus is moving through an arid landscape. Cacti lean toward and away from a burning sun. The driver of the bus sweats under a Stetson hat, and the only passenger is an aging southern belle drinking a margarita from the end of a long straw. And Morgan.

Morgan is at the back of the bus. He is wearing jeans. At the crotch you can see the outline of his knob, the material worn here, comfortable against its shape. Morgan appears to be asleep. His eyes are closed, his stomach rising and falling within his T-shirt.

I am thinking that Dr. Kruge is wrong, that this is no fantasy, when the bus stops and I get on. It is me, dressed in a poncho and eating a Granny Smith apple. Morgan appears to wake up. We catch each other's eye, something seems to flare between us, and I go and sit near him at the back.

In dreamtime long periods can pass in an instant. It is like this now, looking into Morgan's arse. The sun moves across the sky, the desert outside the window cools, the driver removes his Stetson and runs a wrinkled hand across his bald head. The outline of Morgan's knob in his jeans remains a constant. This is the epicenter of the dream.

At some point the bus stops for a comfort break and Morgan and I head out to the urinal together. It is a brick shed, four walls open to the sky above. Flies buzz, making patterns in the air.

Morgan and I stand side by side and as Morgan is pissing I look down at his cock. He holds it one-handed and doesn't shake it before flipping it back into his pants. Back on the bus I take the seat next to him.

Night comes and the southern belle reaches up and flicks on her minispot. She opens a large, hardback novel. Something by Barbara Taylor Bradford, I see.

Morgan spreads apart his legs so his thigh is touching mine and he pulls a zip-up fleece across his lap. On the bus I am wide awake, as I am here in this room, my eyes pressed against the binoculars.

In dreamtime outside the bus, the desert is silent. I watch as I stretch my hands up in the air and bring them down on Morgan's lap. I can feel his cock there, beneath the layers of material. It is hard now. As is mine.

Morgan moves his own hands under the fleece and he is undoing the top button of his trousers and lowering his zipper.

I push my hand under the zip-up top and run my hands down Morgan's stomach. I find the waistband of his underpants and I slip my fingers under that too and brush against the tip of Morgan's cock. He groans gently, sleepily, or with desire, and I move my hands further down and grip the shaft more tightly.

At the front of the bus the old driver scowls into a wing mirror. The southern belle turns the pages of her book. I face forward and so does Morgan and my hand is moving up and down.

Morgan cums quickly, inside his underpants. I feel the cum slide down over my hand and my hand stays there and I fall asleep and like the end of a film the image flicks flicks flicks and is gone.

"That is your fantasy?" I say to Morgan, standing away from the binoculars. I am stunned. This friend who has done everything thinks of me!

"Can you get that baguette out of my back passage?" says Morgan. "It hurts like fuck."

Gently I pull back the baguette and watch as it slides out of Morgan's arse. There is a residue of lubricant there and, boldly, I scoop it up on my fingers and press it to my lips.

"It can be my turn now," I say. Then I echo Morgan's words. "All's fair in love and war."

"I already know your fantasy," says Morgan, and he tells me to go and pick up his underpants. They are the ones he has been wearing all week. I stretch them between my hands and gaze at the map of stains.

"That is just a fantasy," I say unsurely.

"Sometimes you can make your fantasies come true," says Morgan. I look at him and our eyes lock.

I think, *Maybe Morgan is right and maybe he isn't.* I am not sure exactly how fantasies relate to the way we lead our life.

No bother. You only live once. I take a step toward Morgan.

My Place
Alpha Martial

There's always a moment when I think about murder. It's not important. Like the moments when you fancy a smoke even though you know you gave up years ago, it soon passes. But I think it's something about the light in this place in the early evening—especially in the wintertime—that mingles with the complete peace and lack of noise. It makes me think of death, but in a nice way—someone else's death, someone who means nothing to me but for their trophy value. Preferably someone who would die for me willingly if given the choice.

One of the problems I've always had is that I don't like bloody human tissue. Making small traces over flesh with a sharp blade—just enough to create little drips and draw a wince from the boy—now, that's sweet. I love my delicate equipment, but the idea of outright gore doesn't do much for me. I remember too vividly the time my sister had her thigh ripped open by a dog when we were young; I think that's the problem. That, and the crash at which I was a witness. Sinews and that disturbing and mysterious whitish goo that explodes from beneath the skin…it's upsetting to think we're all made of that. I've no desire to see it again.

As for other methods, well…guns aren't sexy other than the shape and the shine. Shooting someone has to be the coldest and least satisfying way; besides, the gore is probably as bad, contrary to the movie romance. There's no point in poison. Electrocution kind of appeals…but to take it to death? I don't think so; there's no begging at that point.

Whatever. The fact is that if I killed the boys, I wouldn't get to see their faces on screen later and say to myself, *You carry me inside you*. Instead I might be in jail. Or, worse, I might have to see them become some Jim Morrison–esque martyr-legend. As it is, they always sing my praises afterward; I'm pretty good at judging who's bought the myth enough to protect me, come what may. There's an endless stream, thanks to that. It's a game and I'm always aware of that, even as I sometimes ponder breaking my own rules. The thing is, I'm not sure I've ever won the game; I dream of the perfect opponent, but they've all turned out to be charlatans so far. And now I'm hoping….

Just as I'm examining the sunset through the pale amber of my Jameson's, there's a slight noise. Casey's waking up, or just dreaming a nasty dream, maybe. When I look around, sure enough, I can see his left hand twitching feverishly. I started out the usual way, cuffing his wrists separately and suspending each from on high—just so that his knees were almost dragging on the floor but not quite. Midway through the first night, however, he started making such a racket that I couldn't sleep so I gave in and strapped him up by the shoulders and just cuffed his wrists behind him. It's been almost three days now and, this afternoon, he finally passed out from exhaustion. Most of them sleep the second night—resigned to what's happening, I suppose. It's not as though they don't get a break for their tired limbs; all the while I'm busy with them, they're supported and they can always stand up when I'm not. But I knew, from his very first mail, that Casey was going to be the supersensitive type.

That was the main attraction, to start with; I've become very bored with boys who come over all repulsed and then, too quickly, pretend to be playing along with me—whatever they think that means. It's all bluster, simply play-acting. Some of them make a point of feigning pleasure whilst others quite evidently enjoy it, no matter how I step up the pain. I don't need that; I have Adam to satisfy the part of me that wants a constant with whom to enjoy occasionally rough consensual sex. Meanwhile, he has his own things to do and he's never begrudged me mine...safe down in my place. He's never even been here.

I had it designed especially. Most of the house is just an old minichâteau, classic in the style of the southern French Compte of yore. I had it completely gutted and done out, then worked on this part. It's quite cleverly designed because you can't see the dome from outside other than from the air. The house is on top of a hill. Not that many people come here, anyway. I do my business in England still. Press, etc., come to my respectable Islington pad. Anyway, half the dome is windows, a semicircle that allows natural light to saturate the place from dawn till dusk. In the dark side of the circle lies all my equipment, including the enormous mirror in front of which Casey is presently hung.

The light is a golden pink, even without my whiskey filter. I noticed it last night, though he was thrashing about so: his skin is perfectly complemented by the color. I didn't actually find myself attracted to him in the least before I got to know him. He's the stocky rocker type—tattoos and piercings all over—so he'd usually have been instantly interesting to me; it was just his coloring that put me off. Yet having had the time to browse his body, I find it quite special. He's *almost* freckly, but not quite. His skin doesn't have that translucent, redhead's quality about it, but rather a porcelain-type fineness. Better still, when I examine it, he flutters his long, fair lashes closed in exquisite but completely pointless protest at my touch. Better yet, when he gets particularly upset, he tosses his head back a little, sending his tremendous mane of golden curls cascading even further than normal down his tensed spine.

Casey's beautiful, I've decided. One of the best yet.

He confided to me, in his mail, all about his upbringing; he was raped by a stepfather over a period of two years before running away from home and becoming a drug addict and prostitute in New Orleans at the age of fifteen. A classic tale, especially for a rock star. But there was something so terribly credible about him...and now that I've met him, I don't doubt it. I can't imagine him lying about anything, let alone something like that. Earnest, is the word. *It's* delightful. So when he said he's sat and pored over my words for literally hours on end, whilst, before, I was dubious, now I think maybe I've found the Real McCoy. He looks up to me in a way that I've never thought possible before, I now realize; there's always been something missing from the others.

I wrote back to him straightaway. He seemed to be looking for something—some kind of fatherly reassurance on his chosen path. I'm just a poet; I never pretended to anything else, and I never claimed the moral high ground, either. He wanted me to be some kind of mentor; I wanted to explore him. It's a type of exchange. "*...I never felt truly confident in myself, despite the fact that I'm just a singer in a rock band (so I shouldn't need qualifications, I mean). I always felt myself cringing in the dark, alone. I always wanted to finish school, in truth. It means a lot to me and it will never stop smarting that I didn't get through it and get my college degree—at least. I feel* *a constant need to prove myself, intellectually. It's embarrassing because I feel it showing sometimes...as though my fly is undone but I'm holding two drinks."*

He has the cutest way of expressing himself—and he's right; he's bright. It shows. But so does his insecurity. I can honestly say that my lack of formal qualifications never occurred to me as a barrier to what I felt driven to do artistically. Maybe it didn't occur to Casey either but he seems a lot more chewed up about it, in a general life attainment sense, than I've ever been. Maybe it's partly an American thing, too. I came from a good family but just couldn't be arsed to toe the line; in England, that's almost normal. Class is about breeding far more than letters after your name. I fully admit that I've been able to achieve fame almost solely because I had the connections—and Father didn't want me to "come to nothing." Maybe that is the same in the States, judging by certain presidents, but I've a feeling there's more pressure on kids to attain, academically. And if you're a kid from the wrong side of the tracks in the first place, the gap between you and the elite is bound to feel vast.

The light's fading. I've found myself staring at him again, hanging there...golden pink. I feel an overwhelming desire and I have a feeling I can fulfill it without risking anything. I unstrap him, supporting his sturdy form, and he lets out no more than a sigh in his slumber. I drag him, backward, to the chaise longue and lay him out, spreading his full-muscled thighs over the end. He cries as I push inside him. I never even had to think about preparing myself, or him; just thinking about him makes me ready and he's so moist up there from the last time...

...and to take him gently now....

I could have done it in the first place. I could have wined and dined him and watched the faux-shocked expression flit across his face before he acquiesced, as I know he would (a he said he would). But to take him gently *after*....

When he arrived, he looked like a giant orchid, transported to colder climes than those to which it was native and likely to wither as quickly as such. He's not especially tall, like so many stars, and stocky, as I said. But some Americans—particularly those from the central states, I've found—don't need size to make them come across larger than life. He's one such. I greeted him as he made his way from the taxi, up the dry grass path, a khaki holdall flung over his shoulder. He smiled so beautifully that all misgivings I'd had about his looks were gone; he was so transparently giving...and so transparently mine.

I have a little cabinet of various medications I can use to subdue them if they look likely to struggle. I'm a young guy still, and fit, but all the same even someone of Casey's stature could probably floor me given the urge. I slipped him a downer in his whiskey and Coke (he'd asked for Jack) and watched his clear blue eyes start to glaze over. He was talking about how much he'd looked forward to coming here, even started talking about how he'd never really had the chance to see the landscape when he'd been on tour around here, how much he still wanted to learn about and experience the world and all the different beauties it had to offer. I know the feeling. But anyway, he was just getting on to how much I meant to him again—and I wasn't about to contest his reasoning—when he started to have trouble propping his chin on his elbow.

"It's really good of you to invite me down here, Ant, but I think I'm gonna be really impolite and fall asleep on you...I don't know why I'm so tired...." I smiled at him and reached out to touch his workmanlike hand.

"Come upstairs with me. I'll show you your room."

And I'd brought him up here. He was still aware enough to

register the leather straps and the mirrors, the lack of any bed-like normalities. I steered him toward the biggest mirror, stood solid behind him, chin resting on his shoulder. His lids were becoming very heavy by that stage. I kissed his hair for the first time. He started to lean into me and I could feel the power almost gone from his muscles. I began to pull his clothes from him; he'd left his jacket downstairs so there was only the Black Sabbath T-shirt on top. I felt his breathing stop as I unbuttoned his jeans and let them slip to the ground. A pair of black designer boxers remained. I buckled his wrists in the shackles directly on both sides of the mirror, just at the right height so that he could stand and support himself with his arms perpendicular to his body. Restrained, he was breathtaking—something Christ-like about him. I kissed into his warm neck, took time to examine the designs on his chest and arms, the little cupid just below his belly button contrasting with the scary fantasy images on the rest. Meanwhile, he stared at me via the mirror with increasing difficulty.

He could talk ten-to-the-dozen, as I'd quickly found out. So it was particularly rewarding to shut him up, and I sensed that I *would* have shut him up with or without the drugs; he seemed to babble through nervousness and the need to prove his powers of communication. I could sense his fear, the danger he felt with the realization that I'd been premeditative enough to knock him out with he-knew-not-what. I could do anything, as he knew.

"I'm going to fuck you, Casey," I whispered close to his ear.

"Why didn't you say? I don't mind...I'm not blinkered."

"I know...but asking is so boring, darling."

"You can't rape me, Ant—you know what they say; I'm willing...."

"That's not what your body language is telling me, Casey."

I ripped the boxers from his lightly-golden-haired buttocks, transfixed, momentarily, by the enormity of the almost-erection that greeted my eyes in the mirror. "Not even that fools me, but it's quite nice, all the same." As I pushed him onto his knees and helped gravity part his thighs, I decided to give in to the desire to see him come before getting stuck in myself, so to speak. Kneeling snug behind him, I started to touch him—no lubrication, no niceties save a few tender kisses and bites to his shoulder and neck. He straightened his arms against the wall, resisting the urge to collapse forward. I sensed his need to convince me he wanted this in any case, even as his fading consciousness demonstrated his manipulation and lack of consent. I reached forward to get the KY from the floor next to the mirror.

Working him with my hand, I could see his head drooping just as his tensed arse pressed back into me. I stroked him hard, desperate to keep him awake, then pulled his head back by the hair to watch his half-open eyes watching himself and my greased fingers. In his drowsiness, it was easy to bring him to orgasm. I wanted him spent beforehand; he'd have had too much physical pleasure in being fucked otherwise. But he still tried his best to convince me:

"Screw me, Ant. You know I want you to." His glazed eyes stared into mine in the mirror. The struggle to keep his cool was valiant and impressive, more so than his pseudo-educated talk beforehand. I sunk into him, tasting his neck again like a bloodsucker, wallowing in warm locks as I let the viciousness take me over. I could feel his insides give way to me, hear his heroic stifling of the cries as the pain hit in—pain, not only of the penetration itself, but of the leather slicing into his wrists as my thrusts pushed him down and into his own reflection. I trailed fingers, still sticky with gel and his cum, through his finely conditioned curls, and felt a flinch. Finally, as I shot into him, he let himself collapse into the wall, a slight sob escaping his gentle mouth.

It was after that that I first strung him up like a carcass; he was so passed out that he stayed mute, eyes shut, for around six hours. I sat there and watched him for about half of that time, lost in the delicate trail of blood down the inside of his right thigh, the way his thick neck gave way to a broad yet finely muscled back, the way his legs remained parted. I could see his impressive biceps straining automatically to counter the drag of the shackles on his wrists, could sense the pressure building in the knees that were so cruelly—and only just— robbed of their rightful position on the ground. It was a false rest, of course. I never waste good drugs on my boys after the first requirement. Besides, it spoils the entertainment.

The distant village clock was striking midnight as he started to come round. I'd enjoyed a fine Bourgogne and my favorite speciality from the local charcuterie by that time. I offered him some food, but all he could say—rather patheti- cally—was "Let me down?" and "My head's killing me." I love the way he's so lacking in pride like that. I moved a bench around so that I could position it under him, twisting his arms around till they were crossed and contorted above him and his thighs were neatly straddling the wood.

"You must like a bit of torture, Casey, judging by those great piercings you have through your nipples?"

He shook his head slowly. "What's the safe word?"

I shook my head in turn. "There isn't one around here, Precious."

"So why are you asking me?"

That kind of talk is simply begging for a nonverbal response. I lubed my electric probe and set it next to his left nipple. He gasped and shrank back, a faint burn mark evident on his chest already. "Want it inside you?"

"...don't...."

He made it so much more fun than usual. I have to confess, I've never stuck the thing inside anyone; I don't know what it would do. But I've often threatened. Even the hardest cases tend to turn to jelly at the prospect. But with Casey, it was more about how many sweet noises I could wring from him without actually hurting him much at all. There was something so wronged about his expression all the while. Most of them have forgotten who I am by that stage; if they worshipped me before, they'd long since stopped—at least, until they wanted to keep up with the image at the next interview. Casey radiated submission and, somehow, I knew that what he thought of me, I'd know. Me and no one else.

A while after, I gave him some wine, serving it to his mouth as though to a minor goddess. He gazed into me, seeming to search out the meaning of my actions. I followed the wine with a kiss—very gentle. It was the first time I'd touched his lips with mine.

There was no reluctance on his part; he accepted my tongue almost greedily. I'd stripped to take him the last time and I ground our nakedness together, aware of the strain on his sturdy wrists as the pressure of my body bore down on his. He dared to escape my lips.

"Let me go, Ant. I'll be your boy. You can hurt me."

He was driving me mad with this stuff. Missing the point completely. I knew I had to break him, convince him of my intentions, that night. I don't want him like that, you see. And to resist him and to disappoint him—and myself at the same time—is a challenge and an ultimate pleasure. I could even kid myself that lying on him naked like that, kissing him softly, was just another way to offer him false hope that I'd give in and make love to him.

I pulled back, strapped him up, feeling his feeble attempts to use his weakened limbs to push his point. I didn't need to say, "I don't want you to be my boy, I don't need your permission to hurt you." It was hanging in the air as I switched off the light and left him to stare at his own exquisite form in the reflected moonlight.

Sometimes I ponder whether what I do is actually a crime. It's this doubt, on reflection, that makes me stop short of murder; murder *is* a crime, without question...but what I do? If the "victim" never takes you to the police—when, in fact, they tend to leave your house almost as serene as they'd been when they'd entered it—are they a victim at all? Rather like Schrodinger's Cat, it's not a crime unless it's witnessed as such. Surely. But then that would equally mean that Casey's stepfather was entitled to rape his boy-charge—so long as Casey never complained. And as far as Casey's stepfather is concerned, Casey never complained. He saved it until now, until the likes of me came along to offer comfort and sympathy, a father figure. History repeating....

As I hang him up again, the gentle fuck over, he doesn't bother to so much as wriggle; I've broken him, finally. He's mentally and physically sick of the challenge to be anything more than an object for me. He can't imagine how much more than that he is, which is perfect beyond words. His head hangs forward, the golden ringlets aspiring to the floor like a waterfall shielding its almost paradoxically calm inner sanctum. There's a barely perceptible shudder running around the muscles of his entire body—first his right thigh, sending a current through the down, then up the contour of his waist; a twitch of the fingers; a slight, involuntary shake of the mane. He shakes it for me even more as I reach through and fondle his soft balls, whisper his name....

It's fully dark as I settle down on the sofa again, tapping future memories into my laptop. I stop to turn the heating up a little. The lack of nourishment over several days has left him cold as well as weak; I can almost hear his teeth chattering.

I was in a band when I was in my late teens and early twenties. We got some attention and it was only fifteen or so years ago; it's not as though I have no clue about the lifestyle. I was the lyricist and singer, just like Casey, but I soon became bored; I never found my musical soulmates, I suppose—people who'd wait for me to write something I loved and love it too. It's not a problem, because so many artists ask for me in a guest capacity that I still feel connected to the music world without the pressures. And I still enjoy the perks of celebrity status, including the few peculiar ones of my own making. I never liked performing anyway; as a poet, you don't have to do too much of that.

Casey, on the other hand, loves to be on stage. He must have mentioned it at least once in every mail he sent me. Not that I needed to be told, in the first place; you can see it from any live footage. He's not a cock rocker—just a plain old-fashioned singer with a big voice and leather jeans, belting it out and making love to his audience between every song. I watched him much more attentively after he wrote to me the first time, intrigued but not sure why. I even saved a few videos. Maybe I tasted a little bit of that mystery charisma that's made him one of the highest-earning, most adored singers of his generation? Or maybe I just knew he'd be easy and enticing?

It's simplistic, in any case, to talk purely in terms of what he is now—which is, after all, only a product of what he was aged five, ten, fifteen, and twenty. That's exactly what makes him easy, but not for just anyone. No, he chose to sacrifice himself to me. We've never spoken about his man-on-man experience as an adult, but I've a feeling it doesn't amount to much, if anything. I may even be the first man to have had him since his last client, ten years or more ago. What a thrill.

I look at the document in front of me and focus, just as I hear a groan and glance around to see Casey's head thrown back, the muscles in his arms tensing visibly, if frailly. What happens next shocks even me; he starts up a kind of primal howl, as though he's given up on all words. I knew I was pushing him beyond the usual, but I never expected that kind of sound to come from anyone as a result of something I'd done. For long minutes, I sit, head craned around, watching his strong fingers curling and clenching, his eyelids screwed up, his lips stretched to their widest capacity…and listening to the noise of pure despair, completely within my control. It's as though he's oblivious to my presence in the room, maybe delirious through lack of food and proper rest. His cries echo in my head like something from my very distant past; it's the most exquisite pleasure and pain to hear them.

I wonder, fleetingly, if he might just be finally desperate to perform some natural function other than the liquid kind. But that's clearly not the case; the sound subsides as a spasm ripples down the muscles from his shoulders to his hips. His head's still hanging back, the throat and strong profile silhouetted beautifully against the soft light from the stairway. He looks dead.

I put my laptop carefully aside, as though a noise might alter the outcome of my next move. As I approach him from behind, I can see he's still perfectly alive; the breaths pump shallow, like those of a sleeping animal, visible only when squinting at the peripheries of the body. I touch the roots of his hair, trail my fingers through the length, spreading the small amount of accumulating oil to the silken ends close to the small of his back. He remains silent, unflinching. I'm not sure what makes me decide; usually I've done this much sooner—drained them and extracted a promise before letting them down. Usually they're not this far gone. I wouldn't dream of taking it so far. And now I wonder where I've taken it exactly. But I know it's time to take him down….

I carry him, surprisingly easily, to the only bedroom other than mine that has clean linen. He's barely a contour against the clinical white as I lay him down, and he refuses to open his eyes. His body's beautiful, so broken, the cheekbones prominent in his full face, the blues and greens around his wrists melding into deep red welts just below the palms, the bruising visible between his thighs even as he lies on his back. I find myself gently soothing the salty traces from beneath his eyes and still he doesn't stir. A slight shiver sets in from his lips to his chest. I pull the duvet over him hastily. He's a strong boy physically but is he giving up? Dimming the lights, getting a fresh bottle of wine and some snacks, I settle in for the vigil.

The thing is, I'm not sure where to go from here. If I make the effort to wake him—assuming I can—what am I going to feel if he breaks the spell? Storms out, or worse, does what most of them do and feigns nonchalance? To have him die on me, in that respect, would be ideal. But the thought of disposing of a body and successfully fooling a police enquiry...considering that his wife and friends know he came here, I wouldn't stand much of a chance. I'm not good at withstanding interrogation, as my father told the head of the school to which he transferred me after my "transgression" with Richard at the previous one. "He won't go wrong," he said; "just bring him in here once a month and ask him. If he's guilty, he'll start to stutter." I never found out what happened to Richard—no doubt relegated to some state school; he was on a scholarship. When I bumped into him, ten years later, he was working in a newsagent's shop; he looked glassy-eyed and through me. I'll always regret not having opened my mouth and sparked his memory, if only to have quieted the questions that assail me in my dreams.

I shake Casey's shoulder lightly and he murmurs a kind of protest, wincing a little. I'm now sure he's all right. Physically, at least. I whisper his name and fondle his neck and he finally responds to an extent, touching his chin against my hand. The light from the amber lamp lends a healthy, golden tint to his face and disguises the subtle lines of stress that I know have appeared, albeit temporarily, over the past few days. I bend in to kiss him tenderly on the lips and he lets out a slight sob before extending a weak arm to keep me there. I lie transfixed. I've never felt anything as intimate. With that simple action, he's owning me in a way he'd never imagine. I'd like to tell him but I've too much to lose.

I concentrate on the sensation of his broad fingertips barely touching the nape of my neck. As I draw back and reenter his mouth, the fingers move to caress the stubble that's now covering my head thanks to several days' negligence. There's a certain vacuum of emotion in both of us, I sense. There's a purity in this kiss that's all new—well, maybe not entirely— but I haven't felt it for a very long time. There's no pretense at last. He knows why now and, beyond not caring, he actually understands. It's trivial...and, yet, everything. The warmth that sneaks out from his cold body via his tongue eases open certain dark recesses of my psyche. I'm lost for words.

I feel the cold cut of the hot leather treating the flesh of my back, slicing a neat line across and between my shoulder blades for the seventh time in succession. Yes, I'm counting. And I can testify that Casey has got the strength back in his chunky biceps. My face pressed against the very mirror I watched him in over days, I can see the liberty in his entire demeanor as he builds up for each strike. He didn't have to force me into the restraints...but I let him think he did.

"Did I rape you, Casey?"

He pauses, golden eyelashes flashing briefly down and up over clear blue. "Yes...."

I wait. "But did I beat you, Ant?"

"You did."

And he smiles hugely, throwing his head back to reflect,

perfectly, the lazy evening sun. He looks like a timeless god-head at that moment. But after a gleaming beam, eye to eye, he turns to leave. There's a twinge of regret in my heart. He's a symbol—a talisman. He's put a geography and a scale to things, and for that alone he's special.

The cab sweeps almost silently away, leaving all but his essence in his place.

Get on Your Bikes and Ride!

D. Travers Scott

I'm fat, and I work at a gym. Yeah, the irony doesn't escape me. It doesn't escape some of the snickering queens who priss through this place, either — but I just remind myself *they're* the ones paying *me*.

It's a small chain of gyms called Ripe Fitness. *("The fastest growing chain in Western Washington!")* The owners want to be the next 24-Hour Fitness and mimic their business strategy of hard-core salesmanship. Think *Glengarry Glen Nautilus*. I sign up any and every little birdie with a checking account: teenagers, parents, grandparents, paraplegics, octogenarians, multiple amputees, terminal cancer patients. *("Everyone has a right to fitness!")* We ain't Studio 54.

Our dues are low *("Honest rates for real people!"),* and lots of people drop off after a few visits. We also make some nice coin selling protein powders and low-carb bars. *("It's not just getting rid of calories, it's bringing in* better *calories!")*

It's a used car lot, sure, but I kick ass. I may be shy as fuck in person, but at work something takes over. I can convince anyone that they need to join a gym *("Don't you deserve to treat yourself to the quality care of a facility like this?"),* that it's nothing to be scared of *("There's a place for everyone at Ripe Fitness!"),* that we're the best in town *("We're a gym that cares about you inside and out, not some body beautiful meat rack"),* and that we're perfectly suited to them *("Seriously, I can really see you achieving your goals here at Ripe Fitness").*

Everyone loves a fat man, and I use that to get under their skin. *("Fitness isn't about muscles—hey, look at me! Ha-ha!")* Half the time I think they want to sign up to prove they're better than me. Whatever. I'm a fat fag in my late twenties (really) with an extremely useful Masters in Performance Studies but too much of an anxiety disorder to pursue an academic career. But on the job I'm this badass top, and I make these fucking birdies do what I want: sign on the dotted line.

The downtown location where I work used to be a boutique gym, but we bought them out. Fussy place built inside a renovated 1930s bank building. When you leave the locker rooms, you step through a big, round vault door—like the giant safe on *The Beverly Hillbillies*—to find a waterfall cascading into a hot tub. It's totally gay, but it's good bait. Folks *ooh* and *ahh* when they first see it, then never use it after they join.

The gays loved this gym under the old management. They think chain gyms and their fat suburbanites are trashy. I catch the eyerolls and smirks, hear the clucking tongues and *sotto voce* comments. Lots of old members are leaving. I'm signing up new ones twice as fast. I may be fat and live in the 'burbs, but I pull a paycheck that doesn't bounce, which is more than the previous employees could say.

Between giving tours and sealing contracts, I hang at the desk with Neal, the other fag here. It's low-impact but, hey, if you'd spent the last two years arguing about Gayatri Chakravorty Spivak and Homi K. Babha, you'd be up for a little low impact. Neal is eighteen, bald, adorable, and I think he's a virgin. He's not fat, but he's a good buddy.

Neal and I were alone at the front desk one late afternoon, big chunks of pinky-yellow light slipping between skyscrapers and through our plate-glass windows. Neal folded towels; I waited for my next appointment. The evening crowd trickled in, flashing IDs at our scanner, snatching the thin, white towels from Neal's hands before trundling downstairs to the locker rooms.

"His dick is, like, totally curved." Neal nudged me, indicating a tall guy in his thirties with spiky blond hair. "Bang a boomerang."

Frequently Neal followed guys he was hot for into the locker room. He'd pretend to mop or pick up towels while they changed. Sometimes they waved their dicks at him, but Neal would scurry back upstairs to the desk. He's funny that way, fiercely curious and socially inept. He'd make a good academic.

Neal nodded toward where the rubber-tiled free-weights area met the carpeted Hammer Strength section. One guy was trying to figure out the anterior-delt half of a combined seated pec/anterior-delt machine. Next to him, another guy, flat on a bench, flapped his arms doing dumbbell flys (in terrible form). They studiously ignored each other.

"Caught those two in the dry sauna again last week," Neal said. "They're all, like, 'Don't know you!' on the floor."

"You ever join in?"

"Ye gods!"

Did I mention Neal was a theater queen? He was always quoting *The Music Man* or *Oklahoma!* in the most disconcerting ways.

"Why not?"

"I'd lose my job."

"The fitness team hardly ever goes downstairs."

Neal sniffed. "I just like to look."

He's kind of a prude. So was I at his age. But notice he didn't even bother to ask me if I ever fuck around with clients.

"But hel-lo!" Neal snapped a towel in the air. For a second it billowed in front of us like a childhood blanket-fort we hid inside. He shot me a mischievous look. The towel descended, and a new birdie stood before us: tall, skinny, early thirties, Middle Eastern guy with close-cropped black, curly hair and deep, dark brown eyes looking straight at me.

"Hello," he said. "May I speak to someone regarding membership?"

"That'd be me—Carter," I said, extending my hand with a dumbfuck grin as my role overtook me. "You like a tour? Neal, buddy, if my four-thirty shows up, can you give them a brochure and page me? Great!"

Neal blushed, staring into the towels, and nodded.

"So you're looking for a new gym...?"

"Hanif."

And away we went: Cybex, free weights, studios, meet the spin instructor, cardio cardio cardio, voted one of the top gyms in the country in 1997 (before we owned it but omit that detail), blah blah blah. He nodded but seemed a little impatient. I brought him to my office.

"So, Hanif, are you new to Seattle or just switching?"

I keep a pair of fat calipers on my desk. Like any torture implement, they're rarely used—the mere sight of them usually induces the desired reaction. Eat out of my hand, sexy little desert birdie.

"I just moved down from Vancouver." He leaned forward in the chair, eying me. He propped his elbows on the desk, shoving aside the calipers and now finally smiling, unlike during the tour.

"Well, I think you'll find that Ripe Fitness...."

"Right. It'll do. It's got everything, and my office is across the street. Would you get a contract for me to sign?"

I pulled a birdcage from my desk, three pages of legalese, but felt a little put out. It's no fun when birdies give themselves up like that; I like a little resistance before snaring them. And he wasn't even giving in; he was telling *me* what to do. Not sure what I thought about that at all.

"So, you liking Seattle?"

"It's lovely," he said, ripping his signature across the forms. "But I miss pubs. Seattle has clubs, but not really any proper neighborhood pubs. You know Vancouver?"

I nodded.

"I miss the Royal: big, friendly, unpretentious, you know? Can't find a place like that here yet."

Oh, I thought, surprised. *We're gay.*

He pushed the contract back and leaned in, eyes deep and liquid, his black, bushy eyebrows nestling closer together. I wondered about his hairy chest.

"You can suggest a place perhaps," he told-rather-than-asked me.

"Well, R Place...."

"Carter, you're disappointing me; I thought you a bit brighter than that."

Who the hell did this guy think he was? I rose to the challenge. "Well. Have you been to Madison Pub? Smallish, neighborhoody, mixed, some working boys but not too seedy, pool and trivia, definitely off the map of the A-list queens."

"Brilliant." He stood and brushed off his lap, basically rubbing his crotch right in my line of sight. "Why don't I come by when you get off, and you can take me there."

That was not what I normally hear at work. This was not a typical day for Fat Fag at the Gym.

Madison Pub was one of those dark, long narrow places with a bar and TVs up front, pool table and bathrooms in back. It used to be only a quasi-dive. But during Seattle's dot-com boom all the true dive bars got razed or rehabbed, leaving the Madison to carry the banner. Any dive connoisseur would turn their nose up at it. Yes, there were hustlers, johns, drunks, and slumming straight kids; and, yes, they had no top shelf to speak of and served hot nuts in paper cups. But unlike the old Seattle dives, there were no tranny hookers or amputee drag queens, not even back-corner blow jobs or patio water sports.

Hanif had called the gym before I got off and told me to meet him here. It sounded like the prelude to a brush-off, but what was I going to do, say no? I steeled my nerves, then took a Xanax and an inconspicuous seat at the bar. Amazingly, the TVs displayed not *Friends* but something I had actually studied in college: "This American poet lived most of her life in Brazil." I grabbed a trivia-game handset and selected "4. Elizabeth Bishop" as soon as she appeared onscreen.

"Hey, sexy."

That was not an address I normally respond to, but it was panted in my left ear like some breathless dog, so I couldn't help but turn around, and there he was. His arm encircled me and squeezed; he kissed my lips. There was a sheen of sweat across his face, and he smelled odd. Chemical. It added a new note to the bar's dusty musk of cashews and cigarettes.

"Hi...."

"What's this? Aren't you happy to see me?"

"No! Yeah, very glad. Just—ah, I'm not used to being addressed that way."

"Well, you should, you're a hot fellow."

"Uh-huh."

He was peppier than when I first saw him, bouncing and weaving, as if a little boxer inside him was trying to get out. The bartender came over, and I watched closely for the important first-impression drink. I do bottles of Whatever Lite. I hate it, but wines and white liquors aren't at all butch, only the brown ones are, and I hate those. The things you do to appear fuckable.

He ordered seltzer. Recovery?

"Thanks." He took a sip and looked at me, his head bobbing, and swallowed, then hummed. I'm not kidding, he *hummed* at me laciviously, an "mm-mm good" sort of humming, while checking me out, top to bottom. This freaked me a bit, so I went, "Are you excited about living in Seattle?"

"I'm excited about sucking your dick."

Luckily this was a Xanax occasion, so my shock sat four stools down instead of doing *Riverdance* in my head.

"You come on strong," I told him.

"Yeah, sorry about that. You mind?"

"Are you a chubby chaser?" I asked, point-blank.

He shook his head. He wagged his fingers in the air, searching for words, thoughts racing. He looked like an evil hypnotist.

"F-first off," he stammered.

I turned on my stool to face him and braced my back against the bar.

"First off," he said, "I despise that name. 'Chubby' is fucking *cute,* and cute does not fuck. It's Campbell's Soup kids, Augustus Gloop from *Willy Wonka,* Spanky from *The Little Rascals.* It sounds like some pedophile lurking in the kids' section of a department store, near clothes labeled 'Husky' or 'Pretty Plus'—pretty plus *what?!*"

I shrugged. *Whoa.*

"Second, there's no such thing as a 'chubby chaser.' There are fellows with a hard fetish for obesity, you know—queer and straight, with their own porn and such. There's all that Feeders and Gainers nonsense. There are Joes who wallow about in some bear's hairy, working-class belly. But I've never met anyone who actually referred to themselves as a 'chubby chaser.'

"That's not me. A fetish is finding only that thing hot, like a Asian guy who only dates white guys. Or when that thing makes anyone hot, like a guy who's boring until you hear his Aussie accent.

"Okay," I said, palms up. "Sorry. I'm not used to guys coming on like that."

"I can understand being defensive. Fags are awful. I'm defensive. Am I freaking you out?"

"A little, but it's a nice change of pace."

"Good, because you make me quite hard." He smiled and stretched up on his tiptoes. "But what sucks is telling you that, here, for a second, I feel paranoid, like I'm breaking the law. I'm not ashamed; I've done plenty of fucking that I *am* ashamed of, and I know the difference. But when I'm cruising a fat guy, part of me feels like I need to get all furtive, like what I'm doing is illegal. Is it cool I say 'fat'? I hate being all PC with 'of size' or such."

"I regularly refer to myself as a Fat Fag Bottom," I said, and raised my drink to him. Although self-conscious about his volume, I was digging this guy. And, shit, he wanted me.

"Nice," he said. "Because it's like, you get caught—see? I said, 'you get caught,' like I'm doing something wrong—you get caught checking out some fellow, and your friends or whoever you're with, some asshole will be all, like, 'Oh...?' " He said it with an accusatory fagstyle lilt.

"I'm sorry, but basically, I'm a big slut and find lots of guys hot. Including fat guys. They're not different from other guys I fuck except for how much they freak out everyone else. Hey, there's a booth free."

He grabbed both our drinks and bolted, sliding in one side of the booth. I took the other. He got back out and slid in beside me, rubbing a sweaty palm along the inside of my thigh.

"Sexiness is all about carriage," he said, still talking whiplash fast but deeper, more intense. "When some guy meets your eye with that cold, let's-rut stare and he's *not* sucking his gut in? Hot. When he's so confident, he lets his sides bulge down over his belt, his thick tits sag? He's not all sculpted and defined because he's got better things to do than spend fifteen hours a week at the gym stepping to last year's Kylie megamix. And the fat-equals-lazy thing is crap. Look at all the construction workers with big guts. All a gut means is: I'm a man, not a boy."

I vacillated between taking offense and doing a spit-take, but his hand kneaded my dick through the rough canvas of my Carhartts, and that was the bottom's line for now.

"Picture a fellow in dirty, baggy jeans with no belt, an untucked T-shirt, scuffed trainers. Now wash him up, tuck in the shirt nice and tight with the sides folded, belt those jeans, and what have we? FUSSY. Same thing: a tight gym body is FUSSY. Sloppy clothes are hot because they mean the guy is confident enough to know he's hot no matter how he dresses. Ditto with a sloppy body. You do coke?"

"What?"

He shrugged. "Coke, you want some? In case you can't tell, I'm high, that's why I'm talking nonstop. I'm going to do another line if you want some. Are the bathrooms safe?"

I hadn't been offered coke since college. How bizarre. Right on. "Yeah...no," I said. "They let hustlers work here, but part of the deal is no monkey business in the bathrooms."

"No mischief?"

"No tomfoolery."

"What about hijinx?"

I shook my head with mock gravity. "Not even a *suggestion* of hanky-panky."

"Well," he said, giving my dick a squeeze, "since I'd go for more than a soupçon of shenanigans, let's go out to my car."

We climbed into the front seat of his Volvo wagon, which was a relief because if it had been a pickup, a Jeep, or, worse yet, a Hummer, I'd have known he was a total bottom, too. He chopped up lines with a grocery store savings card on the case of Kelly Osbourne's CD and asked me to roll up the dollar bill. I was charmed that he gave me a single instead of trying to impress me with a large denomination, which would've been the tipping point for this whole doing-coke-in-the-car-in-the-Bank-of-America-parking-lot-where-people-at-the-ATM-can-completely-see-us thing.

He told me to roll it tight, and I thought, *Like rolling enchiladas,* but said nothing because that would've been such a fatboy thing to say. It might have scored me points, but I wasn't sure I wanted to, that way. Despite what he said, I certainly felt fetishized, exoticized, eroticized. But was that wrong?

I looked away as he vacuumed along the CD case; it felt rude to stare. Big globules of rainwater gathered along the lip of the passenger window; I leaned away as they fell, nearly knocking Kelly out of his hand.

"Suck it up, baby."

I gingerly slid the dollar into my nose and pressed the other nostril closed. I snorted a long, hard intake, trying to suck the whole line from Kelly's mug. Everyone's cheering her as a role model for fat kids, I thought, but how come no one claps for Jack?

An acrid drip crept down the back of my throat, bitter like aspirin and vomit—lovely!—but soon I felt really calm and together, not spacey like from my meds. His hand went back to my crotch, unzipping and pulling out my dick. Of course, he was talking again.

"Yeah, fat guys usually have hot dicks," he said. "It's the contrast, the difference, you know?"

"Yeah, difference," I murmured, too high on the coke rush and his stroking to articulate anything more thoughtful.

"Your body's curving and pliable, but your dick is this hard little bitch, this obstinate jackass standing up at attention while everything else is sagging down. It calls attention to itself, like a homeboy's crotch-tugging or a leather daddy's assless chaps.

"Oh yes, and the ass. Big ones are brilliant. You're standing there stroking your dick, and it's wonderful to have this big, meaty target to drive it into. And you can be rougher with a big fellow. You can grab those heavy hips and just ram into him, slapping your thighs against his backside, shoving your dick all up inside, your balls swinging like mad. It isn't fetish, it's physics: You've simply got more leverage."

He proffered Kelly up under my nose with one hand, the other still on my dick. I took the dollar off the dash and inhaled one of the lines, then held Kelly for him. He did the other and wiped her clean, rubbing residue on his gums. We sniffed and sniffed, and it was too '80s, not that I'd know, but when I turned on the radio it was Duran Duran, which really was too '80s, so I spun until I found some downtempo, and he went into it again.

"Fat guys' bodies tell a story." *Sniff!* "They haven't been cleaned up and edited into blandness. Is he the aging jock gone to seed? The fellow who labors at work but not enough to burn off that belly? Plus when I'm with them, I feel all a right little piglet. There's more there, you're soaking in it, wallowing. Because it's so socially wrong to be fat, it feels transgressive, outsider, freaky, and that's hot. You're saying fuck it to Chi Chi La Rue and *Advocate Men,* I'm gonna get dirty with this piggy guy who's confident with who he is. Oh, fuck."

He shoved his face down on my cock and sucked deep and long, and it was fantastic. I raced along with the coke but felt so clear, so focused, and he gave great head, which also shut him up. Only the urge to talk passed to me. I spoke slowly and with secure enunciation. I felt razor-sharp, needle-pinpricked focused, and I loved it.

"But I do not do that," I told his rising and falling head. "I am not confident. I do not carry myself like that. I'm fat. I'm shy. And I hate myself. I'm not some big tough Daddy who can carry it off. I'm twenty-eight, and I'm a bottom. I have Generalized Anxiety Disorder and take Paxil daily, Xanax on special occasions, and Vicodin on very special occasions—and no, you can't have any. I've had too many guys promise sex for drugs then can't fuck because of the drugs. Although, considering this situation, I guess I owe you. Anyway, so what am I supposed to do? I'm not the butchest thing in the world, so why the fuck are you sucking me off?"

My cock slurped out of his mouth, and he looked up from my lap. "I think you have potential."

"I'm not a fucking charity case."

He sat up, pumping my wet dick in his hand. "No, I know. Look, everything I said—maybe it doesn't all apply to you. I mean, those are some of my reasons for why I like fat guys. I have lots of reasons for lots of things. Very rational and orderly but, uh, sometimes reasons are just there to cover up the fact that there are no reasons."

"Huh?"

"Look, I've been rattling off all these reasons why I like fat guys. Honestly, most of them don't apply to you, but I do like you. You give me a boner, and I'd like to fuck you when the coke wears off, and yes, a Vicodin would be smashing, thanks. But you know, I don't know the fuck why. I can't spew forth some thesis on how you're my archetypal fat guy or something. I just—I just talk a lot when I'm nervous."

"And coked up."

"Yeah, well that too."

It was all clear suddenly; I had this guy figured out.

"I think this is how you fuck," I told him. "You fuck with all this talking! I know this game; I do it all day with my customers."

"So maybe you can top after all," he said, way too smug.

"I do—I do it all day. It's called salesmanship. And it's

what you've been doing to me all night. I'm your birdie."

"In case you haven't noticed, I prefer blokes to birds."

"No, your mark—you're trying to sell me. And I don't think it's right."

" 'Right'? Look, we're doing drugs—that's wrong, that's against the law. I'm sucking you off in a parking lot—that's against the law. You're fat, and I want to fuck you—that's against the unwritten laws of fagdom. But we're doing it because we want to, despite legal prohibitions and social codes."

Rain splattered on the windshield; the cab of the Volvo was cold. My dick had shriveled into a wet little morel mushroom.

"The coke can do that," he said apologetically. "Shall we go back to the pub?"

I tucked myself in. I didn't know how long it would take the coke to wear off. I looked at him sideways.

"This has been a trip," I told him, "but I'm gonna go."

"What do you mean?"

"Thanks for everything but, ah, I'm going to go." I opened the door and stepped into the rain. He leaned over.

"I beg your pardon?"

"I'll see you at the gym, I'm sure. Thanks."

I shut the door. He sat inside, and I walked down the parking lot, toward the ATM, blinking past the winter drizzle. The scene appeared outwardly pathetic, but I felt really good. I'd never before walked away from sex—or even suggestions of, or the possiblity of, sex. When I got to the shelter of the ATM canopy, I looked back and saw him doing more lines off Kelly. I took out $40 and felt sober—coke wears off pretty quickly, after all. His Volvo wagon roared out of the parking lot, and I headed back into the bar.

from *Voodoo Lust*
M. S. Hunter

I awoke slowly from a drugged state, only gradually becoming aware of my surroundings and my condition. First I realized that I was lying on a surface that was moving, bouncing about on a rough road. But there was a mat under me, so it was not painful. Opening my eyes and looking up, I decided that I was on the floor of a small van traveling at moderate speed. It was apparently daytime, as dim light filtered through the van's dirty rear windows. I was still naked, but something seemed different. I looked down at my body and realized that something was missing—my pubic hair! I moved my arms and determined that the hair from my pits was gone as well. I had been body shaved! Turning my head slightly I could feel the hair on my head move against my scalp. At least they had left that.

When I turned my head I also saw something else—two pair of military boots. Soldiers? My guards? My questions were answered at once when I heard voices speaking in Creole.

"I think he's waking up."

"Good! Then we can have some fun with him before we get to the turnoff for the island."

"Yeah! And I want to fuck that pretty white ass."

"And I want to eat it. I want to get my tongue up that chute."

The other soldier laughed. "Right! I know you, Carlo. You'd rather eat an ass than fuck it. But let me fuck it first, and you can eat my spunk out of it."

"Sounds good to me, Andre. And you can fuck his face while I do it."

"If I'm still hard enough. Maybe I'll just suck on that big white dick while you're eating his ass."

"Okay, but if you fuck him first, I'm going to swing on that while you're doing it."

They both began laughing, and then one of them said, "Look! He's awake and he's getting a hard-on!"

I was indeed wide awake by now and, despite the obvious fact that I was still a prisoner, I was thoroughly turned on by the conversation I'd been overhearing. It's doubtful they would have been speaking so freely if they had had the slightest inkling that I understood the language.

Now I looked boldly at the two and, as I had suspected, they were the same soldiers who had taken me to the interrogation room and who had sported erections while I was being forced to suck off that disgusting Inspector Moreau. If they wanted to "have some fun" with me while we were going wherever we were going, that was fine by me.

One of the soldiers began to remove his boots and the other followed suit. In short order they were both stripped naked. They each had a rifle that they unhesitatingly leaned against the van's wall back near the door. I thought fleetingly about jumping up, grabbing a rifle, or both of them, and trying to escape. I dismissed the thought at once. Where the hell could a naked white man with a rifle go? And where was

I? Just somewhere in Haiti. I might get out of this van, but that would be all.

Instead, I took a good look at my guards. One, Carlo, was pitch black, smooth as silk with just a tiny patch of pubic hair, and well-defined musculature all over. Swinging between his legs, already half hard, was what looked like ten inches of uncut dick. My mouth watered at the sight.

The other, Andre, was different—taller, a medium-brown color, with body hair—not a lot, just a sprinkling on his chest with a trail of it down to a curly swirl around his genitals. This one wasn't just half hard. His dick was already at full mast and, at a quick guess, about nine chocolate inches.

That was about all I had time to observe before they were onto me. Carlo, speaking Creole as if I was supposed to understand, said, "Don't worry, Peter, we're not going to hurt you." And then his mouth was stoppered as he dived down on my rampant cock, swallowing it all the way in one gulp. This guy was no novice at cocksucking. His lips wrapped themselves tightly around my shaft and began to move up and down. It was as expert a blow job as I've ever received. This Carlo could suck the chrome off a trailer hitch.

Meanwhile, Andre had straddled my face and was ready to plunge his dick into my mouth. I opened up without hesitation and in it went. That's when I realized that it was one of those with an upward curve, all wrong for the angle. It scraped the roof of my mouth. I signaled for him to turn around, and after a moment he got the message. He swung around, facing Carlo, and now the head of his curved cock was pressing against the opening of my throat. After all the cocks I'd sucked over the last couple of years, it was easy for me to relax, suppress the gag reflex, and let that long, thin shaft slide right in. Andre proceeded to give me a most satisfactory face-fucking. That he was enjoying it as much as I was, was clear from his moans and, after a minute, his words to Carlo. "Oh man, this is great. This kid got more of my dick down his throat than anyone, even Leon, ever did." I didn't know who Leon was, but I knew a compliment when I heard one. I'd long since decided that, if I was going to be a cocksucker, I should try to be the world's greatest cocksucker.

Carlo didn't answer. Hardly surprising since his mouth, so full of my dick a moment before, was now full of my balls. When he released them, he pushed my legs up into the air and plunged his tongue straight into my asshole. What a sensation! One long dick down my throat and one hot tongue up my love chute. I was in heaven. All thoughts of my serious predicament were gone from my mind.

"That's it, Carlo," I heard Andre say. "Get it all wet and ready for me."

Carlo lifted his head. "I think it's ready now."

They changed positions, Andre now between my legs, still stretched up into the air, and Carlo straddling my face, facing Andre. Carlo's dick, longer and fatter than Andre's, presented a new problem. It was straight as a die, so in order to let it into my throat I had to tip my head backward. I did, and in it went. His silky ball sac came down onto my eyes and nose, treating me to a heavenly aroma but cutting off all vision. It didn't matter. I could feel what Andre was doing. He inserted first one finger and then another into me, twisted them around, and in no time had my sphincter relaxed and my hole wide open. Then it was the head of his cock that I felt knocking at the gate. I was hoping that the spit Carlo had left was enough lubrication, but that didn't matter either as I felt him pushing some kind of lube into me.

"Oh!" I heard Carlo say, "I see you've got some ju-ju." I didn't have time to wonder what *ju-ju* was as I then felt a double sensation at my midsection. Just as Andre's long shaft began to penetrate me, I felt Carlo's lips engulf my cock. His short, stocky build made it possible for him to do so even though my legs-up position made the distance between my face and dick shorter than it would be if I was stretched out flat.

Meanwhile, as Andre's rod slid into me, that curve at the end drove it right against my prostate on the first thrust, sending new waves of pleasure coursing through my body. So there I was with one big black dick in my mouth, another up my ass, and hot lips sucking on my own cock. What more could I ask of life?

What more? Well, after a few minutes of this triple delight I heard Andre yell, "Oh! Mother of God! Here I come!" Whereupon I felt his dick swell, he shoved it in further and harder than ever, and his erupting fountain of joy bathed my insides with a copious offering of Haitian jizzum.

When he finally withdrew Carlo said, "Now, you know what I want." What he wanted was what I'd heard him say before we began. At once he was off my dick, pulled his huge shaft out of my throat and mouth, scooted down between my legs, and his mouth landed squarely on my asshole. In went his tongue, and it was accompanied by a sucking action by his lips that seemed to be glued to the rim of the hole. It was a sensation I had never felt before. This was rimming at its most spectacular.

"Go for it, Carlo," I heard Andre say. "I put plenty of my spunk in there. Eat it all out." And that was exactly what Carlo was trying to do.

Andre, after a couple of minutes of relaxing beside us, now leaned over and took my swollen dick in his hand. He was slicking some of that lube onto it and I thought it a wonder that I didn't come at once as his hand slid up and down the shaft. Instead it got harder and harder, feeling as if it would explode. But it didn't. Then Andre's mouth went down on it. He wasn't the expert cocksucker Carlo was, but quite good enough.

That didn't last long. Andre had other ideas. He came off

my cock, straddled my face, facing toward Carlo, and, instead of dropping his now resurrected cock into my mouth, lowered his hairy ass toward me. He wanted his hole eaten just as Carlo was eating mine. Fine by me. I stuck out my tongue to meet him and he landed squarely on it. Clean and tasty. I drove in as far as I could, my lips spreading out over those brown buns. With all that kinky hair around his butthole and over his asscheeks, it was a little like rimming a Brillo pad. But I didn't care. I kept forcing more and more of my saliva into him, and that was just what he wanted.

Again this position only lasted a few minutes. Andre turned around, straddled my body, and brought his now well-lubricated ass right down on my rigid rod. Andre let out a moan of delight as I penetrated him and began lifting himself up and down, fucking himself on my cock. His warm love chute clutching and massaging my dick felt divine. With Carlo still rimming me, sucking Andre's earlier deposited spunk out of my ass, I was in a new version of heaven.

It was too much to last long. I felt the vibrations of ecstasy mounting in my body, spreading from my toes, from my head, from my asshole, from everywhere into my throbbing dick. "I'm cumming!" I yelled. Though I said it in English, both soldiers seemed to understand. Carlo at once abandoned his meal between my asscheeks and came around Andre to squat over my face, his dick immediately sinking into my mouth while he took his friend's cock into his. As I felt my cum erupting into Andre's ass, Carlo's spunk began squirting into my mouth. At the same time I heard Andre shout, "Here I cum!" So I knew that Carlo, too, was getting a load of jizz down his throat.

That was it. We collapsed into a sweaty pile, me in the middle—a not unfamiliar position, the crème in an Oreo cookie. Both Carlo and Andre then surprised me by kissing me tenderly. If this was their method of being my guards, I hoped their assignment would be permanent.

Just at that moment we felt the van swerve left off the road and onto a much rougher, apparently unpaved path. We bounced a bit and we all sat up.

"We're almost there," Andre announced.

"Yeah, time to get dressed," Carlo added. "And we have to get Peter ready to become one of General Sanon's slaves."

What the devil does that mean, I wondered.

Of course I wasn't about to be allowed to get dressed, even if there had been any clothes there for me. The soldiers donned their uniforms, and then, with apologies muttered in Creole—that I wasn't supposed to understand—my hands were cuffed behind me and manacles placed on my ankles that allowed me to make only short steps. Carlo and Andre retrieved their rifles, and it was clear that I was back to being their prisoner.

The van came to a halt and I heard the driver and someone else climbing out of the front seats. The rear doors of the van swung open and I saw another soldier, the driver, and Captain René LeClerc. LeClerc looked at me with a strange expression on his face, somewhere, I thought, between pity and lust. He stepped back and my guards lifted me—I couldn't have taken the step alone—out of the van. I looked about. We were in a small unpaved parking lot surrounded on three sides, except where the road emerged, by jungle. On the fourth side was water, sea water I thought, though a body of land, probably an island, blocked most of the view out to sea. Closer, on the shore, was a small building and a jetty. Tied to the jetty was a boat, a small power launch. Standing about, entirely at ease, were a dozen or so soldiers. At once I was acutely aware of my nudity. They were all looking at me as Carlo and Andre, one on either side holding me by my arms, marched me toward the jetty and the waiting launch.

"Hey, Carlo!" I heard someone yell. "What's that dribbling down your chin? Whose load did you just get in your mouth?"

"Andre!" another shouted. "Why are you walking so funny? Just had something stiff up your ass, eh?"

This was followed by laughter on all sides. I looked at my guards. The grins on their faces told me that they weren't at all offended by the jibes of their fellows.

Finally, as I was lifted into the boat, I heard, "That one's a beauty. When do we get a crack at him?" Then the boat's engine fired and we were off toward the island offshore.

The Bad Boys Club
Michael Huxley

Prologue

I was lucky. My initial same-sex experiences began occur-
ring when I was very young, and culminated in sharing, with
my first "lover," both his and my first orgasm. Talk about
timing: I'd never even had a wet dream, and to this day still
haven't. No, after that glorious fix I was hooked, and have
consequently appeased my wonderful addiction by getting off
as frequently as possible ever since. God forbid I would allow
however much time is required to lapse between shooting
loads for such an event to occur!

Interestingly, at his request, I relayed my first-time experience to a French actor I had the extreme pleasure of meeting
last summer while staying in Paris, "doing research" for my
novel-in-progress. On returning to the States, I wrote about
my encounter with this actor, whom I shall refer to as "Alain,"
within a fictional context. Extracting this conversation from
the longer manuscript and placing it within a nonfictional
framework has resulted in the piece you are about to read.

Because it was relayed under such hot and heavy circumstances, I have opted to communicate this tale by interpolating both the conversation with Alain and the situation within which it took place. But, wank assured, the sexual revelation chronicled here occurred in my hometown of Louisville, Kentucky—to me—precisely as articulated to Alain in Paris.

It was launched at Lakeside, the summer after I turned thirteen. At one time a fully operational limestone quarry, Lakeside was, and I presume still is, Louisville's premier swim club, conveniently located on Trevillian Way, within easy walking distance of my old neighborhood. Now I ask you: How else was a boy on the verge to spend the sultry summer days in urban, brain-fuck Kentucky than hanging out with his buds, every day at Lakeside? I was soon to find out.

"The Three Mikes and Chris"—as we called ourselves—were quite an inseparable foursome at that time. One seemingly typical Lakeside afternoon, Mike Hannon and Chris Hart had repaired to the concession stand, leaving Mike O'Day and me to our own devises, sunning on the smooth rocks near the deepest end, away from the crowd. Imagine my surprise when, out of nowhere, he asked me: "Hey Michael, you ever like to do…y'know…*dirty* stuff?"

I knew exactly what he was talking about; I'd enjoyed doing what I then considered "dirty stuff" as far back as I could remember, but always by myself. Wasting no words, my pregnant response was a simple "Yes."

"I do too," he continued carefully. "And so do Chris and Mike. We've been thinking that…maybe your basement would be cool for a secret club or something, just us four…."

I remember resenting that I'd been left out of the loop until then, but that subsided after the other two returned, bearing treats. It was then that The Three Mikes and Chris—timidly at first, but with gathering excitement—began laying the foundation of a Boys Club that would forever change my life. Ah, recalling that innocent initiation into the spurting realms of same-sex activity, and how it rendered, and still renders, time momentarily meaningless, tempts me to shamelessly unzip my baggy shorts and free up the heavy cargo straining within. Surely you won't mind my succumbing.

It is at this point that I must also request that you make the leap from Louisville to Paris, where, traveling alone (my lover would join me the following week), I found myself—temporarily writer's-blocked and feeling restless—engaging in a wee bit of infidelity with a late-afternoon trick I'd picked up at the Café La Marronnier, located in the very gay crotch of Le Marais. The humpy, if eccentric, Alain had already proven himself a fantastic paramour. Following a sweaty aperitif of making out, extended oral sex, and mutual masturbation, begun the moment we crossed the threshold of my rented apartment in the Rue des Tournelles, we took a break, drank some wine, smoked a few cigarettes. After surviving a ridiculous argument (you know the French!), we hastily made up and had begun making love again, getting very worked up, when suddenly, pulling away from a round of my finest rimming, Alain announced that he needed to evacuate his bowels, for obvious reasons.

Take it away, Alain! Take it away, as I delve through my zipper and reach into my past....

"Oh *stop,* Baby, *please...*!" he cried. "Michael, I mean it; I must make a shit! I am very romantic, no? Do you have condoms?"

"Well, yeah, of course," I laughed, undaunted by Alain's exuberant madness.

"Get them," he commanded. "We will be ready when the moment is right!" He dashed into the bathroom, not bothering to close the door behind him, calling from within: "We must have more wine; there is no need for us to rush our love! Fill our glasses, Baby, as full as my heart!" A significant moment later he added: "...Mmm, my shit stinks!"

"Jesus Christ, turn the fan on!"

"No no! I *love* my odor! Can you smell?"

"Not yet," I answered warily. "But I'll keep you posted." I refilled our wine glasses and set up the condoms and lubricant on the bedside table. The toilet flushing signaled Alain's beaming, little-boyish return.

"I feel fantastic," he said, tugging his semihard cock and flopping onto the bed next to me. After a moment's pause his eyes brightened. "Michael! Tell me the history of your first sex." He took a sip of wine, reached for the smokes and lighter.

"My first sex?" I said, not really getting it, indicating the cigarettes. "Here, give me one of those."

"Not your first sex," he clarified, lighting a cigarette for me and placing it between my lips before lighting another for himself. "Your first orgasm."

"Leave it to you to ask me that."

"And why not ask about such an important event?" he countered. "It is a moment that changes a man's life forever. What was your age?"

I smiled nostalgically as I brought the memory into focus. "I was thirteen...."

"Were you alone? You must tell me in detail how it happened, Michael, how it felt." He flicked his ash, savored another sip of wine, and settled back against the headboard, fully attentive.

Oh, my...I thought, observing Alain lounging on the bed: naked, idly fiddling his semierect masterpiece of circumcision, the half-smoked cigarette smoldering between the fingers of his other hand, his arm resting on one raised knee. I was getting hard just *looking* at him. He was so bonkers, overwhelmingly sexy, such a babe! Resisting a ferocious urge to pounce on him, I couldn't help but wonder how it would feel to penetrate Alain's ass with my hard-on, thinking: *God, I wanna fuck him something fierce, feel his insides with my big one right here and now, but...first things first.*

"No, actually I wasn't alone," I began my tale. "I'd been playing sex games with a group of friends for months before that."

"Boys?" Alain inquired, raising his wine glass to his gorgeous lips.

"Yes, there were four of us in the club: 'The Three Mikes and Chris.' "

"*Le Club Mauvais Garçon!* I love it," he said delightedly. "You were very bad boys...."

"I don't know how 'bad' we were," I corrected, "but we did share an interest in spending time together naked, with erections—'boners,' we called them. We'd go down in my basement; there was a storage room, set up with an old sofa and a couple of overstuffed chairs. It was perfect. We rigged a lock from the inside and put up a sign that read

---

SECRET CLUB—DO NOT ENTER!

<u>NO GIRLS ALLOWED!!</u>

—not that anyone but the four of us ever went down there."

"And then 'The Three Mikes and Chris' would get naked together?" Alain prodded.

"Yes. We were frisky young boys, and oh-so-willing.... None of us had any hair on our bodies to speak of yet, except on our heads. Our sweet hard-ons were as smooth as silk and so *sensitive,* Alain! But even then I was conscious of size and looks. Chris had a small dick, even when hard. Too bad, because—next to me, of course!—he was the best-looking one. Mike Hannon's cock was average, I guess, and he was average *looking*, but Mike O'Day was much cuter, and had a really nice dick—as big as mine, maybe even larger in circumference. He and I were the ones who really enjoyed the club. After a while the other two could take it or leave it.

"Anyway, we'd go down there, strip naked, and get turned on and hard and compare boners and touch each other and talk about sexy stuff—about how people fuck like animals in secret to make babies and all that. We used to wonder what it would have been like had Eve not enticed Adam to eat the apple, and people walked around naked and fucked in the streets whenever they felt like it, for all the world to see. We talked about how much we wanted to fuck girls in that decidedly 'better' world, all the while playing with each other's cocks. In retrospect, for all our talk about hetero fucking, go figure why we put 'no girls allowed' on the sign. We knew nothing about homosexuality, really, only that calling someone a faggot was a bad thing. But I loved our club, Alain; *that,* I did know! It was so much fun, such a turn-on, felt so dirty, so taboo.

"As time went on, our games became more serious. We started to experiment with jerking off and sucking dicks, just figured it out. Jerking off was okay, although we never came, never 'got the white stuff' like Chris said his older brother did. But sucking cock: *Man,* did that ever feel great! Still, even doing that, we never came. I just assumed we weren't old enough, but the truth was, we never did it *long* enough. The one sucking would become impatient to get sucked, so around and around we went, getting hotter than hell and winding up deliciously frustrated time and again."

Watching Alain play with his no longer *semi*hard cock compelled me to break from my story. "Good god, Alain, you're as hard as limestone! C'mon, man, fuck this. Let me suck your dick a little," I implored seductively. "C'mon...."

"No, Michael. I am very much liking your bad boy story." Alain crushed his cigarette in the ashtray, then grabbed the container of lubricant. "Will you mind if I play while you continue? I promise not to come. I want to prepare for when you fuck me, hm?"

"Whoa, don't say that, or I'll never finish the damned story! Look at this: I'm in *pain,* man. I'm dripping like mad."

"I see that, Michael." He reached over, pumped a dose of pre-cum up and out of my many rigid inches, and spread it over his middle finger, commenting: "Mmm...perhaps we will not need the bottled stuff." And then, damned if he didn't raise a leg and work the shiny finger up his ass! "Oh, I am so clean inside, so warm and smooth," he taunted. "It will be like paradise for you.... What happened then, Baby? Tell me, while I play. Did you experiment with fucking, you and your friends? Tell me more, Michael."

Continuing my tale proved an interesting challenge from that point forward, as Alain reinforced his erection by tenderly finger-fucking himself. "All right, then," I said, clearing my throat, my eyes beholding him from behind a mask of Eros, as if through the medium of fever. "Experiment with fucking...?" I absentmindedly mumbled, backtracking. "Yeah, we did, but that went nowhere; we couldn't handle the pain. But sucking cock definitely changed the club's dynamic. We paired off. Of the three, Mike O'Day was by far the best at giving head; he did it longer and slower, really seemed to enjoy it. He and I...."

"Became lovers," Alain interrupted, correctly finishing my sentence.

"Yes. The other two fell by the wayside, became secondary. One day, when we were alone...I don't know how it came up, but I asked Mike if we could kiss. I remember being incredibly afraid to ask him that. It's funny...."

"Not funny at all, Michael, to be shy about asking for something as intimate as a kiss," Alain responded throatily, utilizing a bit of "the bottled stuff" to slip a second digit into his ass-play. "Mike said 'yes' to your lovely request?"

"Jesus Christ, Alain...." I paused, twice as inflamed. "Yes, he did; he loved it."

"You found each other's tongue?"

"Right away. We knew what to do, somehow."

"The human animal knows," he said with a smile.

"It was wonderful. We made out all the time after that, whenever we were alone; we couldn't get enough. Naturally, kissing would get us big-time in the mood for sucking, but we *still* weren't quite ready to come yet."

"When did it happen, Michael?" inquired Alain, studying me with half-shut eyes. "How was it that you came with your Mike?"

"He was at my house for a sleepover—spending the night, like friends do—some weeks later," I continued. "Both of us were going through fairly dramatic puberty changes by then, growing pubic hair, the whole bit. Our cocks were getting bigger too. Oh, he had such a pretty *cock,* Alain!

"I remember it so vividly, now that I'm called to task to tell it. My bedroom door was locked. The television was blaring, but we weren't paying any attention to it. Hell no, we were naked, on my bed, making out, holding each other tightly, dry humping, very, *very* turned on, like never before. We knew from the onset that the whole experience was different from other times, was far more focused. We had to be quiet; I didn't want my mother to hear us moaning, which excited us even more. It felt unbelievably better than usual when he began blowing me. I recall whispering, 'Mike, don't stop this time; it feels so *good,*' and him responding, 'I don't even *wanna* stop!' And to be sure, he didn't; he kept *doing* me and *doing* me, on and on. I was sitting up, my back resting against the pillows, my legs stretched out—like you're sitting right now, Alain—quietly freaking out, *whimpering* with pleasure. Mike was kneeling to my side, balanced on one arm, just *going* for it. My god, that kid could suck cock! I was watching him jerk off, his gorgeous dick so big and veiny and hard in his hand. All at once, he struck me as looking...so much like a *man*. Watching him took me to a level I didn't understand, had certainly never experienced before. I couldn't *believe* how fantastic Mike was making me feel! I was breathing hard and sweating; my heart was going berserk. I began to think that maybe something was going wrong, but kept whispering, 'Don't stop, Mike; don't *ever* stop...' even though I knew he was super-into it, that no way was he going to stop.

"My *cock*: My god, it was bursting with increasingly intense waves of pleasure! My first orgasm escalated in such an unexpected way, there was no time to analyze it, no time for anything but to experience it. And that's when it happened: I came like a *motherfucker* in his mouth. Totally overwhelmed, I cried out, god knows what, but loudly, and Mike bellowed like a wounded steer when he shot *his* first load on my bedspread, gagging a little and coughing. I never suspected that a physical sensation could offer so much joy, and wanted more than anything for that feeling to last forever, but then again—don't we all? This may sound strange to you, Alain, but I knew right then that there was something besides reading and writing to live for. I wasn't afraid of becoming an adult after that."

Alain withdrew his fingers from his rectum, filled his palm with lubricant, and, reaching over, smoothed it up and down my impossibly erect penis. "Oh, *Baby,* thank god..." I swooned. Wordlessly, he tore open a condom and rolled it down my glistening, prized possession. Adding another layer of lube, he said: "We aren't little boys anymore, Michael. What do you want from me?"

"I wanna fuck you very badly, Alain."

"Tell me *how,* Michael. How do you 'wanna fuck' me?"

"Lie on your back," I replied. "Raise your legs. Yeah...."
Mounting him, going for broke, I eased myself through his compliant, puckered circumference into unimaginable ecstasy. Such a *relief....*

Epilogue

Yeo! I should have grabbed a towel first. Would you hang on for a second? Seems I've "procreated" quite a mess here, rather close at hand, that needs cleaning up....

...There now, that's better. Whew! Okay, where were we? Oh yes....

From that momentous evening, Mike's and my affair lasted a mere six months, but within that time frame we made love many, many times, keeping our secret sweetly exclusive.

Later that Parisian evening, after we had shared what can only be described as a mystical sexual experience, Alain asked me: "What happened to your first love, with your Mike?"

"My family moved to Cincinnati, about a hundred miles away, the following summer," I explained. "Mike and I cried and cried and cried."

Indeed we had. Unfortunately, Mike and I lost touch, both figuratively and literally, after those tears were shed. I am confident, however, that Michael O'Day will fondly remember, as will I, our budding passion, our poignant, transitional time spent together, until the day he dies, for who could possibly forget their first true love?

Dejected and hopelessly addicted, yet finding no substitute for Mike in Cincinnati, I settled into a sad subversion of watering the societally sown seeds of guilt sprouting in my closet, non-stop masturbation, obsessive fanaticizing, and...well, *nonstop masturbation,* which lasted until my junior year in high school. Subsequently began my three-year experiment in denial—with heterosexuality—that proved such a fabulous disaster.

Not to sound too *Will and Grace* about it, but Vicky was my best friend. I loved everything about her, except having sex with her. Yes, I "lost my virginity" with Vicky, and she with me. When, early in my sophomore year at college, I told her—before I'd even fully admitted it to myself—that I was homosexual, Vicky was rendered speechless with disbelief, utterly shattered, and ultimately heartbroken. So it was that I lost my best friend, but gained a much healthier life-perspective.

Enter, the following semester, my new roommate, Marc: a theater major....

I've had many "first-time," same-sex experiences in the years since college. With luck and perseverance on my part, perhaps you will read about them down the often blurry line that separates fiction from non-. Whether so or not, however, it is through embracing the innate, biological imperative of my loving cock, of loving men, of loving myself, that I now celebrate my capacity to fully experience love, and resolve to continue the composition of my life's story accordingly, as nature intended.

Thank you, Alain, for asking.

Derelict
Steve Berman

Bravey Boy stood where strawberries once grew. He nudged the earth with the toe of his worn sneakers, disturbing browned weeds and cigarette butts. October in Philadelphia could be fickle. He had left his tenement building wearing a jacket, but as the sky darkened the air turned warmer, so he unzipped, letting the sweat cool on a bare chest the color of dark coffee.

Some years back, a garden had filled the lot where he stood. Nothing grand, a site large enough to bring the community together to plant a few greens and build a place for the kids to play safely. Then six months back, the mayor chanted *safe streets* to every news camera, newspaper, and council meeting. The cops descended on the street corners, forcing the dealers to move on. They had found the garden an earthly delight, where they could lounge during the day and sell at night. Parents had boycotted the garden, keeping inside at all hours, and the lot quickly fell into despair. When some other crime crisis drew the mayor's attention, the cops turned their attention elsewhere and the dealers reclaimed the street corners.

So an entire city block was abandoned, except for dying brush and a sickly couple of trees along the rusty fence.

Then the men and the boys came, looking for sex—another addiction.

Bravey heard the normal sounds of the night: hip-hop music banging as a car floated by, someone somewhere yelling, a bloody fight between feral dogs. A breeze blew, carrying a deep, musky odor, a touch of old sweat on an unwashed body. Bravey closed his eyes and shook his head even as he breathed in deeply. *Please,* he thought. *Not him, not tonight.*

A muttered "Yo, my brotha" came from behind. The smell intensified. He turned around to see Demonte shuffling up to him.

He hadn't seen Demonte in more than a week. The boy didn't look so good. His left eye was swollen half-shut, blood crusted one nostril, and the blatino's strut had more limp than swagger. Yet he swung his arm around Bravey as if nothing were wrong.

"What's up?" Bravey kept his tone steady and cool, though in his head he urged Demonte to *move on, get lost.* If Lashon saw them standing there....

Demonte shrugged. "Same shit." His breath smelled sickly-sweet, of flavored cheap wine. He reached over to tug lightly at Bravey's jacket, revealing more smooth, toned chest. "Heh, what have we here?" Fingers scuttled over one nipple.

"Don't." Bravey slapped Demonte's hand away.

"Oh, I'm not good enough a lay for you?" Demonte plucked at his grungy '76ers jersey. "Didn't complain on your first fuck, 'ese."

Bravey Boy could not stop staring at Demonte, admiring every bit of muscle on display, aching to touch the skin under a cotton tank top and baggy pants.

When he got up the nerve one night to follow Demonte, a

winding route through sinister back streets of the neighborhood, they ended up at the derelict garden. An old man seated on a bench muttered a greeting. When Bravey looked down, he saw the man's hands busy below his belt, stroking his cock. That almost sent Bravey running. But Demonte had walked by without breaking stride, so he did, too.

It took a while to navigate the garden; in the dark it seemed the size of a park. He glimpsed men standing, or sitting, or strutting about. Their stares made him tremble.

He found Demonte leaning against the thin trunk of a sorry-looking willow. One of the brother's hands lifted up his T-shirt, obscuring half the marijuana leaf drawing covering the front, and scratched at his flat belly, offering a peek of the waistband of his boxers.

Demonte nodded at Bravey, who forced himself to walk over to the object of his obsession.

"Yo. Didn't know they let little boys in here."

If the guy hadn't been grinning, Bravey might have been hurt, instead of slightly stung. He stepped back.

"Don't leave. Come closer." Demonte reached out to the younger boy's belt loops, and pulled Bravey closer. The boy's hands reached for Demonte's chest. The heat from solid muscle coursed through Bravey's fingers, making him sweat, and yearn.

"So, what do you want to do?"

Bravey's face burned. "I-I don't know." His mouth was dry. Words came out in a hoarse whisper.

Demonte laughed and grabbed one of Bravey's wrists, leading him toward a clump of scrawny bush. Demonte's boxers slid to show a hint of asscrack. Bravey swallowed hard, turned on by the speed of what was happening, more excited than he ever thought possible.

Behind the cover of vegetation, Demonte pushed him roughly to the ground. Bravey tensed, worried he had been played, that he was going to have the shit beat out of him. One dead faggot. In this neighborhood, who would ever care?

But instead of fists pounding Bravey's face, Demonte's hands were quickly, deftly, zipping down his jeans.

A warm wetness engulfed Bravey's dick, the greatest sensation ever. He squirmed in the dirt, biting his lip not to cry out and let everyone in the garden know what was happening to him.

Cool night air replaced the warm wet. Bravey looked up to see Demonte tugging his pants down. A thick cock pushed out of a forest of black hair, leaking a strand of pre-cum that caught the moonlight and turned silver before breaking.

"Have to get it wet," Demonte said, directing Bravey's spit-slick dick toward his furred crack. He grunted a few times, eyes closed, as the tip went in, and then sat down, forcing the boy deep inside him.

Bravey's first time being sucked was intense, but this first-time fucking was a thousand times hotter, tighter, more demanding. He instinctively pushed up as Demonte rode him hard and slapped his chest. Neither of them lasted long and when it was over, they lay in a heap, sweaty and sticky, and quiet, listening to each other gasp for breath.

Demonte didn't date or even fuck the same guy regularly. That had been made clear in the awkward aftermath, as they parted.

Still, that didn't stop Bravey Boy from finding his way back to the garden on nights to come, hoping he might change Demonte's mind. But he was dissed, ignored, and ended up jerking himself off in the dark, listening to others get laid.

He told himself he was done with the garden, but two nights later he was lying on the bad mattress in his room and could not stop thinking about what happened there. He closed his eyes, but couldn't fall asleep. So he threw on shorts and a tight T-shirt and snuck past his snoring grandma, cursing with every step but knowing he had to go back.

He didn't find Demonte, but an older guy, in his thirties, with muscles that only came from construction work, approached him. He wanted to kiss the man, discover if the guy's goatee would tickle his face, but the man made it clear he only wanted to suck Bravey off. He let him.

So it went. His craving was satisfied too quickly after every trip to the garden. He needed something more, but he couldn't define it, describe it, imagine it—until one day he bumped into Lashon while on break from bagging groceries.

Lashon. The new stock boy.

Because of the rain, Bravey chose not to step outside. Instead, he headed for the chips aisle, meaning to get a snack. That's when he saw the boy with the linebacker's build, humming as he carefully arranged bags of salty pork rinds. Bravey knew he was wasting precious time; he only had fifteen minutes of freedom from ringing up sales of cold raw chicken and boxes of mac and cheese. But he couldn't break away. He was mesmerized, drawn to the boy's sweet, high voice, as he shifted from humming to singing—not some rap song, but an old R&B tune; he couldn't remember the name, but his grandmother listened to it on the radio.

The stock boy caught Bravey's stare, smiled, nodded hello, but kept working.

They hung out after work, sipping sodas, chatting, every day for a week. Suddenly, Bravey was excited about coming to work. Seeing Lashon, talking with him, brought Bravey alive. He wanted to sing, he wanted to dance, he moved to new rhythms in his head.

But at night, before he could find sleep, he worried. He replayed every moment spent with Lashon over and over in his head, trying to figure out if this look or that gesture or some word said by the fine boy meant that Lashon liked him. More than liked. Did he ache, too? Not knowing drove Bravey crazy.

One day soon after, distracted by desire, he fought with his manager, and was told to go home early. Lashon saw him leaving in a huff and ran out, risking his own job, to ask what happened. Bravey didn't even remember exactly what he said, but then Lashon was hugging him, out in the parking lot in front of everyone. Not just a light squeeze and a fast slap on the back: He held Bravey tightly for seconds that seemed to become hours, and softly sang in his ear, *If I have to sleep on your doorstep, all night and day...just to keep you from walkin' away. Let your friends laugh, even this I can stand... 'cause I wanna keep you any way I can.*

On the walk home, Bravey no longer saw the dilapidated buildings or the trash on the street or the dealers and the drunks lounging lazily to pass the day. Occasionally he shut his eyes, the better to recall the feel of Lashon holding him, the smell of Lashon close to him, and the soft whisper of Lashon in his ear.

Nervous as all hell—maybe he had misread the boy—he called Lashon that night. Asked to meet him, told him how to get to the old garden.

But Demonte didn't seem ready to leave. He stepped close to Bravey Boy, and their bodies brushed. Bravey felt the heat rising off the brotha's body, carrying with it the stink of a dump in July.

Demonte smirked.

"I know you remember it." He reached down and cupped Bravey's crotch, expertly rubbing the tip of the shaft with his thumb. Bravey was aroused. "See, this remembers me, too."

Demonte's touch made Bravey gasp. Unsteady, he leaned

in to Demonte, his head touching the other boy's forehead, damp and feverish. Bravey lifted an arm and laid it on a bare shoulder.

"Please," he muttered.

"Please what?" Demonte said, aping Bravey's voice. He slid his other hand under Bravey's jacket.

He didn't know what to say. He no longer wanted whatever quick fix Demonte once offered. Yet the cravings could not be denied. But when he heard whistling and saw a figure walking toward them through the darkness, the desire threatening to overtake him turned to sick fear and shame. He pushed with both arms, separating their bodies.

It wasn't Lashon—just a man dressed in bad overalls, who looked them over with goggle eyes. "Any you boys want to party?" He held up a paper bag with the tip of a dark amber bottle showing.

Demonte turned back to Bravey. His voice was low, dangerous. "Come on, one more time. You can ride me good. Hard." He slid his baggy pants down, revealing a trail of wiry hair. "Let you bust a nut in me."

The man piped in with a desperate pant. "Let me watch that shit, at least."

"Get the fuck outta here," Bravey said. "Both of you."

Demonte's face fell, a scared boy, no longer a cocky kid. The man next to them wavered, unsteady, obviously drunk.

"There's me." He gulped at whatever was in the bag.

"Yeah, yeah." Demonte grabbed the man's arm. "Too bad, papi."

Bravey watched them walk away. In the moonlight, Demonte's feet seemed never to touch the ground as he led the man deep into the garden. Bravey exhaled, releasing tension, then paced back and forth, worried—sure—that Lashon wouldn't show.

And then his stock boy was by his side.

Bravey hugged Lashon tightly, then eased into him, relaxing in the other boy's arms.

"This is some strange place," Lashon said, shaking his head. "Two guys came up to me lookin' to hook up. Freaks."

Bravey saw the look of disgust on Lashon's face and knew he had been wrong to ask Lashon to come to the garden. What had he been thinking? Wanting? A fast grope or quick blow job or sloppy fuck? No, not with this boy. A smile from him would be enough.

Lashon must think me a ho, Bravey thought. "Yeah, you shouldn't be here," he said.

But his friend only chuckled. "Like you should? Shit, look at this." Lashon motioned at Bravey's clothes. "You acting all sexy for me?" He laughed. "Trying to make me think you like me or somethin'?"

"No," Bravey lied, looking away. He could no longer meet the other boy's eyes. He backed up a few feet, and then turned to walk away, cursing himself for thinking something good could ever happen here.

"Wait up. Why you leavin'?" Lashon started after Bravey.

Bravey shrugged, not sure what to say. The two boys passed an overturned barbeque grill, the metal long since turned to a rusted hulk. Not far away, a man lay on the ground.

"Damn," Lashon said, and nudged the guy with his foot. The man didn't respond.

Bravey saw a paper bag wrapped around a bottle, leaning against the barbeque—it was the man who left with Demonte. The guy's pants were undone but not pulled down. He stank like sour milk and rotten meat. Demonte was nowhere to be seen.

"He's just drunk," Bravey said out loud, more to himself, because he wasn't so sure.

"This is some park," Lashon muttered.

"I'm sorry I asked you to come here."

"I'm not." Lashon's fingers cupped Bravey's chin.

"No?" Bravey didn't dare smile, afraid he'd heard wrong.

"Unless that's all you want." He pointed at the man on the ground. "What everyone else 'round here wants. I'm not trash and won't be treated like it."

Bravey shook his head. "It's cool. I mean, I want…."

Lashon chuckled. "Wanna go get somethin' to eat?"

Bravey nodded, buttoning up his jacket, suddenly embarrassed at how much skin showed.

"Cool." They headed back to the edge of the garden, walking so close they rubbed shoulders or bumped lightly against one another. Lashon pulled out car keys and flicked them playfully into the air. Bravey meant to catch them but only succeeded in knocking them to the ground.

"S'all right." Lashon bent to pick them up. "Damn," he said then, lifting something small and red from the ground near his foot.

Bravey looked at the strawberry. Small, and a bit misshapen. Lashon smiled and lifted it to Bravey's lips. The tiny berry was Elsewhere, sweet and strong, lifting him away.

"How does it taste?"

Bravey Boy leaned in and showed Lashon.

Surf
Andy Quan

I'm thinking about the colors of tanned skin. Sunlight boring
into the outer cells of the body and each body reacting indi-
vidually, changing into different hues, all of them inviting. I
like the way that tanned skin in the sunlight makes you want
to put your hand on it, to rest it there gently and maybe coax
back some of that solar energy into your own self.

It's ten-thirty, a good time to be at the beach. I could get
fried into an angry red if I were to stay out too long at noon. I
wince at the thought: the sunburn wheedling up to the head's
feverish fatigue, the peeling a few days later. My friends in
Sydney go to tanning salons. They're too rushed to go to the
beach, or maybe it's too far. Most people say they can't tell
the difference, but I think I can. There's always a trace of
ultraviolet orange. Also, the evenness makes one suspicious
at a gut level.

A natural tan is best, really. It makes me think of food:
honey, bran, chocolate. But I could easily think of elements:
earth—brown shale, red sand, the tan shade of certain rocks,
parched soil; or metal—copper, bronze, platinum, rust. Even

trees—though the tint of a deepening orange maple tree is probably unknown here, as would be the paper-thin bark of the arbutus tree, narcissist, exhibitionist, constantly stripping itself down to raw green underneath.

I miss those trees sometimes, but I'd rather be here. You wouldn't find tanned surfer boys in Canada. Not like these magnificent packs of young men striding through late adolescence, the particular motion of the body when walking in sand. I'm glad I made the move to Australia and was surprised at how easy it was: the whole world calls out for experts in IT—*Information Technology*—who ever says it by the long form anymore?

Not only that but I get to go to new places, not just stay in Sydney with its excess of men and attitude and beauty—*not that I'm complaining*—but hey, hey, Brisbane-Brisvegas (I don't know why they call it that). Welcome me with open arms. Show me something new in my two weeks here.

It was a pleasant enough journey out here: A train from the center of town, a ferry, a short bus ride, a little walk from the road through some trees and now I'm on this really long, flat white beach on Stradbroke Island that goes on and on. Step out of reality for a second, and you can imagine it stretching out forever.

That's what I'm thinking as I breathe out and watch the salt dry on my body. I'm a bit winded from playing in the surf. The scenery is calming me. There are some cute gay men here: A posse just ambled by in two pairs of Speedos and one pair of designer trunks, box-cut. I'm not as fixated as some of my friends, but my eyes did settle at crotch level in this case. Shiny sky-blue Speedos was well packaged, the light color of the fabric revealed a good contour: Big balls, it looked like. Black Speedos was harder to see, seemed like he'd tucked himself off to the left. The box-cut got my prize: Through a geometric pattern on white, he had his penis pointing right up against his belly. I love that habit, and the shape that results. And it was fat.

A lot of the surfer boys are wearing board shorts. I'd complain that they're covering too much but it's not a bad look. Tight little waistbands slung low on the body. Hugging a contour like two hands touching at the wrists and forearms and pointing away from each other, stretched out, forming a wide shallow cup. And in the space of this cup is a beautiful alcove where tanned, muscular backs slope into the shorts and then jut out suddenly and modestly to round, tight buttocks. And these butts are ready. Ready to be part of a balancing system to stay upright on the waves, the long board underfoot and now a part of their bodies. A great big hard long extension.

Other guys are wearing wet suits. I don't mind them either. I like the thought of men, young or old, squeezing themselves into tight rubber like a cock into a condom. I imagine myself as a pair of arms, a throat: Either embrace. They hold up both sides of their suits, put one foot in, then the other, shimmy it up so they can slide in their arms. I picture myself as that material so I can press against all parts of their bodies. Funny, I don't get the same thoughts when I see a man in a nice pair of jeans. Maybe I should.

I was just playing out in the surf. I'm not a strong swimmer and there's a sign warning about the undertow here so I stayed close to shore. It was hard to be far out. The strength of the sea rolling in on big constant waves: Swells would lift me five feet off the bottom and put me back down, a wave would break over my head and fill my ears and nostrils with salty water. I tried to figure out body surfing but I'm not sure Canadians are naturally suited to it.

So here I am, resting up on my shoulders, checking out all the cute young surfer boys through my sunglasses when Brian walks by. He's tall and lean with long rectangular muscles. His surfboard is in his right arm behind him so his silhouette is a chunky cross. He notices me looking, or senses my lust, or his gaydar goes off. Something. But he glances over, and with his smile I forget everything: my name, my country, my present location.

"Hi," he says, though it might have been "G'day." Whatever he says, it's in the most natural way in the world, as if he always talks to strangers, and as if there's nothing unusual about somebody checking him out—which there isn't—since with that kind of beauty, I'm sure it happens all the time. I look left once and right and no one else is watching him, or us.

"Hi," I reply, because "G'day" would sound forced, too chummy, a colloquialism that doesn't quite sit right with my Canadian accent. No foreigner ever learns to say "G'day" here correctly.

He stops and I tell him I'm here for work. It strikes me, while we're making small talk, that I hadn't considered the possibility of a gay surfer. Not that the two things would be opposed: homosexuality, balancing on a board in the waves. But my image of the sport was of young, virile boys filled with straight testosterone. It's ironic that I try to fight against stupid prejudices but hold them myself.

"What do you do when you're not surfing?" I ask.

"I'm a florist," he tells me, grinning. I sense he grins the same way any time he tells this to another gay man. "Stereotypical, huh?"

No. His physical charm to me is so completely original that the word touches me for only a second before it flies off.

I could sit and talk for hours, but he informs me he's starting work at 1 P.M. today and should be on his way.

"You ever surf? I bet it's not a Toronto kind of sport," he comments, and my silent half-shake of the head indicates no. "Do you want to learn?"

Yes.

No.

Not really.
I'm scared of sharks.
And the water.
Anything to see you again.

My eyes come out of a blur and I'm looking into his smiling eyes. I don't know what I've said.

"Right, then. I can't tomorrow. So, Monday? Ten A.M. You're willing to come out here again? I do all the time; it's worth the trip. I'll meet you near the public toilet and change rooms over there. I can bring you a board. A nice big flat steady beginner's board." He winks at me and walks off, that surfer walk again. If I ever had an Australian fantasy, this is it. If I didn't, this is it.

He arrives on time. I was early. I couldn't stay away.

The first lesson is on dry land. I thought we'd be in the water right away, paddling around, but instead we sit on the shore. He's describing the waves to me, pointing out patterns and where you should paddle out, how you should ride across the whitecaps, never go in front of someone else, watch out for swimmers, not that they should be out in that area anyway. *Is this information important?* I'm having problems concentrating. When he lifts his left arm to point out to the surf, part of his chest pulls out from his body, like the fabric of a kite being stretched on a frame. It forms this sail bordering the hollow of his underarm, which I'm guessing he probably trims. The hair is neither bushy nor sparse. It's a dark brown bloom, one of these new Australian flora I'm trying to learn the names of.

"You'll have the board attached to your leg anyway, never panic, it's not so rough out there. You might not be able to stand up the first time, but we'll see how it goes, first you can just try to get the motion lying flat, then kneeling. We won't stay in too long today. You don't have a wet suit. I don't want you to get too cold. Or too burnt. Lotion?"

"Uh, right," I say. "Forgot." I take the bottle from him, a waterproof variety and SPF36: He's predicting that Canadians fry in the Aussie sun. I slather the lotion onto my legs and arms, chest and stomach, self-consciously, then neck and face. He dips his finger in a small container and reaches out and paints my nose.

"Pink zinc. Gorgeous."

I hold out the lotion to him and can't even get the words out but he grabs the bottle, squeezes, and efficiently rubs it over the parts of my back I can't reach.

More, please. All over. Lower. Higher. All around. That's what I'm thinking, at least. I'd suggest forgetting about surfing, but if surfing is why I'm here, I'll carry on.

"Um, um…. You," I comment. It sounds like an accusation.

"Oh, I put mine on already. Let's go."

I can't even seem to carry the board properly, so I'm relieved when we get to the water's edge. Then, instead of getting in the water, he makes me put the board flat on the sand.

"Okay. Last lesson. You've got to learn how to pop up."

I look down at my board shorts. I didn't tell him that I bought them especially for today, and I hope that he doesn't notice. But I'm checking whether I've still got the half-erection from when he was rubbing me down. I could pop that up.

He looks at me curiously, wondering what I'm doing. "You've got to be able to stand up in one clean motion. If you can't do it on the land, it'll be a lot harder in the water. You want to be able to do it without thinking."

I look at him, and the board, and the sand. "You want me to do this?"

"Yep." He seems serious.

"In front of these people?"

"In front of me."

"Uh, okay." I lie down face first on the board, tense my legs, and then hop up and draw them underneath me. I end up with my hands in front of me as if I'm trying to catch a ball. He says it's fine for a start. I look around. No one is watching. I do it again. And again. The fourth time, I lose my balance and fall over on my butt. He doesn't laugh, just shrugs, and the slight rising and falling of his shoulders sets off small ripples in the muscles in his upper body. I forget my task, or my role as student, and just look at him. I must look like a fawning idiot.

"Just a few more times then."

My first lesson is a minor success. The waves are small but steady. There aren't so many people out in the water that I run into anyone. I mainly paddle around and try to catch the rhythm of the waves. I attempt to stand up, and fall over. Actually, numerous times, but I manage to do it once. The wave carries me in so slowly that I soon tumble into the water. But I am proud of myself.

"Bend with your knees, not your waist," I hear as I duck my head out of the water and swim toward my board. "Keep your weight over your feet. Crouch for control."

He paddles over to me.

"Can I bend over with my waist after?" I ask hopefully. I'm not sure if he hears me.

I'm tired, but I ask him if we can go to where it's a bit rougher. I don't want to surf. I want to watch him surf. "Just a few times."

He agrees. I paddle my board in the water, awkwardly, trying not to obstruct others, but wanting to remain out in the ocean, as close as I can, to watch him. The waves look far too easy for him but I marvel at how someone so tall can remain so upright. The sun above drapes small shadows on his long torso; his muscles shimmer like the sea below him. He catches one long wave and heads far off down to the east. I get the full view of his body. First his torso facing me as he catches the wave, then the side of his body as he picks up speed, and finally his long back as he surfs away from me. Every part of his form lustrous in motion, steely and strong, confidently traveling on his long, flat carriage.

Even though I paddle in his direction, and he in mine, it takes a while to meet in the middle.

"Enough?" he inquires.

No. I could never get enough of you.

We exit the water. "I'm exhausted," I say, then add, "and thankful."

"Don't mention it." We're in the men's change room, and somehow we're alone.

"Hey, have you ever been back here at night?"

He looks at me quizzically.

"Or, you know, done it here, in the change rooms, or even...in the surf?"

He takes his time in answering. "When I was younger, a few times, maybe. You know, it's not comfortable at all. The sand gets everywhere, the salt water stings. Some of the beaches have pretty sharp rocks and you scrape your skin. Out here, there's just sand, nothing to lean onto. It's a bit boring. I know something much more comfortable." He leans over me and blocks a shaft of sunlight that is coming at an angle through the doorway. Even his shadow feels good.

His room. Spacious. Curtains drawn. Smatterings of dusk seeping through. The walls are white but clothed in shadows. His bed is covered in crisp white sheets. There is a huge bouquet of roses in a crystal vase in front of a mirror on a low set of drawers.

"Do you always have roses in your room?"

"I cannot tell a lie. I hoped you'd be back here today. They're for you."

"Not daffodils or lilies? Or Australian natives?—not that I can remember the names of any of them."

"Well, you're not an Australian native." He takes me in his arms.

Height. Did I confess how much I like tall men? Not all the time. In fact, I kind of like all sorts of men. But a tall man will make you swoon just because you have to look up. Then the blood tilts to the back of your head. He leans over to kiss you. *Wham.* Hopefully he stops your fall.

"I'm going to take a shower first." His voice has some command in it. First roses. Now what? "You can relax in here." He enters the bathroom, which opens directly onto the bedroom, and shuts the door.

I sit on the edge of the bed at first and listen to the sounds of the taps and spray, the echoing timbre of the insides of bathrooms. I'm both exhausted and raring to go.

When he comes out, he's wrapped his midsection in a white towel. I grip his sheets in my hands so I don't tackle him to rip it off.

"Your turn."

I'm quicker than him. I let it all slide down the drain: the last remnants of the ocean and beach, the day's lessons, the heat.

I come out and he's lying back with his head against the pillows, a long silhouette, his legs slightly parted and the space in between a long triangular arrowhead that I follow, dropping my towel on the floor and climbing on top of him. It's like finding the ideal place on a beach and lying down, the give of the sand below your body, how it molds itself to you.

We kiss and kiss, and then he leans forward, slowly easing my back down to the surface of the bed. I swing my legs out from under me until they wrap around his thighs, and then he is on top of me.

"Let's fuck," he says, and even in those two short words there's that Aussie accent that I love. Lube has appeared out of nowhere, wherever he keeps it—his arms were long enough to reach without my noticing. He squeezes some into his right palm and reaches behind him to smear it between his but-tocks. I must look quizzical, and he reads my mind. "No need to warm me up, I'm an expert at this."

I can't believe how still I'm managing to keep when my insides are waves crashing against rocks. There's a speedboat in my head but I'm breathing out and in, shaking only slightly as he slides a condom onto my cock, which is as hard as it's ever been. Unwavering.

He straddles me, kneeling, and I can feel changes in pres-sure and texture as he lowers himself onto me in two short breaths. Then he starts to ride, slowly at first, up and down, his eyes closed tight and his head thrown back slightly, as if sensing a signal from a far horizon. His hands rest on the fronts of his thighs, every muscle in his body warming up, moving, joining into a rhythmic motion. He opens his eyes and stares into mine.

I'm reluctant to look away from his long torso, the tops and sides of his thighs, but I hold his stare and see in it: plea-sure, satisfaction, desire.

He rides me and rides me, his torso twisting back and forth, side to side, balanced on top of me with a reckless knack for the sport, an instinct. Bouncing on a wave, he is surprising me with his intensity. The sight of him makes my mouth go dry just as the rest of my body is covering itself in sweat.

I am about to ask him whether his legs are tired and if he's okay but it strikes me that this is what he does: standing up, squatting, a position halfway between. These are surfing muscles he's using.

I am gasping now too, and as he lifts his body up, he squeezes his anus tighter against the shaft of my cock. On the downward cycle he grinds against my pelvis and I feel the head of my penis jostling against his inner sphincter. I think we've reached as far as we can go—can the elements get stron-ger than this? He leans forward, places his hands on my chest, and arches his back so my cock slides out of him. He whips off the condom, tosses it aside, and lies back. He's already got a condom out and is working it onto his cock, which is gorgeous and erect. He leans forward, then pulls me into a position where I'm kneeling above his head.

"Let's warm you up." I lose track of his progress with the condom and lube as I feel his hot tongue inside me, thrusting up into my anus. I have to grab my balls and tug so I don't shoot, right then, all over his face. He rims me for ages, then grabs my hips in his hands and guides me down toward his cock. "I like the hair on your arsehole. It tastes…" he licks his lips, "…textural."

Then, without a chance to think about it, he's inside me. I'm not used to being fucked in this position, but I like it. The best way to learn something is to watch someone who is good at it and try to do the same. I'm looking at his face, and at his torso pumping underneath me, and superimposed is the image of him, not moments before, being fucked in the same position I'm in now. My shoulders, hips, thighs are moving the way he moved. I think I'm getting the hang of it.

Not for long, though. I've been excited too much, for too long. The wave forms, the white foam turning over onto itself. The curve of it rises, pulling everything from underneath it toward shore. My legs are getting too tired to hold me up. I'm only a beginner at this. I rest down on his cock, grinding, rubbing. My hands reach out to grab the handles of his chest. My cum sprays in all directions. I arch myself over him as he grabs his cock and pumps, a few decisive strokes. One of my hands still rests on his chest, the other is now next to his head. He turns his face, kisses my wrist, and groans. Salt from one ocean mixes with that of another.

After we finish making love, we shower. Together this time. We squeeze into the shower cubicle—it is rounded actually, like a space capsule—and take turns soaping each other down. I get hard again, and take him in my mouth, my tongue and cheeks responding to his penis swelling with blood, softening, different degrees of firmness. We dry each other with big, comfortable, square white towels.

We walk into the bedroom again and I face him. His skin holding that quality of just being toweled down.

I tell him there is a square of his body I like. Not a small square. I stand in front of him and draw it in the air with both hands. I start between his pectorals, move my fingers outward in opposite directions about two inches above his nipples (the nipples are the best part, the angels in the corner, the whole way the painting is lit) and two inches past, then down the same distance, and back toward the middle of his abdomen. He is so tall and long and lean that this square shows not his whole belly but just the top part. So: the nipples, the line of his chest underneath, the division between right and left pectoral starting to soar, and then these rectangles, one on top of each other. I picture a hunky bricklayer putting them into place, this wall of stomach muscles. If I were to traverse it, I wouldn't hop over; I'd gently ease the bricks out and replace them behind me as I entered.

"This," I say. "This makes a beautiful picture."

He laughs at me, a gentle laugh, and gives me a hug, strangely nonsexual, the same reaction you might get when you can't help yourself and tell your woman-friend's boyfriend how hot he is, and he's cool about it and he even puts his arms out to you.

He looks into my eyes, and I picture my perfect square as a photograph mounted on the wall of my apartment in Sydney, right in the entranceway so it would be the first thing you see when you come in.

I drop by Brian's shop before I leave Brisbane, and there he is, looking so different, an efficient florist in a cool room. I'm looking for a phone booth that he can change in, back into his surfer-boy persona. Or he could keep his Clark Kent flower-guy shtick: Either is fine with me.

"I'd buy flowers from you, but I'd give them right back," I say.

And right there, in the middle of his store, he grabs me and pulls me into his tall frame, and into a kiss, a subtle, long, two-tongues-entwined kiss that doesn't break, even when the tiny bell on the door chimes and a pretty, young woman walks in, breaking into a mischievous grin.

"How 'bout I call you when I'm in Sydney next?" he says, and walks calmly behind the counter. I hear the conversation start and fade like the sea caught in a shell.

"Brian, Lily got a promotion at work, I'd like the most beautiful bouquet of flowers...."

And as I'm out the door, I'm surfing.

Light offshore, blue skies, and a thirty-foot swell. I'm driving into the shore, and I'm on it without even a wait. I don't know how big the thing is, but I know it's the heaviest wave of my life and I'm gonna ride it. My largest tube to date.

It spits as soon as I'm inside it and I can't see a thing for the entire ride. The board is part of my body, I'd entered the zone long ago, and the long appendage beneath me is doing what I need it to do: holding steady, riding fast, keeping me upright, my knees supple and bent, my shoulders and arms sensitive to changes in the ocean beneath me, balancing me out.

The whole time, I have my eyes closed, thinking, "I'm coming out. I'm coming out." I'm thinking myself through the wave, envisioning myself exiting the barrel. And I'm making it. Riding the most powerful wave. Somewhere far below is sand and earth. But here, right in the middle of things, is me, balanced at the most perfect and unique place between the water and the sky.

from *My Name Is Rand*
Wayne Courtois

It was 3:05 P.M. when I took the turnoff into Granger's neighborhood. To the southeast lay the city, crowded and noisy, but you'd never know it from these quiet streets and small, well-kept homes. Each front yard had one or two trees. The lawns were uniformly clipped, free of fallen leaves or stray toys. They were white houses, mostly, including Granger's, so square and bright in the afternoon sun that it seemed to hover a few feet off the ground.

I pulled into the driveway, turned off my engine, and listened to it ticking as it cooled. It had been a long drive across the state, with not much to see and a lot to think about. Picturing myself at this very moment, about to meet Granger, ready to discover if I'd taken the right path. But readiness wasn't something I'd packed in my small bag along with a change of clothes and tape recorder; at the moment it was such a foreign concept that I touched the ignition key, more than halfway inclined to slip into reverse, get away while I still could. Instead I stared at Granger's screen door, and realized in a minute or so that he was standing there, his outline assembling slowly, a tall broad man wearing white, his face a grayish mystery.

I rolled down my window. "Am I okay here," I called, "or should I park on the street?"

"You're fine." His voice was loud and deep and welcoming, as if I were an old friend or relative. "Come on in."

"Thanks." Always self-critical, I felt a surge of pride, as if I'd passed a test: voice normal, nerves normal. It was possible to feel ordinary as I slid out of my SUV, bag in hand, and approached the door, Granger still a ghost behind the screen.

I set my bag in the living room, and Granger gave me a tour of the house, which he'd just moved into a few weeks earlier. My first really clear look at him was from behind as I followed him down a hallway. He was an ex-Marine, with a short gray crew cut and strong frame, his T-shirt stretched taut across a muscular back and shoulders. His white shorts contrasted well with his tanned furry legs, the kind of legs that could carry a man into and out of all kinds of trouble, legs that would always land a man on his feet. His face, his eyes were still mysteries.

The house was much larger than it looked from the outside. He led me through a generous sun porch down to the basement, which he'd had finished in oak. Half of it had once been a party room, judging by the counter that could easily serve as a bar, and in the other half sat a white washer and dryer. "Also," he said, "I want to build a room over here. For a rack, and some stocks, and a few other things."

"You could have yourself quite a decent torture chamber down here," I said.

"It will come. In time." In the weak light from the basement window Granger's smile, framed by a closely trimmed mustache and beard, was confident. He wore a small gold ring in his left ear. I still wanted a good look at his eyes.

We sat out on the front stoop for a while, facing the sun

that had dimmed just perceptibly, nudging the clock toward late afternoon, enriching the lawns and houses with a light more gold than yellow. A few neighbors came and went, some of them waving as they got in or out of their cars. It seemed like a pleasantly integrated neighborhood, a far cry from the redneck suburbs that surrounded the city where I lived.

"It's been years," I said, "since I've seen a neighborhood this quiet."

"It's quiet all the time, too," Granger said. He was wearing sunglasses now. "Even on weekends. No kids on this block."

"And your house is soundproof?"

"Bet your ass." Again that smile, not only confident but also anticipating something good.

"Was that the first thing you asked your real estate agent—whether anybody would hear guys screaming in this house?"

Granger laughed. "It wasn't the first thing, but it was high on the list."

I almost asked him then if I could see his eyes. But how do you ask that question? I was working to make every gesture and word project self-assurance, as if I constantly traveled to meet strangers for intimate encounters and this was just one more.

"Let's go inside," he said finally, as the sun came close to touching the tree line.

In the living room I accepted the beer he offered. He had switched on a lamp and as he handed me the beer I got my first good look at his eyes. They were light-colored, a hazel that was almost gray, but their size made up for their paleness—that, and the way they searched my face as if every part of me was to be found there. Eyes that could seek and find anything, with or without cooperation. *Escape proof.* I was close to picking up my bag and retreating while I still could.

"Sit down," he said. "Let's talk."

Like many men I had known, Granger could talk about

his erotic history the way others talked about their banking careers or hunting dogs. He took it for granted that I was an expert in homoerotics, had handled male bodies and let them handle me with a familiarity that bred an appetite for more. He assumed I had fucked myself raw, sucked cock till my face turned inside out, and jacked off dicks till my palms were callused. It was when he got to our mutual obsession that my heartbeat sped up and my dickhead stirred in my jeans.

He had learned at an early age that he could make other boys helpless by tickling them, and that it was almost unbearably exciting. As he grew up, reducing a boy to breathless laughter and eye-rolling panic became the central ritual of his life. It got him in trouble, the way he single-mindedly pursued his victims; but it also gave him an expertise in stimulation that few others were able to obtain in a lifetime. He explained this to me, not as a braggart but as a man who need make no apologies for what he has diligently earned. He couldn't relate all of his experiences, but he told me enough so that, after a while, my tongue felt dry and swollen, and I realized I'd been sitting and listening to him with my mouth hanging open.

As he talked I watched his eyes, those all-encompassing eyes, and was somehow unaware that he'd moved from his chair onto the sofa beside me until his hand brushed my arm and I jumped. I was everything he wanted, everything that excited him, and the more I realized it the more I shrank away, as if I could retract my ticklish nerve-ends the way a turtle hides in its shell. I was certain that I couldn't stand to be touched, not by him, not anywhere.

"Down at the end of that hall," he said. "Get going."

I sat and blinked at him. If just one of his large groping fingers touched my naked skin, I'd die.

"I said *move!*"

The bedroom had light green walls, small shaded lamps, and a double bed with an immaculate white spread. It was the kind of room you'd find in a B&B, comfortable and inviting, not threatening in the least. But my knees shook as I looked around, because the harmlessness of the setting seemed to *add* something threatening to it.

Granger grabbed the center of the bedspread with his fist, snatched it off the bed, rolled it up in a ball, and tossed it in a corner. From a drawer he took some cloth restraints—surgical restraints, he said, the kind they used in hospitals. He didn't look directly at me as he spoke, as if he were speaking aloud to his obsession, stoking it with words. "Some tools," he said, taking a box from a chest of drawers. I saw hairbrushes, regular and electric toothbrushes, feathers, some wicked-looking hair picks, thick pipe cleaners. I reached out to touch one of the brushes, one he had told me about the first time we chatted online. Called "the widowmaker," it had steel bristles with rounded nylon tips, and was deadly on the soles of the feet.

He was getting out yet another bag of tools when the doorbell rang. He left to answer it. I was having trouble getting my excited breathing under control. I paced in the narrow space between the bed and the shuttered window, then moved out into the hall. Granger stood at the front door, talking to someone—a solicitor?—standing outside on the stoop. While they chatted I could barely take my eyes off Granger's left hand. It was in constant motion, the fingers stiffening, then springing into claws, then wriggling ferociously—tickling, tickling the air. Was it a signal to me, or did that hand really have a mind of its own, independent from the judgment and will that normally made it run?

I lay naked on the cool sheet, my head propped up enough so I could watch Granger peel off his shirt and shorts in a couple of neat stripper moves. His dick—the kind of dick that can stop an argument—preceded the rest of him from then on, bobbing and swaying as he performed his bondage chores.

He grabbed my ankles and easily pulled me down toward the bottom edge of the bed, where he tied my ankles together, first wrapping them in a towel so the black cord wouldn't cut into the skin. A second length of cord led from my bound ankles to a fixture on the floor at the foot of the bed. Next he slid toe-rings over my big toes, metal rings that tickled as he fitted them snug, making me gasp. It wasn't a good sign: If my toes were that ticklish, what kind of chance did I have? He tied cords leading from the rings to the cords securing my ankles, so I now had feet that couldn't move up or down or side to side, soles that couldn't flex, toes that couldn't clench. By the time he had fastened the wrist restraints, stretching my arms to the limit, and blindfolded me with a tight dark cloth, I knew the utter helplessness of a victim, unable to fend off the merest threat.

He showed me how easy it was for him, reducing me to blind laughter within a matter of seconds—playfully, using a big soft feather on my nostrils, violating my nose, shoving tickling sensations up into my brain till I was begging him to stop. From there it was a short trip to my ears, feathering all in and around them as I felt them grow, my ticklish ears becoming all of me, then expanding into the room, the street, the city. The tickler and his feathers grew, too, keeping in step with sensation as my laughter, already hoarse, swallowed up all other sound.

I was half out of my mind, and so far he had only touched my nose and ears. He had a lot to teach me just by moving as far down as my neck, where the feathers had me giggling and sputtering like a child, twisting my head, exposing new spots, new angles to the torture. Now my body was a map of the known and the unknown, and I gasped as he reached each frontier, my shoulders, my upper chest....

When he reached my armpits I began to beg in earnest. His strong, quick fingers whirred like eggbeaters in those tender pockets, and I was twisting my head again, choking out laughter that rose in pitch and volume, then babbling whenever my breath could find room, an automatic string of *stop-it-please-stop-it* and *don't-do-it-don't-do-it....*

Then he jumped whole continents, moving from my armpits to my feet, and I realized how much power he had, how he could turn me into anything. I screamed as his strong fingers raked my soles over and over; it was as if it had been ordained long ago that these were the fingers that could tickle me to death. He paused only to soften up my feet with some kind of lotion. Catching my breath, I pictured that deadly brush—the widowmaker—heading toward my soles, and cursed my imagination for conspiring with the blindfold to scare me witless. But the scare was nothing compared with the actual moment when those stiff bristles ground into my arches. My head exploded. I screamed at him, said I was going to die if he didn't stop. I spent my precious breath begging him, using every dirty promise, every filthy bribe I could think of, pledging to be his dick-slave, to jack him off, suck his cock, lick his balls, massage his prostate if only he'd stop tickling me. I promised him everything I could think of short of letting him fuck me in the ass, which I'd never let a man do. But my mouth could serve him, I swore I'd make him come like he'd never come before, honest to Christ, he'd never be sorry he took mercy on me....

"*Mercy?*" He laughed like hell as he scrubbed the flesh beneath my tightly stretched toes. When he finally paused just long enough to say, "Now I think I'm gonna work *between* your toes for a while," I pictured again what he was doing, taking up a handful of thick pipe cleaners.

Much later, when I was finally free and had had a chance to recover, and we were sitting on the red sofa in his living room, he called me on those promises. I pointed out that they had been pleas for a mercy I'd never received. His counter-argument was convincing, though: "You better get to work, or the next session will be even worse."

To make his point he grabbed my feet and used his finger-nails on my soles. That flipped a switch and I was instantly helpless, writhing and sputtering about how good I could make his dick feel.

"So do it," he said.

I sank to the floor, took him in my mouth, and, excited by the feel of his dickhead against my palate, sucked as if my life depended on it, which it probably did. I sucked and jacked his dick, licked his glistening balls, soaked his groin and navel with my tongue. He lay back, his eyes closed, moaning seri-ously. I sucked his achingly hard dick again till he was at the point of coming, then moved back to his balls. His moans were louder than ever. I spread his thighs wider, the more easily to reach down and manipulate his prostate with my fingertips. Unable to resist his hairy thighs, I let my fingers roam there too, stroking, then lightly squeezing. His moans grew shorter, sharper. As I continued working his dick with my mouth I let two fingers explore between his cheeks to find his asshole, prying and rubbing and rimming it.

When he was close to coming I started jacking his dick for all I was worth. His dickhead popped free from my mouth and he came in an explosion so long and hard that it left me sitting against the wall with my face, neck, and chest soaked with cum. I was so fucking wet, I thought his dick had literally blown up.

Then I got in his face. He seemed barely conscious, moan-ing and shaking his head in disbelief at what I'd made him feel. But I knew he was hearing me as I said to him, "Now here's what I want you to do. Tie me up and tickle me, and keep it steady. Don't stop for a second, till you've tickled me out of my mind. Make me your slave."

In no time I was tightly stretched, tied down, and blind-folded again. I knew whatever he had done to me before was now going to be ten times worse, but it turned out I was wrong. It was a hundred times worse. His tickling was relent-less, keeping me in such steady laughter that I couldn't speak. Even when he stopped to lotion up my feet for the widow-maker, I couldn't beg for mercy because I was panting so hard. Those bristles dug into my soles again and I was screaming, a steady hoarsening wail that rose in pitch and intensity like a siren gone haywire, taking all my breath, threatening to burst my own eardrums. I screamed for what seemed like forever as he scrubbed my slickened feet all over with those bristles, and I was no longer tied to a bed but floating, suspended in endless space, held aloft by nothing but agony.

When that particular torture was over I had no time to recover, for he was at the rest of me again, from my neck to my knees, and my screams subsided into steady, hysterical laughter as his strong, quick fingers seemed to move every-where at once. When I could get out a word, finally, one exhausted word, it was "Don't!"

"Don't what?" he asked. "Don't what?" But of course he wouldn't stop long enough to let me get out another word, I was off on another course of breathless laughter.

"Don't!" I managed to say again, perhaps an hour later.

"Don't what?" he asked again, jabbing my belly with all ten fingers, my laughter so shrill now that it sounded like the keening of a madman throwing himself against the rubber walls of his cell.

When the widowmaker came again I broke completely. The time when I thought he *couldn't* totally break me belonged to ancient history, when the earth was flat. Now, with those bristles as merciless as fire on the center of my soles and beneath my toes, I knew, for the first time, what it was like to lose the will to survive. Through my struggling the cords had loosened enough so I could clench my toes a bit, but now, after another long, high-pitched wail, I relaxed them for the first time, allowing them to spread, *surrendering* them to him. Immediately bristles forced themselves where they couldn't quite reach before. I was laughing, babbling, and wailing all at the same time.

After my feet had been totally destroyed, broken down into ticklish molecules and down again into nothing, he moved back to the rest of me, kneading, squeezing, pitilessly poking and pulling the lethally sensitized flesh from my neck to my thighs. I was reduced to panting with my tongue hanging out, drooling down my chin like an idiot.

The session lasted all night.

The next day, after we'd slept a few hours—I'd stayed on the bed, too weak to move from the sweat-soaked sheet—we had eggs and toast, sitting naked at the kitchen table with a pot of black coffee, then ended up on the red sofa again. I lay on my belly with my feet hooked over his thigh, which let him play with my soles with his right hand as he jacked himself off with his left. After a while he said, "Now I want your ribs," and like the obedient tickle-slave I'd become I rolled over, got to my knees, and raised my arms above my head. The unspoken rules of engagement demanded that, if I wanted to get him to stop tickling my ribs, I had to beg him to tickle my belly; and in order to rescue my poor sore belly I had to beg him to tickle my armpits. "Please, master," I said again and again, offering up my feet, then my lower back. Soon we were writhing together, slick with sweat and pre-cum, and I had his dick in my mouth. It seemed even bigger today, as if it had swollen with use. He had to admit that he liked my dick too, showing it in his own way: no obliging hand jobs or sweet suckoffs, not without a lot of agonizing apple-polishing first. Did it make me more ticklish? Of course it did. Everything did—breathing the air, processing oxygen, replacing dead cells with new ones.

Sometime in the afternoon we got stoned. I was afraid at first, but fear had also become as standard as breathing. Being with Granger was all about fear, because I was so scared of being tickled to death and he was so ready to make it happen. The grass that we smoked was moist, as if he grew it himself in the backyard. Maybe he did; a hidden plot of marijuana was no more subversive than a torture chamber, which he did a pretty good job of improvising even if he didn't have all the equipment yet.

Being stoned *was* dangerous. My buzzing brain kept losing track of my skin. There I was with my feet in his face, shoving them against his tongue and teeth; how'd *that* happen? And how did I ever allow him to wrap me in plastic like a mummy? Not that it was much work for him—he had only to spread the thick plastic sheet on the floor, have me lie down on it, grab an edge, and roll. His work consisted of tying ropes to keep the plastic in place, making absolutely sure that I couldn't move my arms, hands, or even fingers. As I lay on my back, completely helpless, he put toe-rings on my feet and secured them. I was breathing hard, out of panic. This was an advanced stage of bondage, much different from being tied spread-eagle to a bed, where it was at least possible to move enough to prove to yourself you were still alive. The only part of my body I could move at all was my head, and that not very much. It didn't seem to count, anyway, when there was little my head could do but measure the devastation to come, like a seismograph.

"Granger?" I asked, just wanting to hear his voice. "Hey, Granger." He wasn't near my stretched, bound feet; where was he? Twisting my head to the left, I could glimpse the kitchen area, the light from the open refrigerator glowing on the tiles. Cellophane crackled, a jar popped its lid. The son of a bitch was making himself a sandwich. Pulling a chair over to the kitchen counter, he sat where I could see his bare feet as he ate, making plenty of slurping and smacking sounds but not saying a word. "Hey, Granger." He was probably reading a magazine, too. "Granger, goddamn it!"

It was tough to appraise a situation where, thanks to pot, my senses lagged behind my observations. I was in deep trouble, its depth revealing itself slowly, like layers of a dream. While most of me could do nothing, my pot-sensitized feet perked up like a retriever's ears, registering everything—air currents, particles of dust, sound waves from Granger's squeaking chair. Idiot feet, bragging about how sensitive they were, as if to reassure me. "Hey, Granger?" I said. Maybe it wasn't too late to call this off. "Granger." I was growing warm in my plastic cocoon, my sweat seeming to tighten the sheath even more. "Granger," I said, twisting my head toward his bare feet on the kitchen floor, all I could see of him. Unlike mine, his feet were confident, in control. Feet that would always land a man on his legs. What, what was I going to do? *What could I do?* The unacceptable *nothing* echoed through my mind in a voice very much like Granger's. I shook my head vigorously, like a child throwing a tantrum, until I heard Granger's voice again, for real this time.

"Here you go," he said. As if he were handing me a glass of water, instead of fitting a blindfold over my eyes. "Here you go," and there I went, into total darkness.

What he did to my feet over the next hour should not have been done to anyone, ever. I would never know what he used on them, for he refused to tell me, even after he finally stopped. I assumed it was something from his kitchen, something that was never meant to be used on human flesh. It burrowed into the core of my ticklishness and multiplied like a corrosive virus, flaying my feet down to raw nerves. At each touch I howled a desperate laugh and the touching never stopped; he kept me on the brink of passing out but I never quite crossed over. When he finally stopped tickling me

I kept howling, stuck in my hysteria till he grabbed my chin with one hand, turned my head back and forth. It was then I knew it was over, also realizing that my midsection had become unbearably warm and moist: I had pissed myself.

Something was different in me after that. For a long time I sat across the living room from Granger and looked at him looking at me. He sat with one bare leg hiked up, a forearm resting on his knee, a vaguely satisfied expression on his face, the look of a champion trying to appear humble. Even his dick, which I had rubbed and sucked raw over the past twenty-four hours, looked satisfied, lying on his belly as if it were taking a well-deserved nap. Still half-stoned and hardly sane, I began listening, almost against my will, to the tiny voice in that part of my brain that could still organize thought. The voice was telling me that somehow I was going to have to pull myself together. Somewhere the world kept turning, and I would have to join it again.

"You want anything to eat?" Granger asked.

I shook my head.

"Anything to drink? Water?"

I just looked at him. "How am I going to do this?" I asked.

"Don't worry," he said. "Just take it slow. Do you want to make a phone call?"

Yes, that was another thing that just came back to me: I wasn't going to be able to make it all the way across the state tonight as I had originally planned. I needed at least another couple of hours before I would be in any shape to drive. I looked at my watch and figured out, with the time-consuming, roundabout logic of someone under the influence of too much stimulation, that David would not be home from his law office yet, even though it was Saturday. That meant I would get his answering machine. That was okay, I could handle being coherent enough to leave a message.

By my watch it was 8:15 when I left. Granger, still naked, saw me to the door. Even in the hallway the air reeked of sweat and cum and piss, and I felt I had his scent on me too—hard to describe, a clean but strong smell, like a no-nonsense soap. In spite of what they had done to me I was going to miss his enormous hands. And his dick, which I stooped down and took in my mouth one last time, clutching it with my tongue. He cuffed me on the shoulder as I picked up my bag and stepped outside. The late evening sun was surprisingly strong.

I was still feeling a little stoned, and drove with the kind of overcompensation that can be so amusing in someone who's high—keeping twenty miles under the speed limit, braking far in advance of a red light. There wasn't much traffic, though, on the quiet streets leading to the highway.

The interstate was a different matter, especially at the point where it merged with another major highway. Suddenly I found myself in the midst of eight lanes of stalled traffic—a thousand taillights flaring at random as brakes were lightly touched, no car moving more than a few inches at a time. Whatever caused the jam lay far ahead, unseen; I couldn't spot even the flashing lights of a police car or ambulance. It seemed like a long time before traffic moved freely again.

The ugly, over-familiar highway offered little to see but gently rolling countryside, flat and featureless. I kept to the speed limit, letting tractor-trailers and anxious SUVs rush by on my left. Alert now, I could see each step of the journey ahead: stopping at a cheap but adequate motel, catching seven or eight hours' sleep and taking off again with a thermos full of coffee, finally reaching home around noon. Calling David, who would surely be at home then, reading the Sunday paper. I'd told him that I was visiting an "old friend." He'd have no inkling of what I'd been through; if I tried to explain that I had been tied up and tickled to within an inch of my life he would only stare at me, wide-eyed and openmouthed, letting his *Parade* magazine fall to the floor.

Traffic grew sparse as I approached the center of the state. With no oncoming headlights or a clear radio station to keep me company, I reached into my bag on the passenger's seat and found the cassette tape player. Granger had turned it on and kept it near me during our most intense sessions. As soon as I pressed the PLAY button my own raucous laughter, so sharp and clear in the dark of night, took my breath away. I was neither seeing him nor feeling him, but at that moment Granger seemed more alive than anyone I had ever known.

All at Sea with Master E
James Williams

Scuba diving near a dying coral reef in the warm Caribbean waters, we gradually lose our colors as we descend: First the reds go, then the yellows, then nothing but fathomless blue remains as we sail out over a steeply sloping wall. The endless depths there call to me as you once called to me, and I feel myself begin to slip below the dive-master's sixty-foot limit as at first I slipped below my own thresholds of sense wherever you were concerned. Afternoon dives are always to forty-five or fifty feet, but morning dives are deeper. Yesterday we dived to one hundred feet in the morning, why not now? Because yesterday there was no wall nearby sliding out of sight, sinking deeper than light, that's why: Among the sandworms and eels and butterfly fish there was no temptation to disappear.

Not quite weightless in the salty sea, I settle like a falling leaf to land. Hands across my chest, I listen to my measured breathing: one, two, one. My depth gauge reads sixty-six, sixty-seven. Preserving oxygen I drift, I do not swim, and drifting with the current I've left the reef behind. Over the wall the blue below me does not seem to end although I know that color too would soon be taken away. Sixty-nine, seventy. This is how I fell in love with you, inching out on another sort of ledge to see how far I might go before I lost my balance, seeking you through a studied darkness much like this watery one, stalking you until you saw me, circling closer for your eyes on every pass, entering your smoky nimbus, rippling the emanations that surrounded you always in those days, making myself more daring so I might fall into the aura of your waves, might disappear into your famous murky depths.

I was new to the netherworld where you had long been famous: the great, the grand, the *notorious* Master E whose expertise with whips and ropes and straps and pain was all seductive legend. Oh, yes: I saw you demonstrate your prowess for the masses in your wide community at conferences and classes, on videotapes turned into DVDs; I read about your exploits in the panting words of women who longed to be your china dolls, your macramés, your footstools, your mattresses, your holes; I watched you play at parties, turning women into slaves and virgins into whores and making other masters play your sycophants: you who anyway did not deign to play with men yourself, directly.

I watched you work the tools of your deliberate trade with narcissistic certainty. You never moved as fast as your women wanted you to move, were never as rough as they begged you to be, never called and never explained, never flourished your blades as loosely as your legends claimed except every now and then, without notice, when the eyes were right that might report what they had witnessed in hushed murmurs to others who had been less fortunate; when rumor and report could mingle in the echoing chambers of your underground; especially on the public street when nothing was expected, in shadows against dark walls at dusk when colors lost their luster in the gloaming red to yellow to blue and left you to shape the delicate awe that was the brick and mortar of your current biography.

But though I was a novice, soaking wet behind the ears and wearing my keys on the left in homage to an old, long-lost tradition, I knew what I wanted and that was you. I wanted you quietly, privately, out of your public's eye. I did not need the world to know you played with men—one man—after all, and I did not want your notoriety: just you, naked and bound at my feet and at my mercy. I wanted to beat you in a measured way: one, two, one, the way I'd seen you beat the women you wanted to make fall in love with you; I wanted to make you crawl when you could hardly even move; I wanted to watch you watch in fascinated, helpless horror while I wrapped your balls in my tight fist and brought them slowly all the way up to what would have become your screaming, open, and very dry lips. And one more thing: I wanted you to want to be there. I wanted to see your pleading eyes all doglike in their helpless, begging, desperate, lunging bid for surrender to my absolutely unknown will. All I wanted was to be lost in the disappearing blue below the disappearing surface of the blue Caribbean sea. That was all.

The dive-master bangs his knife on his tank: the dive is nearly over. Maybe five minutes' air remains for most of the divers. Some are up already, rising like bubbles in the water cooler at your club's meeting house, breaking the surface and bobbing like corks on the pretty waves beneath the pretty, cumulous island sky. I can imagine them at sea level, one eye above and one below the water's edge, removing their masks and mouthpieces, shouting excitedly about what they saw, breathing real air instead of the pure canned stuff we carry on our backs. The first burst of fresh salt spray is always so lively, an inspiration, a breath of life for the mammals we are.

I searched the best outlets for tools and toys and accoutrements, courted famous artisans, then learned to make even better gear myself. I visited the best Masters and Mistresses

I could find, as well as the ones with odd skills that set them apart, and what they could teach I dutifully absorbed, making every special technique my own. I was flogged and strapped and paddled and punched, tied and chained and hoisted and caged, cut and pierced and bitten and bludgeoned, used for sex and used for labor, used as a table and used as a toilet, used as a pony and used as a slave, bought and sold like trash for a cigarette, slept with the dogs and woke with a senator—happily: happily. I wanted to know about everything, and I practiced what I learned on any unsuspecting piece of party flesh, all against the someday coming when I would have a chance to use it with you. But what I learned from you, oh, that was different: That was something no one else could teach, and it had nothing at all to do with all that made you famous: From you I learned patience; I learned to simply wait.

Ninety feet down I hover, immobile as an object in the deep, rocking waves. Three barracuda thirty feet away hover like this also, like readied torpedoes, aware and wary of me as if I were a bigger fish. Everything is wary here, everything is prey. Above me I see our group of divers all buddied up, the last ones rising behind their bubbles. The tropical colors of their bright dive suits, red, yellow, and blue as reef fish, fade in the greenish distance of water, dim brightly, as it were, against the thinned, milky light of the filtered sky. Up there I see you as you look around and look around again, and spin, and spin until your movements seem frantic and antic and then when you see me so far away, so far below the surface, you motion and move at once: *Come*, your arm calls, and *I'm coming*. You swim, you do not drift, down and out across those dozens of watery feet, reaching out your hands to come mask to mask with me. You arrive out of breath, out of air. I see your chest heave, see your grasping hands as you stare wondering into my eyes. I could let you buddy-breathe from my tank. Below me the wall disappears in blue. I wait.

Doll Boy
Jonathan Asche

Jed Bolshear got home after midnight. Mama and his cousin Doyle were already asleep. He tried to move through the dark house silently, wincing every time the stairs creaked under his feet, even though he knew Mama wasn't likely to hear him over her snoring.

He went straight to the bathroom, stripping off his clothes as soon as he shut the door. They stunk of smoke and oil. Shoulda' thrown those in the fire as well, Jed thought. He'd have to get rid of them in the morning.

Jed started the water running for a bath—he reeked of smoke and oil, too. The rust-stained tub filled slowly; there was barely enough pressure for the water to win its fight against gravity as it ran through the pipes to the second floor. After ten minutes there were only three inches of water. Impatient, Jed turned off the tap and eased his thick, muscular body into the tub anyway.

With cupped hands, he scooped warm water, splashing it onto his face. It turned gray as the soot rinsed off his body. The guilt did not wash away so easily.

"I shouldn't a done it," he whispered, his face buried in his hands. In the same breath he reminded himself it was only right. He was just taking back what had been his family's livelihood.

"Oh, sorry, cuz'n Jed. Jus' needed to pee."

Jed looked up. His cousin Doyle stood in the doorway, his boyish face—so pretty he'd been nicknamed Doll Boy—peeking inside.

"Well, c'mon," Jed said impatiently, motioning for Doll Boy to step inside. "No need to be shy. Ain't got nothin' I don't."

Giggling, Doll Boy padded into the bathroom, wearing nothing but a pair of dingy, threadbare boxer shorts. Jed followed his cousin with his eyes. The two men may have had the same parts, but to Jed's eyes, those parts—sinewy arms; bulging pecs; smooth, flat torso—fit together real nice on Doll Boy's compact frame. He was built like a brick shithouse; hard to believe he was but eighteen years old.

Doll Boy stood at the commode and yanked down his drawers. From his position in the bathtub, Jed only got a rear view of his cousin while he pissed, but Doll Boy looked just as fine from this angle as he did head on. Jed's gaze glided down the spine of Doll Boy's muscled back, down to the curve of his full, round butt, where just enough crack was showing to spark Jed's imagination and awaken his cock.

"What'cha doin' takin' a bath so late, Jed?" Doll Boy asked as he shook the last drops from his dick.

"Was up at Joe Willard's, helpin' him fix that dang truck of his. Leaked oil all over me."

"Guess that's why it smells like gas in here," Doll Boy observed, pulling the chain on the toilet. He started for the door.

"Since yer here, you mind scrubbin' my back?"

Obediently, Doll Boy moved to the tub instead, his eyes widening at the sight of his cousin's naked body. Jed was only five years older than Doll Boy, yet, with his face and chest covered with coarse, rust-colored hair, he seemed so much more grown up.

Jed handed Doll Boy a grimy bar. "Soap up my shoulders and back, would ya'?"

As Doll Boy lathered up his broad back, Jed closed his eyes, his mind drifting from tonight's crime to more pleasant plans of mischief. He hadn't been too thrilled about his cousin's coming here to live when Doll Boy's mother, Aunt Tizzy, finally drank herself to death two months ago. It was just one more mouth they couldn't afford to feed. But after they picked him up from the bus station, Jed warmed up to the idea of another man around the house.

The Bolshear house was full of holes—holes in the roof, holes in the windows, holes in the floor. One of those holes was in the wall between Jed's room and Doll Boy's. Jed spent a lot time at night peeping through that hole, hoping he'd catch his cousin changing clothes, or, even better, jacking off. That hadn't happened—if Doll Boy beat off, he did it with the lights off—but Jed had caught enough glimpses of Doll Boy's body to flesh out his jack-off fantasies. Jed often imagined his cousin's full, peach-colored lips wrapped around his hard cock; or he thought of sinking his face into that smooth trench between his fleshy buttocks and....

"Gosh, Jed, you sure got a big one!"

Jed opened his eyes. He didn't have to ask what Doll Boy meant. His cock stood at full attention, quivering with anticipation. "You like lookin' at my pecker?" Jed asked.

Doll Boy's face reddened, and he looked away. "Sorry," he mumbled.

"Naw, that's okay. You can touch it if you like."

Though a flash of interest crossed Doll Boy's face, Jed's young cousin made no move to reach for the swollen rod. Jed cuffed Doll Boy's wrist, making him drop the soap into the tub. He guided Doll Boy's hand down to his boner.

"It feels warm," Doll Boy burbled as he wrapped his fingers around Jed's cock.

"Wanna suck it?"

Doll Boy recoiled, wrenching his hand away. "I don't know, cuz'n Jed. I'm pretty sure that's a sin."

Goddamn Mama for takin' the boy to church! "It's only a sin if you're caught," he said.

"I don't think we're s'posed to be touchin' each other that way," Doll Boy said, getting up to leave. Jed grabbed his wrist.

Jed's eyes filled with an unsettling urgency. He stared into Doll Boy's face. "Don't look like all of you agrees," he hissed.

Doll Boy's free hand moved to cover the pitched tent in his crotch. "Jed, leggo of me," he whined.

"How's 'bout this: If it's wrong for us to touch each other, how 'bout we touch ourselves?"

Though Doll Boy was sure this wasn't right either, he wasn't quick enough to say why. And even if Jed's suggestion was immoral, his dick sure needed some release. In the big scheme of things, Doll Boy reasoned, jerking off in front of his cousin was not as big a sin as sucking his cock. He pulled down his boxers, exposing his stiff dick.

Jed's lips curled into a lecherous grin as he feasted his eyes on his cousin's thick tool, admiring its plump head and the way the shaft bowed slightly. Just looking at it made his cock jump. He took his own rod in his hand, stroking it as he stared at Doll Boy's dick. "Play with it," he commanded.

Doll Boy, his face crimson, slowly circled his hand around his cock. "Ain't never done this with people watching before," he stammered.

Jed said nothing, just eased back in the tub, his hand on his dick and his eyes on Doll Boy's. Doll Boy was watching him, too, though he'd look away whenever his eyes met his older cousin's. "You can look," Jed said, his voice low and deep. "I want you to." Doll Boy became less self-conscious about watching Jed jack off, though he still wouldn't look him in the eyes.

The two stroked their dicks with greater speed. Jed lathered his hands with soap for extra lubricant, while Doll Boy relied on his own spit. Pleasure burned through Jed's body. For a few seconds he forgot his poverty, the mistake he'd made, the revenge he'd wreaked earlier in the night.

His eyes popped open when he heard Doll Boy's sharp, whiny moan: "Oh, I'm comin'." Jed leaned forward quickly and cupped a hand under Doll Boy's dick. But Doll Boy's cock erupted with a fierce geyser of jism, shooting straight up and landing against his own abdomen, missing Jed's hand completely. The next few spurts had less velocity, and Jed was finally able to catch some cum in the palm of his hand.

"Oh, yeah," he gasped, bringing his palm to his face and dipping his tongue in the pool of Doll Boy's sweet spooge. Smacking his lips, he grabbed his swollen cock with his cum-slick hand. He jacked off wildly, grunting and thrashing in the tub, creating a mini-tidal wave in the gray water. It was a wonder he didn't rouse his mother, still snoring downstairs.

Suddenly, he froze. He groaned, but tried to inhale it before it left his throat. He fired his load, ejaculating with such force his wad landed in his chest hair. Doll Boy's lower jaw slackened in awe.

Jed caught his breath, and glimpsed Doll Boy staring at his furry torso, splattered with cum. "Kinda' makes you wish you sucked it, don't it?" Jed sneered.

Doll Boy fumbled for his drawers. "Ah...I...gotta get to bed," he mumbled guiltily, hiking up his shorts and scurrying out of the bathroom, not even pausing to wash the cum off his belly.

Jed shook his head. "Shee-it," he chuckled, absent-mindedly poking one of the globules of his own cum floating in the water.

Doll Boy woke up to an empty house. He vaguely remembered Jed's waking him up earlier, long enough to say he had to take Aunt Wanda—Jed's mama—to town. It was early and Jed was grumpy. When he slammed Doll Boy's bedroom door behind him he was mumbling something about "that goddam bitch."

Doll Boy slept another hour before he got up. Though it was early, the summer air was already hot and heavy. He spread fig preserves on a cold biscuit, poured a glass of milk, and stepped onto the rickety front porch to eat his breakfast.

The car—shiny, black, and foreign—pulled into the Bolshears' driveway as Doll Boy chewed the last of his biscuit. The driver cut the engine and stepped out. He was dressed as if he was going to church, wearing a tailored gray suit. Shielding his eyes from the sun with his hand, he looked right at Doll Boy. "Excuse me, are you Jed Bolshear?"

"N'sir," Doll Boy said, wiping crumbs off his face with the back of his hand. "He's took Aunt Wander to town."

"Do you know when he'll be back?"

"No tellin'. Probably not till after dinner."

The man grimaced, looked away, and cursed. He stared into the bleak horizon for several minutes before his gaze returned to Doll Boy. "Are you here by yourself?" he asked. Doll Boy nodded. "Mind some company?"

"Guess that'll be all right," Doll Boy said.

The man stepped onto the porch. He was tall and filled out his suit nicely. His handsome face reminded Doll Boy of someone he'd seen in a movie, though he couldn't remember the actor's name. Doll Boy wasn't good with names.

"I'm David Castell," the man introduced himself, offering his hand. "I'm one of the owners of the paper plant."

When they shook, the man looked directly into Doll Boy's face. Though he wasn't quite sure why, the man's gaze gave Doll Boy butterflies. "I'm Doyle," he said sheepishly. "But people call me Doll Boy."

"I bet they do." David Castell smiled.

Doll Boy realized why the man's gaze was making him feel funny: Jed looked at him the same way last night. He withdrew his hand. "What you want with cuz'n Jed?"

"Just some business," David Castell said, taking a handkerchief from his coat and wiping his hands and then his brow. "Seems I could use his services to haul pulp wood, like he did before my company bought the plant and set up its own hauling service. Someone set fire to my trucks last night. Not a one of them worth a damn now. Even poisoned the guard dogs! Can you believe that?"

"Why'd they do that?"

The man exhaled. "Don't know exactly, but I have my suspicions." He lightened his tone. "You mind if we go inside? I'm burning up out in this sun."

Inside, in the living room, the man took off his coat and carefully draped it over a chair. "You've got the right idea, I think," he said, nodding in Doll Boy's direction and loosening his tie. "It's not the type of weather for wearing a lot of clothes."

Doll Boy, wearing only a pair of cut-off jeans, folded his hands across his smooth, bare chest as if he were cold. David Castell removed his tie, and then started to unbutton his shirt.

"Just us guys," he said, noticing Doll Boy's surprise. "Don't worry, I'll be decent before the womenfolk arrive," he added with a wink.

David Castell had a body like Jed's, thick with muscle and hair—though his body hair was jet black. Sweat glistened on his bronzed skin, yet he smelled like he just had a bath.

"Never seen a man without his shirt on?" His voice was mocking.

Doll Boy wasn't aware he'd been staring and looked away. "Sorry, sir," he muttered, his face growing hot.

"No need to apologize." The man's voice was soft. He

stepped closer. "I don't mind. Hell, I can barely take my eyes off you."

The visitor's admission sent a surge of excitement and fear running through Doll Boy's veins. Like when Jed asked him to suck his cock last night.

"You're cute when you blush." David Castell stepped closer. Doll Boy stepped back.

"Maybe...maybe you should go, sir," Doll Boy said, his voice wavering.

"After I drove all the way out here? Your mama taught you better manners than that."

"My mama's dead, sir."

Undeterred, one of David Castell's hands settled on Doll Boy's shoulder. Doll Boy flinched at the touch. Only moments ago the man was several feet away; now there was barely two inches between them.

David Castell's warm, soft hand slowly descended the slope of Doll Boy's firm pecs, sliding toward one of his hard, rosy nipples. "You have a very nice body," he whispered, pinching one.

Trembling, Doll Boy exhaled. This stranger was making him uncomfortable. Yet despite his apprehension, his dick was like iron in his pants.

His hard-on did not go unnoticed. David Castell's own stiff prick poked at the front of his trousers. Circling his arms around Doll Boy's athletic body, he pulled the young man against him, their bare torsos and bulging crotches pressing together.

Doll Boy started to protest. "I don't think...."

"Sssshhh. Just relax." The man's hands cupped Doll Boy's full, round ass, gently squeezing it, as if he were testing the ripeness of fruit.

This is wrong, this is wrong, this is wrong, Doll Boy thought, though he couldn't think why, exactly. The more the man fondled his butt, the less clear his thinking became.

When David Castell started unbuttoning the boy's shorts, Doll Boy didn't protest. He slid them off, breathing a barely audible "oooh, yes," as Doll Boy's full-grown boner emerged. He curled his fingers around the shaft.

"That feel good, Doll Boy?" David Castell asked, pulling on the swollen cock.

Doll Boy gasped and nodded. Another wave of guilt shot through him, followed by Jed's voice from the night before: *It's only a sin if you get caught.*

"You won't tell nobody 'bout this, will you, sir?"

His plea elicited a hearty roar of laughter.

"Just call me David," was all he said, before leading Doll Boy back to the faded sofa and forcing him to sit down.

Doll Boy sat, motionless, as his visitor took off the rest of his clothes—not as carefully as he'd removed his coat, tie, and shirt. He didn't even bother draping his pants over the back of a chair, just dropped them to the floor. He yanked off his silk boxers. The man's long, thick cock transfixed Doll Boy. It was even bigger than Jed's—but something else intrigued Doll Boy.

"Yer pecker...looks different," he stammered. "Ain't seen one like that before, with that extra skin on it."

"You mean uncut?" David stepped closer to Doll Boy, who was sitting, legs splayed, on the sofa.

"You want to play with it?"

"Um, I...I...."

David rested one knee on the sofa, his fat, uncut cock bobbing inches from Doll Boy's sweet face. "Go on, touch it."

With some trepidation, Doll Boy reached for the dick. Its pulsing, purplish head bloomed from a sheath of tan foreskin. Doll Boy carefully rolled the skin away from the glans, marveling at the nuances of an unsnipped cock. "Now it looks normal!" Doll Boy exclaimed at the dick's transformation.

"Put it in your mouth." Doll Boy looked apprehensively

at the strong, handsome face above him, and rightly saw little chance of reprieve. Sucking cock was an order, not a request.

Slowly, Doll Boy brought his lips to David's dick, taking a deep breath before closing his mouth over the head. His tongue pushed against the engorged glans. Doll Boy, who'd expected a dick to taste funny, was relieved the taste was not bad.

"That's it. Try to take as much as you can in your mouth."

Doll Boy managed three more inches before his throat rebelled. He pulled back an inch before he choked, then concentrated on sucking the first third of the cock. That was enough to please his visitor, who rolled his hips, gently pushing his big dick into Doll Boy's virgin mouth.

"Yessss," he moaned, placing one of his hands on top of Doll Boy's blond head. "Feels so good."

Doll Boy pushed at the thick foreskin with his tongue, tracing the deep groove that marked the separation of the cockhead and its collar of skin. David sucked his breath in sharply. A lightly salted fluid oozed out of his piss slit and onto Doll Boy's tongue—the boy's first taste of a stranger's pre-cum. The man was close to shooting his load. Abruptly, he pushed Doll Boy away. Strands of saliva hung from his cock as it popped out of Doll Boy's mouth.

David then crouched on his knees, taking Doll Boy's hefty, curved dick in one large, strong hand. He stroked it, squeezed it gently, milking it for the first drops of pre-cum. Doll Boy closed his eyes, drifting on a cloud of pleasure. When David's mouth closed around his cock, his eyes flew open. "Oh, mah Lord!" he squealed, as if he'd just been goosed.

David's mouth moved down Doll Boy's shaft, his lips stopping only half an inch from the base, the tip of his nose tickled by Doll Boy's golden pubes. With well-practiced skill, he slurped on the young man's tool, and played lightly with his pendulous balls.

The oral stimulation was more than Doll Boy could bear.

He writhed and squirmed, moaning and whimpering, begging his visitor: *Stop, stop, please stop, no, don't stop, please, ohhh....* He was on the verge of shooting his load when David abruptly pulled his mouth off Doll Boy's prick.

"Turn around," David instructed. "Kneel on the couch. I want to eat your ass."

Doll Boy considered the command: *Eat my ass?* It sounded nasty—but not so nasty that Doll Boy refused.

His hands gripping the dusty backrest and his pert butt turned invitingly toward David, Doll Boy was ready for whatever came next. Breathing heavily, David kneaded Doll Boy's succulent asscheeks roughly, slid his fingertips down the channel between Doll Boy's smooth buttocks, and paused at the wrinkled pucker of his furry asshole. "I don't know about this..." Doll Boy protested meekly.

David ignored him. He pressed his face into the warm, musky trench and began lapping at Doll Boy's hole. Doll Boy offered no further resistance as the man's tongue circled and prodded his butthole. He moaned softly. And when the tongue plunged deep and hot inside his ass, Doll Boy cried out so loud he startled the chickens resting in their coop outside.

"Oh, yes! Oh, yes!" he hollered like a repentant sinner at a revival. He pushed his ass back to meet the wet stabbings, his body trembling with ecstasy. David feasted on Doll Boy's ass so enthusiastically he sounded like a hog at a trough. He pulled his mouth away, and Doll Boy begged him not to stop.

"Don't worry. You'll like this just as much."

Spitting into his palm, David lubed his pulsing dick with his own saliva. He positioned himself behind Doll Boy, pressing the head of his cock against the young man's asshole. Doll Boy resisted.

"Don't! It'll hurt!" he wailed.

"I'll start slow."

"Don't stick it in," Doll Boy insisted. "Just...rub up against it?"

"We'll start that way," David said patiently. He spit on Doll Boy's butt crack and smeared slick saliva into the fleshy crevice with his drooling dick. Doll Boy's pliant buttcheeks enveloped his schlong. He humped Doll Boy's ass slowly, his cock pressing against the young man's hole. The friction was intensely pleasurable, and David all but forgot about fucking Doll Boy's ass.

The smoldering excitement of David's sturdy cock rubbing his asshole had Doll Boy reconsidering the idea of getting fucked. His second thoughts came too late, however, or else David came too soon. Letting out a monstrous howl, he fired his load across Doll Boy's back. With David's dick pressed against his ass, Doll Boy felt it pump out the last heavy drops of cum.

Save for the heaving of two chests, there was no movement. Doll Boy hoped this wasn't the end of their encounter. He still had to get off...and then David told Doll Boy to stand. He then lay on his back on the sofa. His next instruction: "Sit on my face."

Doll Boy positioned himself astride the older man's face, stiff cock swinging over his forehead, drizzling it with pre-cum. David clamped his hands onto the younger man's muscular thighs, and guided his ass down to his waiting mouth. His tongue slid past the twitching sphincter, lapping up the salty, sticky vestiges of saliva, sweat, and cum.

As he rode the eager face, Doll Boy stroked his engorged cock, coming closer to orgasm every time his fist traveled the length of his shaft. He twisted his hips, rotated his ass against the counter-swirl of tongue, hissed, whimpered, and whined as the tingling pleasure—more intense than anything he'd ever experienced when he jacked himself off—overtook him. His body jerking as if he'd been struck by lightning, Doll Boy came forcefully, his jism raining down on David's forehead, matting his dark hair, even spattering the sofa's upholstery.

Spent and light-headed, Doll Boy slid off David's body and stretched out against the full length of his solid, manly body. For the first time, man and boy kissed.

Eventually—who knew how much time had passed?—David urged Doll Boy to get up. "I need to clean up," he said, gathering his clothes. "Where is your bathroom?" Doll Boy directed him upstairs. When he returned, dressed and scrubbed clean, he was carrying Jed's dirty clothes, reeking of gas, oil, and smoke, found in a pile on the bathroom floor.

"Tell me, Doll Boy," asked David, holding the soiled, reeking—and incriminating—clothes away from his clean suit, "do you know where your cousin was last night?"

There were two cars in the driveway when Jed and his mother returned. One he didn't recognize. The other was easy: *Pearl County Sheriff's Department* was emblazoned on the door.

"What's this about?" Mama gasped. Jed knew.

The sheriff and his deputy appeared at either side of the truck. " 'Fraid I'll have to take you in for questioning, Jed," the sheriff said, almost apologetically. His deputy helped Jed's astonished mother from the passenger side of the truck.

Sitting in the other car, the one that was shiny, black, and foreign, David watched as Jed Bolshear was handcuffed and hustled to the police car.

Doll Boy was by his side. "Don't worry," he said, squeezing Doll Boy's thigh. "Everything will be much better for you now."

Romulus
Bruce Benderson

The bedroom in Syracuse, New York, where I'm lying is boxy and low ceilinged, but the space around my codeine-fueled fantasies is tall and drafty. At the best of times, the drug undulates in and out of nerve cells; my whole body disintegrates into a low-resolution image; my tipsy cells sacrifice their binding power to new Technicolor pictures of Romulus, the Romanian.

The silver shovel of Romulus's face leaps out, like an old-fashioned photographic instant when the flash powder goes off, to show me sucking the nipples of that pallid chest, until that image, too, is devoured by a black swarm of flies. His sullen rosebud mouth tightens; in a grainy, black-and-white twilight we're huddled on the creaky bed of that tall, drafty room I always rented in Budapest.

We must be ever so careful not to make any noise, not to wake his two brothers who are staying with us. What if they see us while....

The dark bedroom in Syracuse pops back into hard focus. The obnoxious thought sweeps away the drops of fantasy leaking from neurons, scrapes away the bright emulsion. My very old mother is lying in the next room. Our doors have been left ajar all night. With a twinge of guilt, I imagine her reaction to these fantasies I'm having, then feel guilty enough to rise unsteadily and tiptoe into her bedroom to check on her yet again, a glimpse of the bundled form I've known since childhood, so still now and surrounded by foreboding; and then I come closer, bend with held breath until my face is nearly touching hers, to be sure she is still breathing....

It's hard to push these worries about her out of my mind by falling into another dream about Romulus. He must be on that clanging train from the Communist period, not headed east to Romania, as he'd promised when I sent him money, but west, to Vienna, where he thought he could sneak across the border. The train pulls in, he's probably crouching in a crawl space over the toilet ceiling, and his half-bent knees are just starting to shoot pain as the Austrian border guards march through the cars checking passports and visas. Now a wooden baton is banging on the slightly ajar partition in the toilet ceiling, and when it won't budge, the guard calls a colleague in to lean on, climbs onto the toilet seat, and bangs harder, jamming Romulus' head against an iron beam and shouting in German, "Come out, you vermin!" When a foot finally dangles from the crawl space, they grab for it, yank down roughly; Romulus lands on the small of his back on the toilet seat and slides to the floor.

Here in Syracuse, my thoughts tarantella around that image, realizing that he was probably already in that Austrian holding cell when I called his home on Christmas Day, while here I lie in this clean, powder-blue room with a full stomach, and he has only an empty belly and the overheated cell to rely on. This fearful yet excited thought is almost like a sub-urbanite's thought of a rat in the cellar. Overfed and feeling strangely confined, you toss and turn on suddenly intolerable permanent-press sheets; everything is safely tucked away, the wall-to-wall freshly vacuumed, but there is that rat down there. You heard it scurrying. With a strange kind of envy you think of that alien heart in that pelt-covered body beating and beating beneath the warm, leathery skin, and those triangular, hair-pricked ears listening for your breathing. How can the two of you exist on the same planet? Maybe your skin deserves to be penetrated by those sharp, black-gummed teeth merely from the fact that they exist, it occurs to you in a half-dream, for what is the reason you yourself exist? The difference between you and that vagrant in some inaccessible place gnaws at you like teeth you can't locate.

Is he thinking of me while he is in jail? Is he dreaming of me hovering in space like some abstracted cushion of comfort? Certainly he can't think of me where I am, on this absurd four-poster in suburbia. But maybe he pictures me in a New York gleaned from old movies, spider-black skyscrapers against a tarnished silver sky, gangsters and amber liquor, while he crouches there in his cell, angry and depleted like a rat in a cage.

The thought makes me consider the musculature and the sinew of that underfed rat. The energy lurking beneath its sharp, glinting eyes, its twitching nostrils, its brain being drenched in cataracts of dopamine, the layer of fat on its belly to protect its rapidly metabolizing organs. It's compelling enough to make you get out of bed in the middle of the night to go downstairs, seek out the humid trail left on the concrete cellar floor by the tail....

At this point, the whiz of the tires of the Syracuse city plow on wet snow loosens the luminous grip of these ideas. The ray of a headlight brings the insipid blue of the bedroom curtains into view. Restless, I think about getting up to check on Mother again, but merely recover the image of her chest rising and falling, her frail form bundled in blankets.

Then the curtains are swallowed back up by the darkness. I creep back to my bed of drugged, guilty fantasies; the half-dreams begin their rippling again, coaxed into larger and larger waves by the trails of codeine.

Against my will these fantasies make me think of that girlfriend of his, the prostitute I know about, a little bloated from her late nights and beers, in a cheaply furnished room in a concrete high-rise, struggling against the drunken hand of a Chinese client whose pants are open at the fly. His hand is fumbling with her head in an attempt to pin it against the hollow-sounding plasterboard, and all because he wants to fuck her without a condom. When she finally bites the hand that is trying to muffle her screams, he lets go of her, but as she is straightening her ripped dress, a glitter of steel driven by an irrational flash of anger plunges between her ribs, after which protectors come running, the client is ejected, and the girl taken to the hospital.

I don't know it yet, but little by little I am arriving in her psychic space, becoming more and more like her. Black is leaking in from the hallway like tar. In the four-poster, my hand slides across my hip and a white hiss begins to travel up my legs. It is as if my shameful body were dissolving into these sharp flashes of pleasure, pulverized into black-and-white dots by my pumping heart.

Afterward I stumble to the bathroom to wipe the come off with a paper towel. When I return, I stare out the shoulder-high window. That stray snowflake stuck to the pane seems something strangely apart from the scrim of falling snow. The storm lets up, revealing the huge evergreen across the road whose branches are piled thick with snow before the air becomes a prison of swarming white again, obscuring everything.

Could my wish-fulfillment fantasies ever do any good? Or are they merely pathological? According to St. Ignatius, whom I happened to be reading before turning out the light,

God's grace is absorbed like a drop of water striking a sponge, whereas for those inured to God, grace is repelled like a drop of water ricocheting off a stone. But he also said that those open to Satan suck in evil like a sponge sucks up water, whereas the righteous are as indifferent to evil as a stone to a drop of water. Only loving, neither as sacrifice nor as selfishness, seems to bring any good.

To be perfectly honest, these thoughts occurred to me only the next morning, at the breakfast table with Mom, in the midst of an opiate withdrawal headache, but they disappeared as I lay back against the seat that afternoon, on the train to Manhattan, two big spoonfuls of Hydrocodone flaring fantasies into scenarios of Romulus's betrayal. Like a sponge polluted by unclean water, I soaked up pathetic notions, which replayed endlessly. From my mother's home, I had called him in Sibiu again. He told me he planned to strip for the whores at the club where his brother was a bouncer. This sounded like a harmless idea but snagged my attention, the way a piece of yarn from a sweater catches on a casement nail and has to be worked off slowly in order not to unravel the whole thing.

However, that afternoon, before starting the five-and-a-half-hour train ride to New York, I kept trying to clear my throat but couldn't. I figured that a couple spoonfuls of the Hydrocodone would relieve it.

Working emphatically with the train's chugs, those opiates lulled me into repeated hypnogogic snatches, from which I'd come to with a start, before diving back in, finding the same scenarios gone no further in time, waiting to torment me, the beloved leaning over the balcony of a formerly Communist high-rise in Sibiu to the soft explosions of a beaten rug. Since it was a week before Easter, the beaters in this eastern country were at it from morning until dusk. Next to him on the balcony was a big blonde whose blue-veined skin seemed infused by the lead-ridden air. From the look of her skin-tight jeans and impossibly clumsy platform heels, they were on the way to the club for the striptease, which suddenly began to overlap...that meaningless noise of a beaten rug becoming a musical beat charged with aggressive sex, as brazenly parted legs lowered jeans to reveal pubic hair inches from leering female faces. His strip to celebrate his brother's birthday.

The images flared up in some white-hot kiln, wilting sullenly into something taunting and sticky in the mildewed corner of a bedroom, which must have been the bedroom of his apartment in a concrete ex-Communist project. Inside, Romulus was gyrating on a bed like he did during the best times his cock was in my mouth. But into the bedroom came that same mercury-skinned blonde, her rubbery breasts bouncing gently in a harsh shaft of light.

The dream clung like molasses as I forced my eyes open. The light in the train compartment tried to strip the images from my eyes as if it were picking off insects. Then once again black syrup coated my vision, my head began to sink into a cone at the end of which his brother the bouncer leered. His face was a slab of meat with the forehead bandaged from a boxing accident. As the club MC, he gloated through a fish-eye lens to announce over and over that the one and only Romulus was about to get naked for the whores, whereupon the body spread open in the jabbing spotlight, the bluish skin of the girl stood stony against all the other female faces.

I flailed away from the image and tried to stand, but couldn't unstick myself. Now the dank bedroom featured a nest of undulating hips and slapping thighs, until the train finally pulled into that satanic, rubbery smell of rot that greets you each time you come back to New York and jerked to a stop.

Two weeks later, in Budapest, in the very room I'd imagined, his pungent cock dangles over my face as I sit on the floor between his legs and nip at the foreskin. His dick smells strongly of vagina. He'd disappeared for six hours, hooking up with his pleading girlfriend, I later found out. He took her to the movies, but then, he added, casually, fucked her in the toilets. And there I lay in bed waiting and waiting and growing progressively more anguished, more angry, watching CNN, whose images, seen through the haze of the codeine tablets I took, one after another, somehow faded into this girl I'd imagined: the watery hair, the easily bruisable skin...and I no longer identified with her, nor felt I was becoming her in that abject sense I'd felt before and she becoming the enemy.

When he finally came back, it was getting late. The river and the cable car stop below our window were awash with golden light. On the balcony, the gusts of wind were surprisingly balmy. White shirts under jackets glimmered on the black bridge across the Danube like white blossoms in liquid tar.

By four in the morning, after we had argued for hours about the girl, he was asleep, and I, despite the codeine, was wide awake. It's true that night seemed to cradle us like black cotton wool and that the air was lazy with cigarette smoke nudged by gusts of river wind rattling the French windows at the balcony. Certainly things were tinged with doom, even if night seemed also to make a false promise of permanence. His leg on mine felt light as a wing. But when he moved away only an inch, it was like watching his body through the wrong end of a telescope.

I just couldn't sleep, so I left the room and walked to the edge of the Danube, whose waters seemed like a kind of rush into a fate I no longer had any choice over. When my eyes fixed on the black meanderings of the water, I thought I saw a flicker of light that suggested a glimpse of a white shoulder or a ringlet of wet hair, or young legs twirling. Limbs twining in a dark, cold place. It suddenly occurred to me that Romulus hadn't even gone to the movies or taken her into the bathroom; he had probably found a street-level window open in an abandoned building and slipped inside.

She was angry and confused and suspicious about this pitiless American, who Romulus said was his "uncle" and demanded every moment of his time. But she loved the way he pulled the wet lock of hair away from her eyes. The mattress looked horrible with its huge stains, but first he took off his coat and made a sort of mat out of it, and then he took off his sweater and covered her with it. And then his strong hands began to wander over her body, slip inside her blouse, cup her breasts as if they were made to fit them.

It felt so good to be caressed by the lips of that hawk-like face. The zipper of his jacket cut into her buttocks and she accepted it, it was like him entering her. All his hardness pushed against her, like metal the temperature of a body.

Now he was kissing her and biting her at the same time. She sucked the nicotine off his tongue, hating its acrid, metallic taste. The idea of the American who didn't want to meet her was making these hard, insistent kisses more valuable. The sudden sting of cold air on body parts felt good; it was as if she was mocking the cold, or as if the cold was fucking her. Suddenly it was like the room flipped upside down, she was on top of him feeling powerful, straddling his narrow hips with her thighs, her breasts swinging above him as he lay underneath lean and pale, moaning with pleasure. Reaching down she could touch her clitoris with her fingertips, and then she took hold of that sharp weapon and pierced herself with it fast enough to hurt. After the first stinging insult, it belonged to her, sliding past her fingers as she massaged her clit, and she watched his face, usually so contained and compact, open as it would during torture, until his hips began to lunge upward as if someone had applied electroshock.

I went back to our room and climbed into bed. Romulus stirred, made a childish mew with his lips, began to drift back into sleep. I remember thinking at the moment that we were nothing but statues in some utopian tableau. And then I made a little sigh and thought, *The character you think you rescued keeps being pulled back, inhaled again and again into those landscapes of deprivation.* But for now, in the dark and middle of the night, we had escaped the premises of our respective cultures. So I sat there watching him plunge back into unconsciousness: that sweet prelude to betrayal.

The Bigg Mitkowski
Davem Verne

You gotta see my dick. It's *bigg*, like my name with two *g*'s. Big enough that my pants bulge every minute and my pastor makes me say ten Hail Marys for every inch of tool I don't use. That's a lot of Hail Marys! He says God bestows an extra half-foot on the lucky ones to teach us a lesson, but the only lesson I ever learned was how hungry my dick gets. I call that penis fever: when your cock is perpetually pumped and needs daily satisfaction. Father Murphy urged me to join the military and get my dick under control, so I left confession and marched to the recruitment office, and along the way my shaft got swollen for days.

"Hey, Mitkowski!"

Someone was dogging me as I walked up Ninth Avenue, strutting my thick thighs and large ass like a Polish bronco. I grabbed my crotch just to remind myself how good a cocksuck might be right now. You know you're really huge when you can never get more than half your length between a pair of legs. Father Murphy says in God's kingdom one size fits all. What I don't tell the good Father is that I find use for all of it anyway, every inch of my Polish manhood. This huge dick finds all the room it needs in a guy's mouth.

Basic description: eleven-inch boner with a thick pink head, wide-veined shaft like a marble column, and fueled underneath by two huge balls, mega-sperm engines that blast proliferating Polish cum at high-octane levels. I like to glide my cock in my hands, lather it with spit between two palms, watch it get moist and swollen, and then let it hang awhile like an overdue guest. I do this five times a day—at home, at work, at the gym, and twice after hockey practice. It only takes a minute. And I never come. I leave it alone and let my nuts suffer. That way I can walk around all day and the next with a hard-knocking pussy-banger on top of fat, aching balls.

My admiring crew is strictly Hell's Kitchen blue-collar trade: sweaty, stiff-necked, hard-working sons of Ireland with flushed faces and meaty hips. There's Flannery, Keegan, and Manny, all part of the same horny pool: dickheads ready to plug any Brenda McFadden hole. And in the middle of this New York City brood stands the Bigg Mitkowski, the Polish Pick-of-the-Litter, with an eleven-inch ass-cracker backed by almighty hips muscular enough to bang open the gates of Heaven! In short, I am the model among men and a blessing to my father.

And make no mistake, I've never touched, fondled, or sucked another guy's pecker. This is a fact. For the simple reason that I've got more batting between my legs than my whole gang put together, so why reach for some other guy's Ready Ryan when he'll be stripping his jock and hopping his West Side ass up and down on my beef anyway?

"Mitkowski!"

Manny chased down the sidewalk with his low-rent girl-friend, Molly. She and her sisters have sampled my wieldy woody with a two-handed jack job each, but the ghetto girls always want a little more. I hurried into my building and ducked inside the elevator, but Manny dumped Molly, jumped in, and the doors closed behind us.

"So what's up, Bigg? When's boot camp?"

I looked away from Manny so he could get a fair view of the package broadcasting through my sweats. I was comfortable with being ogled by other guys. It didn't bother me. I'm a lot of man all at once, you understand.

I spread my legs. The elevator was dingy like a cage in a zoo. I smelled something funky. The pale fluorescent bulb bathed us in low-income lighting. Whatever the smell was, it didn't leave. Maybe it was my balls raring to explode. My cock was leaking jism, saturating my sweats. I kept my eyes sealed as my hand reached under my jock, tugging at my groin. I kept tugging for cum, like I was playing hockey with my balls.

"Gee," Manny said, his voice soft and sulky. "Can I be honest with you, Bigg?" Manny was shorter than me; in fact, he was the shortest guy in my crew, but he had the best build, solid thighs, and a braveheart chest. "I never thought this day would come, Bigg. You enlisting to be all that you can be, fight the war on terrorism, get behind our leaders." He stammered and his face turned red.

Manny was searching in the dim glow for more than words. He could see my hard-on pressing out of my sweats. The dickhead stared at him blankly. Both of his milky blues fixed on it in a trance. Cum was seeping out of my shaft like spillage at a factory. Its spawning stream dripped down the elastic band of my sweats. Salty and impatient, my raw head was making his mouth water.

"God, I want to suck your boner, Bigg."

"Then suck it, stupid."

As the elevator jumped past the fourteenth floor, Manny fell to his knees and whipped out my cock. My robust root brainwashed him. He mouthed a Hail Mary as his greedy fingers divided the forest of dark hair and excavated the sparkling nutsac. His dimples peeled wide as he swallowed my balls into his face. He rocked his tongue back and forth and mined each nut, before sawing his teeth down on my tough timber.

I let my ham-handed friend jerk and polish the Polish pole as shiny as he could. The elevator light descended on us. I didn't mind that it was Manny jacking for juice from my big dick. The other guys in the neighborhood knew just how abundant Bigg Mitkowski's cock was. They regularly appeared on my stoop every Friday night, smashed and lumpy-faced and wanting a copious cum shot. I invited them up and gave them a few, then sent them home glutted, but I always kept the lights off because the lot of them were just plain ugly.

"This is too good," Manny muttered. Manny pulled my sweats down and handled my humpy hips. A mischievous finger sought the sacred hole between the rumps of beef. But my erect penis sprung out at him, those eleven inches of hung man-meat slapping him hard against cheek and chin. Manny learned to tame it quickly with his mouth, going at it gently with his teeth, loosening his jaw. "It's bigger than Molly said," Manny barely breathed.

Manny opened his mouth wide open as I force-fed the whole milk bottle down his throat, fat free. His tight Irish lips were too thin for a sensuous suck, so he tightened his grip and squeezed the shaft, stubbornly keeping me from coming while he gloated over the long inches pounding back and forth, in and out of his maw. He kept smoking the pipe until we got to the twentieth floor, where I was about ready to blow my load in his face.

"I want it up the ass," Manny said suddenly. He had gulped down enough pre-cum to get a good taste of the dominant Polish seed, and now he wanted the rest of it planted elsewhere.

"Bend over, then," I said.

I jerked my long dick, keeping it hard as he unzipped his jeans and leaned against the rattling elevator door. His ass was wet with perspiration, round and strong-flavored. That lusty smell I mistook for me was baking between his two healthy mounds of firm Irish butt-meat. Manny, straight and stupid, produced the strongest undiluted ass-scent that I had ever encountered, warming his rear for a full-throttle fuck. I quit the formalities of fingering his manhole; instead, I thrust my prick between his hips and stuck it up dry, up his rump, up hard enough to make him squeal.

"It's too big, Bigg!" Manny shrieked, his pink face pressed against the aluminum door. I was only half in, crowding his manhole, waiting for the heroic sphincter to accommodate all of me. I braced my hips against his, spreading his cheeks apart. Our balls clamped together like good friends. My long cock edged in three-quarters, then plugged his man-chute to man-max, making Manny's heart beat to exhaustion, "Okay, fuck it!"

I fucked Manny as we rode up the elevator at full speed. His squirming butt grew hot-as-hell. His ass abandoned the lazy afflictions of the couch and flushed bright red as I bullied him into the corner, screwing him like a bottomless bitch. Each time I pumped, his cheeks jettisoned sweet Irish juice, betraying the nights Manny had cried himself to sleep, fingering his hole in the dark, praying that one of his drunken brothers would clog him with cum during the night.

My thrusts lifted him off his sneakers as I plowed deeper into his ass. I could feel my inches greasing the length of his chute, growing longer and wider. I was getting too big to pull out erect, but I didn't tell him. I kept my hands on Manny's back as I humped my hard-on into him, beating his brawny bum silly. By the thirtieth floor I was ready to heap my load in his jammed ass.

"I'm going to come!"

That wasn't me; that was Manny. His fist beat his numb knob and ejaculated his creamy load over the elevator tiles. I lunged out of him and rode my cock between his thighs, snaking my aching dick between his pink balls and spraying a stream of potent Polish cum. He wailed as he saw the white juice shoot straight out from underneath his balls, like the bigger cock he wished he had, and plaster thick streaks of man-muck on top of his gooey sprinkles.

The elevator doors opened.

Manny looked at me like a dog that had suddenly lost his bone, and floated down the hall. Transported to another level by my fast fuck, he wobbled on his feet, pulling his jeans up over his sticky ass and wiping his lips and cheeks. He didn't even wave good-bye as the elevator doors closed.

I guess Manny was embarrassed because he liked it too much. I should have given him more. Thirty stories down, with the rattling elevator all to myself and the sweet smell of male cum filling the cabin, I beat off twice more just to get the bubbling, frothy top layer of jism out of me. When I got to my floor and in my crib, I put my favorite CD on and swung my dick like a baseball bat in the thick creases of my Yankees glove. Two more times then the steel mill closed, ready to begin Saturday with a clean slate of Bigg brew for my crew.

Flannery and Keegan are my hockey buddies. We're on a team that plays once a week down at the Chelsea piers. There's an ice rink there where a lot of guys from neighborhoods all over Manhattan compete in a league. Flannery is strictly from mean Irish stock, with ruby cheeks, blue eyes, and light brown hair. He's the goalie so he's been shot up a lot by pucks and hockey sticks. Hence, he isn't much to look at. Neither is Keegan, who's built like a truck. But they're inseparable: best friends, hockey mates, and horse-powered gym buddies.

"Take your pants off, Bigg," Flannery said.

We had won Saturday night's game and celebrated in our favorite Ninth Avenue bar. Everyone was at the Garden watching the real thing, so we headed upstairs to a private room surrounded by photos of Gretzsky and the Rangers.

"It's your last Saturday as a civilian, Bigg," Flannery said. "Get comfortable, you know what I'm saying? Right, Keegan? Do as you fucking well please."

Flannery smacked his lips. His eyes fed on my crotch, begging for a drink. Keegan was already whacking his tool. He looked down at my mound demurely. Sensing a need to free my cock, he unzipped my pants and pulled out my eleven-inch rod, which sprung erect and pointed up like the Empire State Building. He squeezed the ridges like they were floors leading up to the beet-red antenna.

My white briefs concealed my balls, but Keegan freed them by gently tugging the elastic band with his little finger. They ripped out of my shorts, two huge balls for my huge buddies. Each took one in hand to weigh carefully. They knocked my balls, playing billiards, pinching the scrotum just to know in detail the Bigg Mitkowski.

Their hands slid down my inner thighs and felt my thick, firm legs. They even found the hole between my legs and took turns sniffing and licking the crack like they had never seen a West Side manhole before. First Keegan, then Flannery lost his face below my balls, eating my ass, getting to know my Polish chute quite well. I beat off loudly, waiting for one of them to get the clue that the granite rock was ready to get scrubbed.

Immediately my thick dick found residence in Keegan's mouth. I could tell it was Keegan because it rode smooth in and out on account of his teeth being small. He didn't have much of a bite, but he had a persistent suck.

"That's it, Keegan," Flannery said, warming me up by swallowing my balls. He was a scrotum sucker. Most goalies were. Ball bums, appreciating the little fellas, tongue-feeling the jism as it vibrated through each testicle. He kept them in his mouth because he liked their heat.

Together, their lips kissed my cock, sliding up and down. Their jock faces were cool and mean with the same expression they wore on the ice, but they ate dick and worshipped balls like it was nothing new. Watching your two best friends choke on your dick is the greatest thrill a guy could have. Though I have a crazy-huge cock, Keegan and Flannery, conjoined at the lips like Siamese cocksucking twins, made my dick seem gargantuan, an Egyptian obelisk, a Bavarian maypole.

Usually I lasted for hours, but this time I shot my load sooner. Their lumpy cheeks forced me to score an early goal. The man-milk jumped, spilling and spraying white seed into the air, over their hair and faces. It showered my abs and navel, dripped down my testicles and between the crack in my ass.

"Phew, that's a big load," Keegan muttered, diving to lick up the hot current and coming up for air with a white mustache. He slapped my marble balls. "Isn't that the best cum we've had, Flannery? As good as Brendan's?"

Immediately, Keegan looked at Flannery.

"Let's show him ours," Flannery said, changing the subject. Flannery and Keegan stood up and faced each other, whipping their pricks to erections. They pointed them at me and within thirty seconds looked ready to come. I made an apology and left the bar, not interested in seeing my two buddies spray their Hell's Kitchen sorbet all over my trunk.

Brendan? The only Hell's Kitchen dog I know called Brendan is a scrawny kid on Fifty-Second Street, a brain geek whose goal in life is to study pre-med in an Ivy League college and join the glee club. I'm off to enlist, while Brendan is packing for biology and a cappella.

I gotta come clean. Even though I said I've never touched, fondled, or sucked another guy's tool, I got a secret pre-army wish: to taste a cum-shake. The Irish, I have heard, brew the best cum in all of Manhattan. Once the Bigg Mitkowski gets in the army, he'll have a reputation to uphold. All those greenhorn recruits will be staring at his Midtown horse-dick, wanting a piece for their saddle. I can't be letting on that I'm just as thirsty as the rest of them.

"Mitkowski." I heard my name. Who's dogging me on Sunday? Enlistment was a day away. A sea of hungry people crawled uptown for the Ninth Avenue Festival. I was obliged to show the Bigg hide one more time before shipping off, so I wore a green tank top and wrapped my ass and crotch in tight, tanned shorts.

Brendan tagged me in the crowd. He drank a seltzer for his glee club voice and expected my respect.

"Is it true? You're going to enlist tomorrow?" he asked.

The Festival was crowding my senses—the muted roar of people in the neighborhood, people on the street, stopping to say good-bye, wish me well, kiss my cheek, and pray for my dick. I found myself staring at Brendan's slight frame and wondering what kind of package was neatly folded in his groomed layers. I could just see Brendan chasing after some Ivy League varsity player, cheering and chewing on that college meat like he never did me. He's the only one who hasn't sampled the Bigg Mitkowski. But this time I wanted to get some. I needed to taste dick!

"Time out," I said.

"Can't call time out when you're defending your country," Brendan observed.

He headed toward Fifty-Second and Tenth Avenue, his block, his home. I couldn't think straight. I followed Brendan back to his place like a rottweiler on a leash. We climbed the stairs to his mother's apartment, and Brendan welcomed me inside his book-laden room with Ivy League banners everywhere.

He was all angles and chiseled charm, thin enough not to worry about exercising and handsome enough not even to care.

Brendan pushed me onto the sofa. "The guys told me about you. Everyone in the neighborhood seems to have gotten his or her hands around the Bigg boner. They wet their pants just talking about you. I also pack a big cock. You want to see?"

"No," I replied.

Brendan slid out of his slacks and yanked his cock from his boxers. The red pubic hair sprang all over the place. I looked away in masculine angst as he stood in front of me getting harder. In fact, Brendan was getting very hard, and very long. He kept jerking until his cock was sticking straight out at me.

"See it?" he said. "Before I pack it away."

His cock filled my vision, ripe and fleshy.

"Taste it. One for the road," Brendan said. "The tasting is all yours. You can either taste it now, or taste it later. But you're going to have to taste it sometime because I know you, Mitkowski. You're begging for it and it's dogging you crazy. Hurry before it cools."

I drew Brendan's huge prick into my mouth. I closed my eyes and sealed my lips around the shaft. I swallowed it whole. The boner propelled a course into my throat. Finally, a cock in my mouth! The head was hot, jogging my tonsils and jabbing against my teeth as it pulled out then jammed back in. My tongue went on alert. I was amazed at Brendan's width. It lunged inside my mouth, filling the cavity with its large head. I could taste the salt at the back of my throat, just as I could smell Brendan's sweaty ball sac.

"Now focus, Mitkowski," Brendan ordered.

I closed my eyes. Brendan shot a load of pre-cum that swept inside my mouth. My mouth became hot and sticky. Before I could complain, Brendan humped my face. The dick-head plugged my throat and grew larger. He slowed down as I moaned, sensuous at the dick-feed. His hips nudged my face. The more I sucked, the more I felt my own cock ready to burst. It was strangled in my briefs, reticent to come up for air, shy to be compared to Brendan. I rode my palm over the large crease in my shorts, jerking myself numb until I came. I bit hard on Brendan as I shot my load against my thigh.

He pumped my lips, whipping up a smoothie like nothing previously tasted in Midtown. His balls lifted high against the base of his shaft and released their bounty. My mouth filled with smart cum, silken and sweet, as he shot his spunk down my gorged throat. Again. More. I ate it as he finished his load and kept his prick in my face. A few more drops spilled out from his shooter. When he withdrew his big engine of dick-flesh from Mitkowski Station, I could taste his jism spilling over my lips. It trickled along the corners of my mouth, dribbling down my chin and onto my tank. I sat in awe.

"Satisfied?" Brendan asked, shoving his prick back in his slacks and buttoning his fly. "Now you've gotten everything this neighborhood has to offer. You know how to keep the dicks in the barracks happy."

I stood to leave, dismissed, his taste clinging to the roof of my mouth. His cock and cum had tamed me, made me feel wonderfully ordinary, like a good soldier. As I exited his room, I heard Brendan remark in a high-pitched voice, well rehearsed for the glee club, "Hey, Mitkowski, did Father Murphy ever tell you you've got a big butt, with two *t*'s? Stop by my dorm when you're on leave. I'll be waiting."

About the Authors

JONATHAN ASCHE is the author of the erotic novel *Mindjacker* as well as numerous short stories. His work has appeared in *Torso, Men, Playguy, Inches, Mandate, In Touch for Men,* and *Indulge,* as well as the anthologies *Best Gay Erotica 2004, Buttmen 2* and *Buttmen 3, Three the Hard Way,* and *Manhandled.* He lives in Atlanta with his partner of nine years and a host of mentally unstable pets. He is busy writing his second novel. You can contact him at ascheland@hotmail.com.

BRUCE BENDERSON is the author of two books of fiction about old Times Square, *Pretending to Say No* and *User.* His manifesto about the decline of urban bohemia, *Toward the New Degeneracy,* was featured in *Rolling Stone.* He is the author of *James Bidgood,* a 1999 book about the author of *Pink Narcissus.* He has written for the *New York Times Magazine,* the *Village Voice, nest,* and other publications. His erotic-noir memoir, *The Romanian,* has just been published in French by Payot & Rivages.

STEVE BERMAN wonders if Mr. Right might be as much a figment of the imagination as any apparition. His stories have sold to *The Big Book of Erotic Ghost Stories, The Faery Reel,* and the forthcoming *Skin and Ink: Hot Tattoo Tales,* as well as been featured in past issues of *Strange Horizons* and *Velvet Mafia.* His collection *Trysts: A Triskaideollection of Queer and Weird Stories* contains more uncanny and erotic fiction. He lives alone in New Jersey and might be scared of the dark.

TEH-CHEN CHENG is the pen name of a Taiwanese-American writer living in Los Angeles. When not busy with home renovations and gardening, he tries to get his lazy ass out of bed and into the gym where he uses a mental image of the title character Yang-Qi as inspiration. The first story of a series, "Yang-Qi" was initially published in *Best Gay Asian Erotica.*

WAYNE COURTOIS is the author of *My Name Is Rand.* His story "Taurus" earned him a Best New Voice award from the Erotic Authors Association. Webzine appearances: *suspect thoughts: a journal of subversive writing* and *Velvet Mafia.* Fiction anthologies: *Of the Flesh, Love Under Foot, The Big Book of Erotic Ghost Stories, Out of Control.* Nonfiction anthologies: *Walking Higher, I Do/I Don't.* He lives in Kansas City, Missouri, with his lover of sixteen years, and is working ambidextrously on his next two novels. Visit him at www.waynecourtois.com.

JIM GLADSTONE avoids boredom and repetition by writing a variety of cool and eccentric things. He has occasionally tried to liven the process up by typing with his toes…but it's awkward, and makes the keyboard get a little slimy. He is the author of the Foreword Award–winning novel *The Big Book of Misunderstanding* and the popular compendium of competitions *Gladstone's Games to Go;* coauthor of the *Access*

Philadelphia travel guide; editor of the anthology *Skin and Ink: Hot Tattoo Tales*; and a widely published contributor to newspapers, magazines, anthologies, and even a comic book. He can be contacted through www.GoGladstone.com.

DREW GUMMERSON is thirty-three and lives in Leicester, England. His first novel, *The Lodger,* was published in 2002 and was nominated for a Lambda Literary Award. His short fiction has been published in *Death Comes Easy, The Gay Times Book of Short Stories 4, Serendipity: The Gay Times Book of New Writing, Aesthetica* magazine, www.thisisitmag.co.uk, www.openwidemagazine.co.uk, www.thegayread.com, www.pulp.net, www.blithe.com, www.megaera.org, and www.forbiddenfruitzine.com. He is now working with Zuluspice to turn a number of his short stories into short films. Reach him at http://freespace.virgin.net/d.gummerson.

GREG HERREN is an author/editor who has published four mysteries: *Murder in the Rue Dauphine, Bourbon Street Blues, Jackson Square Jazz,* and *Murder in the Rue St. Ann.* A fifth, *Mardi Gras Mambo,* is forthcoming. He is the editor of four anthologies: *Full Body Contact, Shadows of the Night, Fratsex,* and *Upon a Midnight Clear.* He has also published a collection of his erotic wrestling stories, *Wanna Wrestle?,* from which "Wrestler for Hire" is taken. He tries to live quietly in New Orleans with his partner and their bipolar cat.

M. S. "MAX" HUNTER, after earlier careers as a lawyer in Boston, Washington, D.C., and Saint Thomas, U.S. Virgin Islands, and as a restaurant owner/manager in Barbados, made his home on a small eastern Caribbean island in a house overlooking a white sand beach and the sparkling blue sea. The stories and novels he wrote reflected his experiences during many years of life and adventure in the West Indies. His published novels are *The Buccaneer, The Final Bell,* and *A Killing in Paradise,* published shortly after his death in July 2004, at age 72.

MICHAEL HUXLEY, editorial director at STARbooks Press since 2002, has thus far compiled four anthologies of literotica: *Fantasies Made Flesh; Saints and Sinners; Men, Amplified;* and *Wet Nightmares, Wet Dreams.* His most recent work appears in the poetry collections *Van Gogh's Ear, Volumes 2 and 3* and the anthologies *Friction 7* and *Walking Higher: Gay Men Write About the Deaths of Their Mothers.* He resides in Sarasota, Florida, with his long-time spouse, Paul Marquis. Feel free to contact him at mhux@flf.org.

ALPHA MARTIAL is a thirty-nine-year-old ex-pat Brit, now living in France with his long-term partner and four cats. He is an artist's agent by profession and, in another life, an academic researcher specializing in issues of sexuality. Past jobs include seven years as a computer analyst/programmer. He has been writing fiction for many years but only recently began submitting work to publishers. With a collaborator, he is now writing the first in a series of unconventional murder mysteries, and has completed a less genre-specific novel.

JAY NEAL: When it comes to men, his favorite adjective is "husky," and those best described as Big Lugs are lovingly treated in his fiction. Basically a geeky, vanilla kind of guy, he enhances his sex life by making things up. His dirty stories have appeared in *American Bear, American Grizzly,* and *100% BEEF* magazines, and in the anthologies *Best Gay Erotica 2002, 2003,* and *2004;* and *Bearotica; Kink; Friction 7; Bear Lust;* and others. He and his partner are celebrating twelve years of suburban contentment together in Washington, D.C.

MIKE NEWMAN's first novel, *Secret Buddies,* is back in print in a new edition from GLB Publishers, with the entire first chapter available for sampling at www.GLBpubs.com. His short story "Wolfie," about a werewolf on San Francisco's Folsom Street, can be downloaded from GLBpubs for a modest fee. "Wake the King Up Right" is excerpted from his second novel, *Detour,* which he hopes to finish in 2005. He has lived in and around San Francisco since 1970, tirelessly doing research for his stories.

IAN PHILIPS (www.ianphilips.com) is the editor-in-chief (and Mama Bear) of Suspect Thoughts Press. He is also the author of two collections of literotica, *See Dick Deconstruct* and *Satyriasis: Literotica*[2]. In February 2004, he wed heart-throb author-publisher Greg Wharton.

SCOTT POMFRET is cowriter of the Romentics-brand line of romance novels for gay men (www.romentics.com). He is also a writer of short stories (published in *Post Road, New Delta Review, Genre Magazine,* and many others), and his erotic fiction has been repeatedly selected for inclusion in Alyson's annual *Friction* collection. He is looking for a publisher for both his collection of short fiction, *Until the Sugar Is Caramel,* and his newly completed novel, *Only Say the Word.*

ANDY QUAN lives in Sydney, Australia, and is the author of *Calendar Boy* and *Slant.* His latest writing and smut has appeared in anthologies such as *Law of Desire: Tales of Gay Male Lust and Obsession, The Love That Dare Not Speak Its Name: Essays on Queer Sexuality and Desire,* and *Best Gay Asian Erotica.* His first collection of erotica and sex writing, *Six Positions,* is forthcoming. His website is hungry for your visit: www.andyquan.com.

ALEXANDER ROWLSON is a freelance writer living in Toronto. He enjoys knitting, angry female rock stars, and pretending he's married to Kurt Cobain. He spent two years working at Toronto's *fab magazine* as its youth columnist, covering the twink beat with a twist. Retired at twenty, he now divides his time between writing feature articles, working at his neighborhood queer bookstore, and licking ass. Not wanting to deprive the depraved, he has started working on his first novel.

D. TRAVERS SCOTT's first novel, *Execution, Texas: 1987,* was deemed "funny and disturbing" by David Sedaris and "halfway between Flaubert and *Straight to Hell"* by Robert Glück. In 2005, Suspect Thoughts Press will let loose his next novel, *One of These Things Is Not Like the Other.* He edited the anthology *Strategic Sex: Why They Won't Keep It in the Bedroom,* and was guest judge of *Best Gay Erotica 2000.* He has appeared everywhere from *Harper's* and *This American Life* to *Holy Titclamps!* and *New Art Examiner.* He lives in Seattle and runs 9099 Media, a micropress for Pacific Northwest nonfiction. And, of course: www.dtraversscott.com.

SIMON SHEPPARD makes his tenth appearance in the *Best Gay Erotica* series. He's the author of *In Deep: Erotic Stories,* the nonfiction work *Kinkorama: Dispatches from the Front Lines of Perversion,* and the upcoming *Sex Parties 101.* His first short story collection, *Hotter than Hell,* won an Erotic Authors Association Award. His work also appears in five editions of *The Best American Erotica,* as well as more than a hundred other anthologies, and he coedited *Rough Stuff* and *Roughed Up.* He also writes the syndicated column "Sex Talk," and the column "Perv" for gay.com. He lives in San Francisco with his honey and loiters at www.simonsheppard.com.

DAVEM VERNE lived in Hell's Kitchen, New York City, for several years before writing "The Bigg Mitkowski," his love song to that city's Midtown. He has written erotic prose for a decade—stories that are sometimes fanciful, sometimes hard core—but always his work reads true when he is writing from first-hand experience. The men of Mitkowski were his friends, lovers, or objects of sexual inquiry who dwell in his heart, larger than life. More may be written about the flesh and fantasies of Hell's Kitchen, but the author suggests living there first.

BOB VICKERY (www.bobvickery.com) is a regular contributor to various websites and magazines, particularly *Men, Freshmen,* and *Inches.* He has five collections of stories published: *Skin Deep, Cock Tales, Cocksure, Play Buddies,* and, most recently, *Man Jack,* an audiobook of his stories. He lives in San Francisco, and can most often be found in his neighborhood Haight Ashbury cafe, pounding out the smut on his laptop.

GREG WHARTON is the author of the collection *Johnny Was & Other Tall Tales.* He is the publisher of Suspect Thoughts Press, co-coordinator for Project: QueerLit, and an editor for two web magazines, SuspectThoughts.com and VelvetMafia.com. He is also the editor of numerous anthologies, including the Lambda Literary Award Finalist *The Love That Dare Not Speak Its Name.* He lives in San Francisco with his husband, Ian, a cat named Chloe, and a lot of books.

JAMES WILLIAMS is the author of *...But I Know What You Want.* His stories have appeared widely in print and online publications and anthologies, including *Best American Erotica of 1995, 2001,* and *2003; Best Gay Erotica 2002* and *2004;* and *Best SM Erotica.* He was the subject of profile interviews in *Different Loving*, by Gloria Brame, Will Brame, and Jon Jacobs, and in *Sex: An Oral History*, by Harry Maurer. His essay "The Mother and Child Reunion" will appear in *Walking Higher: Gay Men Write About the Deaths of Their Mothers*, edited by Nicholas Hornack. He can be found in the ether at www.jaswilliams.com.

About the Editors

RICHARD LABONTÉ has edited the *Best Gay Erotica* series since 1997. After working with A Different Light Bookstores in Los Angeles, San Francisco, and New York from 1979 to 2001, he moved home to Ontario, Canada, where he divides his time between a communal farm near Calabogie and the rural town of Perth. He shares both with his partner of twelve years (and his husband of one year), Asa Dean Liles, who can't take the winters, with their loving pooch, Percy, who has never met a squirrel he didn't hate, and with puppy Zach. He reads many books, writing about some of them in the syndicated review column "Book Marks," for Q Syndicate (www.qsyndicate.com), and in the Gay Men's Edition of the *Books to Watch Out For* newsletter (www.btwof.com). Reach him at tattyhill@sympatico.ca.

WILLIAM J. MANN is the author of three best-selling novels, *Where the Boys Are, The Biograph Girl,* and *The Men from the Boys,* with a fourth, *All American Boy,* due in spring 2005. In addition, he's written several acclaimed studies of the Hollywood film industry: *Wisecracker: The Life and Times of William Haines* (for which he won a 1998 Lammy Award), *Behind the Screen: How Gays and Lesbians Shaped Hollywood,* and *Edge of Midnight: The Life of John Schlesinger.* Currently completing a major cultural study of Katharine Hepburn's life and career, he is also hard at work on his first screenplay. He lives in Provincetown, Massachusetts, with his husband, Dr. Tim Huber, and can be reached through www.williamjmann.com.